THE PLANET *on the* DETERGENT BOX

THE PLANET *on the* DETERGENT BOX

SCOTT PORTER

The Planet on the Detergent Box
Copyright © 2019 Scott Porter
All Rights Reserved.

For information about this title or to order other books and/or electronic media, contact the publisher:
Scott Porter
Wichita, KS
jscottporter212@gmail.com

ISBN: 978-1-7326203-0-8 (Print)
ISBN: 978-1-7326203-1-5 (ebook)

Printed in the United States of America
Cover and Interior design: 1106 Design

For more information on the universe of "The Planet on the Detergent Box," as well as a downloadable full-color PDF map of Calema, please go to www.theplanetcalema.com.

CONTENTS

For a detailed, full-color map of Calema, please visit www.theplanetcalema.com.

Chapter 1 • THE PLANET CLERK

MACK GOT HIS planet on his thirty-fifth birthday. The reaction from his parents and all his old friends was the same: "Really? Are you sure about this?" Mack had always been a bright lad, and everyone knew he could land a better job than Planet Clerk.

For a Planet Clerk is a nearly invisible cog in the vast machine of the Gassian bureaucracy. There are lots of interesting things going on in the G.A.S.S.—the Galactic Association of Sentient Species. Science of course. And for those who want excitement in their life, there is always Exploration. With the Gass covering only about the middle 10% of one spiral arm of the galaxy, and a mere ten billion or so stars, the claim of being "galactic" was still something of a stretch. The Gassian Grand Council has been trying for centuries to come up with a motto all the species can get behind. That isn't likely to ever happen of course, but so far, "Ever Outward" has been the closest thing to a unifying theme.

The Gass is nothing if not flexible. This is the great secret to its millennia of steady expansion. Along the way, dozens of would-be "Galactic Empires" have been folded into the Gassian embrace. Some of these were harrowingly warlike and hostile to the claims of other sentient species. "Species-centric," in the carefully neutral parlance of Gassian diplomacy. But everything is negotiable. And the material benefits of membership—"joining the universe" as they say—had proved so far to be, ultimately, irresistible.

One very minor concomitant to this vast, bubbling cauldron of interstellar politics is the Protected Planets Ministry. What to do with a sentient species that Isn't Quite Ready? We can't have them gobbled up (this can be understood literally) or enslaved by a technologically superior species. More precisely, we can't have this done by *some other* species. And so it is that, quite without their knowledge, the members of thousands of enlightened (but some only dimly so) civilizations have found themselves on the rolls of the PPM.

If their planet is strategically located, or if it contains some especially useful minerals, its Accession Day may be moved up. Otherwise, the PPM is there strictly for the purposes of scholarly observation and to Keep Things From Happening.

In the go-go Gassian universe, where opportunities are essentially limitless, Planet Clerk is the ultimate dead-end job. It nicely sums up all the most soul-draining aspects of academia and diplomatic service. It doesn't even pay well. After all, out there, orbiting round and round some planet of savages, what is there to buy? It is traditionally a lifetime posting; really more like taking religious orders than getting a job. Humans, according to the latest data of the Gassian Comprehensive Census (updated every minute), just aren't cut out for it. In the 1500 or so years[1]

---

1   The years are "standard planet years," approximately 321 earth days. "Standard Planet" this, that and the other is simply the average of the thing among the four ancient Original Species of the Gass: Corgurid, Moke, Tumba, and Seedeedeedee. The Mokes disappeared centuries ago. The Sessevians purchased "Moke" as a registered trademark last year. The Sessevian Company is the only registered corporation in the Gass comprised of every single member of the species.

since Earth Accession, only a handful of Humans have ever been appointed Planet Clerk.

But McAdoo Haywood 47 Giraomiuchaeyae 1331 was not like other Humans, as he himself was fond of pointing out. He loved the Gass. He had grown up on Shuxxa, a planet in the very core of the Gass. What Humans there are on Shuxxa comprise a small, prosperous, and thoroughly assimilated minority; he had very liberal views. No speciesism here.

A Planet Clerk must be above reproach on this point. He is, in a sense, the sole representative for his planet to the rest of the galaxy. He must speak only for his planet, think only for his planet. Now every planet in the PPM has its contingent of monitoring species. Officially, they are there to observe the social and technological development of the planet's dominant species, of which there may be more than one. In truth they are there to observe each other. Every habitable planet is a prize of great value to those species capable of living on it. Good spy work—a little political interference here, a little technological nudge there—can pay off big in a few centuries when the planet becomes Accessed. Everybody does it.

The Planet Clerk is the referee. He must not favor Humans, or even Humanoids[2].

Mack first discovered Calema (Kah-LEMM-mah) when he was just ten years old and undertaking that exercise in futility common to earnestly well-meaning youths everywhere of Memorizing the Habitable Planets. (It is futile because new ones are

---

2   The correct term is "Corguridoid."

being discovered faster than any normal person can memorize them.)

It was the picture on the Calema Detergent box that first piqued his interest: a wide-spreading tree overlaid with flowering vines thick with blue flowers, and behind it a stretch of beach leading down to an azure sea.

Some six hundred years earlier, the Gass Preliminary Survey had canvassed this newly discovered planet for items of any particular usefulness. They hadn't turned up much, but they did find, on a string of tropical islands, a small blue flower that grew in clumps along its vines, making parts of the forest appear to be decorated with streamers. The natives called the flower "Calema," meaning something like "breeze off the water." This flower had the intriguing property of not only smelling vaguely pleasant, but also of absorbing all other odors. All of them.

Gassian chemists couldn't figure out how it worked. What seemed to be the exact same compound, produced artificially, smelled nice but didn't mask anything. Only the original aquamarine liquid, pressed from the petals of these flowers, could do the magic.

Attempts at exporting Calema flower cultivation failed. This planet had a peculiar chemical makeup not found anywhere else. The Sessevians swooped in and transplanted vast quantities to the uninhabited islands encircling the Barbarian Lands. They were canny marketers. Their Ninthwave® campaign for Calema soap, Calema spray, Calema candles and Calema shampoo was a textbook example of generating an instant need for something that previously no one had known existed. Calema soap became a constitutional right on more than a hundred planets. It was only natural that the rest of the galaxy would soon call this place "MOR KALEEMA TIM,"[3] "Planet Calema Flower."[4] And then, simply, Calema.

Calema. Dreamy, impractical young McAdoo searched out all there was to know about this planet. He had to dig pretty deep, and even then there wasn't much. It was on the rolls of the PPM and likely to stay there a long time. Its thirty million-odd Humanoid souls were coming along remarkably slowly on the Mankin-Sgrvzz arc of social development. They were projected to be ready for Accession in anywhere from 600 to 1,000 years, barring another dark age.

Mack began communicating with the current Clerk, an affable Neemnot coasting to the close of an undistinguished career. This fellow, Keebleeg, was flattered and a little astonished by the attention. He enjoyed regaling the young Human with anecdotes and semi-factual tales, mostly hearsay, from the odder corners of Calema's Six Civilized Continents. Little did he realize Mack was taking it all down, cross-referencing, codifying, actually trying to make some sense of it all.

By the time he turned twenty-five, Mack was, as far as anyone knew, the galaxy's foremost authority on Calema. He applied to the Protected Planets Ministry, and despite some last-minute strategic bribes from his parents, was accepted. He served his time

---

3   This is Babata, the grossly simplified, made-up, universal language of the Gass.

4   When the Gass finally decided to make contact with Earth, Humans were startled to find that their planet was already known throughout the galaxy as "MOR SAKOATA⋀," "Planet Chocolate."

in low-level posts and cheerfully underwent the years of mental and psychological testing. On his thirty-fifth birthday, the call finally came. Keebleeg had announced his retirement, and PPM Sentient Species Resources, after toiling about halfway through Mack's thousand-page resume/application, threw up their hands (and talons, and tentacles) and gave him the job.

He arrived a few weeks later at the Calema Gassplat, the orbiting platform that was to be his home for, as far as he was concerned, the rest of his life. As Gassplats go, it was a large one, almost a small city, since it also served as the center of Gass operations in this far corner of the Gass[5]. There was a brief ceremony, followed by cookies. A smattering of Humans, spies from the Earthplat, came over to have a look at this novelty, one of their own, a Planet Clerk. But really Mack just wanted to talk with Keebleeg. He soon had him cornered there in the reception room.

"It's you! It's really you!" Mack was trembling with the momentousness of the occasion. Keebleeg blinked his perfectly round eyes, folded his tiny hands into a ball, and smiled and cast a sidewise glance at the faraway door. Neemnots are at the small end of the Humanoid spectrum, and plump and slow-moving to boot. They find Humans unpredictable and a little frightening.

"I have so many questions still! I'm hoping we can get together a lot over the next few weeks . . ."

"Weeks!" Mack should have seen the panic in Keebleeg's gigantic eyes. But then, if Mack had had people skills, he would

---

5   After 600 years, this plat had its own semi-indigenous population and even its own low-rent district, with throughways you shouldn't be out in at night.

never have wound up in the PPM. "I'm leaving—ah, er, ah—right now, as a matter of fact. Transport to catch. Terribly sorry. Can't be helped."

"But I feel so unprepared! What if something happens?"

Keebleeg chuckled. "My dear boy, this is Calema. Nothing ever happens here."

A smile spread across Mack's features. His shoulders relaxed. A slight mist appeared in his eyes as he turned his head to beam beneficently on everyone in the room.

"Perfect," he said.

Chapter 2 • A ROOMFUL OF SPIES

TEN YEARS ON, the only thing about his job Mack had not quite reconciled himself to was committee meetings. Cramped quarters, long hours, alien food—these he hardly noticed. But Tertiary Committee meetings are downright brutal. Sometimes fatal.

In the Gassplat's Hall of Harmony and Understanding, the 301st Biannual Convocation of The Tertiary Committee of Disinterested Observers for the Planet Calema was grinding through what everyone hoped would be the last meeting of the year. The Primary Committee had wrapped up in three days of what were essentially cocktail parties and exchanges of tightly scripted diplomatic pleasantries. The Secondary Committee had taken two weeks to pass a raft of resolutions totaling approximately a million words of high-minded accords for the benefit and guidance of the Tertiary Committee. The Tertiary Committee was content to accept that these accords were on file somewhere and that somebody—most likely everyone's legal bots[6]—had already picked them over and found the necessary loopholes.

---

6   Many species have ruled it cruel and unusual punishment to actually require anyone to read Secondary Committee accords.

The Tertiary Committee had just entered the second month of its labor in the real and true work of everyone in the PPM: frustrating the ambitions of all the other species. This normally took the form of "faulting," that is, presenting evidence of technical rule-breaking by everyone else's Recognized Observers. There was always, of course, the possibility of exposing their Unrecognized Observers, which by conservative estimates comprised 90% of the Gass citizens now emplaced among Calema's unsuspecting population. This was considered bad form and was seldom done. Much better to simply keep an eye on them once you knew who they were.

Timo, a Human and the Secondary Station Chief of the Earthplat, was defending his operatives from an accusation of poisoning the Master of the Ribbons on the continent Brogora. This particular debate had been raging for two hours, with all the raging being done by Maggericki the Bellow. From the bare fact that the death had occurred soon after a fete attended by a registered Human spy, Maggericki had woven a fabulous plot on the part of the Humans for Caleman world domination. Once Timo regained the floor, he delivered a deft twenty-minute riposte establishing that there was a great deal more evidence linking the death to any number of other causes—Black Toe Disease, Moon Fright, bad fish, or for that matter, Bellows—than to his species.

It was all very dry and amusing. Stud Maggericki 1305[7] couldn't stand it. He jumped in over Mack's calls to order and launched

---

7   "Stud" is a high, ceremonial Bellow honorific. It is self-bestowed by every Bellow male.

into his ready list of Human deceit and trickery on Calema in the past 600 years. He had proof!

Bellows are the living embodiment of Kamgit's 14th postulate of social dysfunction: obtuseness as a core principle succeeds, sometimes brilliantly, as long as the correct distance from your fellow boors is maintained. The math is really quite elegant. The Bellow contingent at the Tertiary Committee, like most Bellow contingents everywhere, consisted of one person.

The debate was being carried on in Babata (pronounced "Bubba-duh" by most Humans), the sole legally recognized language for Gassian inter-species proceedings[8]. Maggericki's facility with Babata was poor even on the rare occasions when he did not have himself worked into a literal froth. By this time almost no one in the room could make heads or tails of what he was saying, although the gist of it seemed to be the moral and physical shortcomings of his Human counterpart. There was a great deal of milling around. At their table, the Neemnots had laid out their second late mid-afternoon meal. The Glags were all asleep. Timo the Human had his head down, tapping away on his Reader, no doubt working on a rebuttal.

Mack's heart went out to Timo, but even though Mack was the chairman of this proceeding, there was nothing he could do for

---

8   Babata is comprised of the 12 accepted and universal phonemes: A,U,I,O,B,K,M,T,S,R,H,^. The ^ is a whistle. Of course, given the extreme variety of vocal apparatus in the galaxy, the rules of pronunciation are routinely stretched beyond all recognition. Many diplomats have extensive medical procedures in order to speak "pure" Babata. With such limited phonemes, words tend to be long, and it usually takes an extraordinary length of time to say the simplest thing. This suits diplomats just fine.

him at the moment. The Gass had a short list of moral principles, but Freedom of Speech was somewhere near the top. Mack hated the personal invective that seeped into these Tertiary Committee meetings after the first few weeks. He couldn't imagine being the object of one of these diatribes. Poor Timo must be mortified.

Timo was, in fact, polishing his CV. An old professor at the Academy had given a hint about a new operational arm in corporate espionage. Despite the fact that Timo had made Secondary Station Chief in near record time, he longed to get away from this Protected Planet posting and to the Real Action on one of the major planets. Yes, Calema was still important to the Humans; its climate was mild and quite similar to old Earth's, and Caleman culture, on the six civilized continents at least, had many similarities to 15th- or 16th-century Earth. Leebs, the dominant species on Calema, were surprisingly Human-like. It was of course more sentiment than serious strategic thinking, but there were lots of Humans who hung on to the idea that Calema could someday be that mystical ideal, a "New Earth." Someday. Not anytime soon. Nothing was supposed to actually *happen* on Calema for hundreds of years yet.

In fact, Timo was about to make sure of that. In the last year he had uncovered a Sessevian plot to upset the balance of power on Calema. He had marshalled the meager resources that Human Interplanetary Intelligence had allotted to this godforsaken planet and unraveled the whole deal. He had the goods on them. The little bombshell he was preparing for this Tertiary Committee was going to launch his career to dizzying heights. Maybe even a posting to Corgeer, the Corgurid home world, matching wits with the best spies in the galaxy.

As Stud Maggericki harangued on, Mack kept an eye on the Attention Register in the corner of his lectern. It tracked how many of the delegates were paying attention, in any way at all, to the current speaker. Below 30%, and the matter at hand could not be put to a vote. Below 22%, and all discussion could be summarily dismissed.

The Attention Register hit 22% and lit up, at the same time sounding a cheerful "ding" and a cheerful "buzz" and a cheerful "hoot" and a few other noises—"cheerful" having different meanings to different species. The room stirred to life, and for a moment all eyes went to Mack.

"That's it then," Mack said. He cleared his throat and sat up straight and added, "The Clerk finds that the Assertion of Fault is unwarranted." He touched the button that not only disconnected the Bellow's microphone but threw a muffle of silence over the area all around him. A sigh of relief wafted across the room. There was a smattering of applause.

Mack continued. "This brings us to Assertion of Fault number …" He checked the monitor, "One-hundred thirty-seven. Lodged by," his eyebrows lifted slightly, "the Human delegation."

Timo, that is, Delegate Timotei 101 Sjogren Thyarohhaefii 1331[9] got to his feet again. Timo at this time did not look especially Human. His ears were too large and swept back and ended

---

9 1331 means "Human." The Sgrvzz System of Sentient Species Classification is a sort of Dewey Decimal System for civilized species. The scale goes from 1,000 to 5,999, classifying strictly according to genetic makeup. The 1300-1400 series is Humanoid, with the Corgurids being a perfect 1350. Most Humans, like most of the other relative newcomer species in the Gass, had taken on a last name borrowed from one of the major languages of the Gass. Timo's "Gass" name, like Mack's, was Corgurid.

in a decided peak. His head was unusually narrow, his nose long and strangely arched. In fact, he was oddly proportioned all around. And a great many of the people in the room, though nominally representing widely diverse species, had a similar look.

Timo was most of the way through the process of being "regenned," genetically and physically altered to pass as Caleman, or "Leeban" as they called themselves. It was a rule. Even the most desk-bound plat guys had to log some field time. It was a long, painful, and for most, a traumatic process. Back on the Earthplat, also orbiting Calema, he had already endured most of the surgeries and procedures for the transformation. He was still too tall to pass unremarked among the Leebs. The operations on his legs and spine were due to be done in a couple of weeks.

"Respected Chairman, Members of the Tertiary Committee, this Accusation is very grave. It concerns a clear attempt to change, not just the political situation on Calema, but the very course of its history." The chatter around the room died down a bit, but just a bit. This Tertiary Committee had endured over a month of daily bombast and histrionics. An opening statement like this seemed almost timid. In a far corner, one of the Glags began to snore.

Timo raised his voice. "I will first present evidence of the rapid development, in secret, of potassium nitrate refining techniques in Kamerduk, South Gadgerus. This development is quite separate from any previous technology of the Gadgerenes."

The effect was sensational. "Impossible!" "What technique?" "Is this a royal project?" "What is your *proof*?" For the moment, all order dissolved. Every delegation's science contingent was either demanding recognition from the chair or excitedly explaining the matter to the rest of their people. Mack made a show of calling for order, but he knew enough of this crowd to ride out the noise for a few seconds more. He took the moment to turn and ask Unu for some snacks for the staff. It looked like today's meeting was a long way from over.

With a few taps on his Reader, a flexible, postcard-sized link to the Gassplat's communications, Timo called up the proof on the room's big screens. It was clandestine video (no doubt from an eye link) of well-tended nitre beds being turned and watered by a host of Gadgerene slaves. A hush fell over the room. This was riveting stuff—whoever it was with the eye link was wandering freely around the whole operation, and it was on a tremendous scale. And there was sound. You could hear heavy machinery— machinery in Gadgerus! And every minute or so, in the distance, the wailing call of a priestess Naming the Moment with a passage from the Book of Days. Meaning, as everyone quickly grasped, that this was indeed a Royal Project. Unbelievable!

A red dot appeared in the corner of Timo's Reader. He had a message. This was strange. Communication from the outside should be utterly restricted at a moment like this. It was from Sarah, who managed communications and encryption on the Earthplat.

The message was just text. *"SESSEVIAN MEETING VIDEO FAKE."*

Timo spun and tried to catch the eye of the Earth Station Chief, Javitz, but the old man was leaning over a table whispering something to the Trokee Station Chief. Timo looked at the text again. This was impossible. This was disastrous. Without that video they had a Fault but no one to accuse.

Another red dot. He touched it. *"FAKE. DON'T SHOW."*

On the big screens, the video had changed to another setting, with glimpses now of grand new leaching vats and boilers. And now there was the royal seal plainly visible.

The crowd gasped. The mood in the room was going from disbelief to anger. Everybody knew this level of organization and technology was unprecedented and completely uncharacteristic of the Gadgerenes. Why build a boiler when two hundred clay pots over bonfires, tended by two hundred slaves, would do? And most importantly, the Kingdom of Gadgerus had no use for the vast quantity of saltpeter they obviously were now producing. Hitherto it had figured only in some medicines and a few "magical" effects. Production on this scale could only mean . . .No one wanted to say "gunpowder." One of the many quirks of Caleman history was how very slowly technology had progressed to now. On all the six civilized continents, it seemed that no one had ever felt the need to explore even the rudiments of inorganic chemistry. Caleman plant life was simply too abundant and varied and generous. Why bother to refine lead and turn it into pipes when Zimmer spires provided waterproof, rot-resistant pipes in any dimension you could need? Who needs paper when you have ready-made scrolls of Winding Tree bark? Why refine saltpeter for use as tinder when you simply needed to squeeze a Toop bud to get a drop of quick-burning oil as good as kerosene?

This roomful of spies was angry not so much that someone was trying to direct Caleman development, but that they had pulled off this trick in Kamerduk, the opulent capital of Gadgerus and the most spy-infested city on the planet. Foundations were being shaken. The time-honored policy of MAF—Mutually Assured Frustration—was at risk.

The scene on the screens changed again. The video quality was worse; the camera was jerking around randomly—probably an insect link. It was a chamber. The designs on the wall showed this was the office of a high Gadgerene official. There were voices. The back of someone's head. Timo's fingers did a staccato dance across his Reader. The video paused.

"That's it. That's all the video," Timo announced. Over the uproar that followed, Timo's repeated shouts finally carried through. "Respected Chairman! Respected Chairman!"

Mack's lectern was fitted with a Command Microphone zone, a system which rather frightened him and which he hadn't used this entire Tertiary Committee Convocation. It took him a minute of dabbing at his own Reader to get it on. Suddenly his enhanced, god-like voice rattled the cups on the tables: "THE CHAIR REC-OGNIZES . . . THE CHAIR . . . WHAT IS IT, TIMO?"

"I wish to revise the Accusation of Fault to a Resolution of Inquiry."

"HA!" said Maggericki the Bellow, who had dodged around the room until he had shaken the muffle zone. A great deal more commentary along the same line broke out across the room. Many gathered around the screens and peered and pointed at the blurry, frozen image of a Humanoid just about to turn and reveal his face.

"I have received new information . . ." Javitz, his well-lined face now a tragedian's mask and turning redder by the second, was jostling his way across the room to Timo.

"REALLY?" Mack's god-like voice boomed. It was a funny thing for a god to say. Mack poked at his Reader some more.

Javitz reached Timo and hissed into his ear, "What about the Sessevians?"

Timo, turning away from the crowd and using his other hand as a shield, gave Javitz a glimpse of his Reader. The Station Chief shook his head in disbelief. He leaned in and whispered something to Timo that required additional emphasis from both arms. He turned and glowered at everything in the room. After one last, violently head-shaking remark in Timo's direction, he stalked back to his table, the crowd instinctively parting to give him room.

"Well, there is certainly enough evidence for an Inquiry." Mack's voice was merely amplified now and back to its usual reedy tone. "Authorized Delegates, please take up your Readers while I prepare the Resolution . . ."

The vote passed with only one opposed. Bellows are the main reason unanimity is never required in Tertiary Committees.

Once they got to the business of choosing up the members of the Inquiry Sub-Committee, Javitz took over as Human speaker. He knew everybody in the room, and this was the sort of thing he did best: packing the Inquiry with as many of your own people and your allies as possible. None of this was going to get done fast. Forming a new Sub-Committee called for passing a raft of resolutions, and then every delegation needed to weigh in with their official position. They had hours of dreadfully predictable speeches to sit through yet. Meanwhile, the real work was going to be done between speeches, as delegates milled around the room and huddled up in twos and threes, sounding each other out and making deals.

And this time there was an additional complication: the perpetrator was almost certainly in the room. Who could you really be sure of? Whose interest really aligned with your own?

Javitz usually threw in with the Corgurids. They were a peaceful, artistic bunch, after all, and tended to regard Calema as a charming late-medieval theme park that, with luck, would take another two thousand years to join the Gass. The Neemnots, with their fixation on "outside science"—what most other species called "magic" or "superstition"—seemed unlikely to be pressing for the accelerated advancement of technology here. They loved the rich magical tradition of Calema's Wizards' Guild. The Trokees and Gerts were usually reliable allies for the Humans, too.

And that was about it. Kamgit may have been joking when he had observed that mutual spying was the glue that held the Gass together, but he wasn't far from wrong. It was a jungle in here.

Another mealtime had gone by before Mack rang out the session, the Inquiry still in the preliminary stage of formation. He ducked for the nearest doorway while most of the delegates bunched together around their leaders one last time.

Mack's quarters were on the planet side of the plat. The main room wasn't large, but a wall-to-wall window looking down on the planet made first-time visitors grab for the furniture once they were in the door. Unu and Brab, two of his assistants, were there, sharing a loaf of crackly bread and some sweet Caleman wine. Mack poured himself a cup and tipped his chair back, getting comfortable in preparation for hearing the Daily Pill—all the day's dispatches from the Recognized Observers.

Unu, a Corgurid girl, read the DP. This was done in Corgurid. Babata may be the official language of Gass diplomacy, but civilized discourse among Humanoids was always Corgurid[10]. Like all of her race, she was small and slender, with a round, delicately featured face and widely set grey eyes. Mack thought of her as a "girl," but that was just a guess; to Humans, all Corgurids looked like children at least the first hundred years of their life. It was only the fact that this was her first posting that gave him the idea she was still a girl to her fellow 'Rids.

The daily pill was a landfill-load of disconnected bits of banality unworthy of being kept secret. Unu didn't need any notes. She was delivering the DP in the clear, silvery Corgurid voice that made even this seem almost interesting. Of course, to Mack everything about Calema was interesting, always. In just ten years as Clerk, he had authored a small library's-worth of Caleman archeology, history, biology, sociology, and so on. And on and on.

She was just wrapping up the results of a Villages Council in the back mountains of Melligar (today's issue: how to honor the dragon goddess Paninanina for the mild dragonbug season) when a bird whistled. Mack made a motion with his hand, and a view of the doorway appeared in a corner of the window. It was Timo the Human standing in the hall. Another wave of Mack's hand

---

10   Not that this civilized discourse was done well. Discerning all of Corgurid's 23 major vowels and 41 minor vowels was beyond the reach of any other species. While all other Humanoid species learned Corgurid as schoolchildren, Corgurid youngsters studied Corgurid as butchered by foreigners.

opened the door. Timo hopped in. Since the room's gravity plate was perpendicular to the corridor, it was really the best way.

"I brought some whisky, but it looks like you're all fixed up. Hi, Brab, Unu. Crackly bread!" He set the bottle on the table and picked up a chunk of bread, tapping it on the table to break it into shards. "From the Trokeeplat?" Brab nodded gravely and gave the "you're welcome" shake of his head. Glags saved spoken words for special occasions.

"Is this real?" Mack gave the whisky bottle a turn to view the label. Mogula? Didn't know they brewed anything there."

"They've started growing grains in the canyons. Humantown is almost a city."

"Well, the color's right. Thank you. Maybe we can open it when the Tertiary Committee is done."

Unu caught Mack's eye, and he gave a slight shake of his head. No more DP for now. Mack poured Timo a glass of wine. They talked, in guarded, general terms, about the day's meeting. Mack didn't want to pry into the particulars of the Human strategy. There were rules.

"But you gave away a lot, showing the eye link from Kamerduk," Mack said. "You know everyone is analyzing that bit of lookage to figure out how it was collected."

"We edited out the clues. Sarah is a master at that. We really thought we would catch the . . . I don't know what happened. I'll be reviewing everything my agents ever sent me. Javitz is in a state. He's demanding . . . lots of things. Oh, well. It looks like I'll be here a while longer than I thought."

"That's too bad," Mack said, and awkwardly added, "For you, I mean."

Timo smiled and said, "I know what you mean. It's very pleasant here. All my agents say so. But there's so much happening on the disputed planets! The Human interest is getting out-maneuvered in so many ways!"

"I think I see," Unu chimed in. "It is as if there was a war going on, and you feel you should be at the front."

"Yes! That's it exactly!"

"Well, at least this Inquiry should throw a wrench into their operations," Mack put in. He really didn't want Timo to get going on his "Human interest" stories. "I suppose, anyway. Whoever 'they' are. And you must have picked up some more clues from the reaction today."

Timo shook his head. "Really? Weren't your analytics working? I thought you people kept track of everybody's heart beat and blink rate and pupil dilation and . . ."

"You know I can't talk about that."

"Oh. Right. Spy stuff. Have some more wine. It's Fengali. One of the outer islands. Doesn't that hurt?" He pointed to Timo's hand on the table. The hairline scars were still visible where it had been narrowed and lengthened.

Timo held up his hand and gazed at it critically. "Not at all. They did a good job. It just feels . . . funny. I still have to look at my hands to use them right."

"I don't know why you want to be a surface agent anyway. Everybody says you've been doing a great job up here in the sky."

This was not flattery. Timo was the rising star of the Human Calema station. Mack wasn't supposed to know the details, but he had overheard plenty of chatter of how this new man had shaken up the whole moribund operation over on the Earthplat. For the previous fifty years or so, the Human presence had been pretty quiet here, mostly just going along with the 'Rids. But since Timo's arrival two years ago, the Humans had taken the lead. He had ideas. He was supposed to be some sort of master tactician. He had written a book or something back in his days at the spy academy. Something must have gone really wrong with this Kamerduk business.

"I need to be able to check up on my field agents. It's a requirement." He looked at his hand again and gave it a frustrated shake. "It can be reversed."

"Ouch. You are dedicated to your craft."

"I am. And I won't be here forever."

Mack gave him a sidelong glance. Timo was gazing idly down on the planet and didn't notice. Mack liked this boy. Up here on the Gassplat, most of the spies he met were the plodding, bureaucratic type, plat jockeys, incapable of making the simplest assertion of fact without following it up with a negating qualifier of some sort. Timo was all in. He had a true believer's zeal for the Human interest in the Eternal Game. Mack had even heard him say once, "Make the galaxy a better place," without a trace of irony. It was touching, really. For that he was willing to overlook the boy's occasional strident Humanness.

Mack rose and went to stand in the window. "The sun's coming up over Dabby," he remarked. It was late spring for the northern inhabited continents, and the sun was favoring them as a great, smooth arc of daylight was sweeping over the hills and grasslands of Dab, one of the less civilized of the civilized lands.

"Sure enough. Isn't it strange to be orbiting this close and still see no cities?" Timo said. "I hope I don't end up serving my time in Dab. 'The Little Kingdoms.'"

This was the rather mocking name the other nations had for the continent the locals called, in their optimistic moments, "United Dab." For the rest of the Civilized Continents, the wars of consolidation were centuries past. But Dab was still a crazy quilt of overlapping claims and alliances for every petty noble. "True," Mack said, not turning. "They're having a hard time letting go of the old feudalism. But they have their bright spots."

"I suppose."

"You'd rather be looking down on Corgeer."

Timo smiled at this, a little wistfully. "Well, they say it's good training," Timo said, "Field work. Even out here on a Protected Planet. Plenty of little intrigues going on among the locals, you know."

"And it's a wonderful planet. You'll see." Mack pointed down and to the right. "There's Calema. I mean the original Calema, the island. The sun is just coming up there."

Timo got up and joined him. Mack pointed out a small volcanic island on the fringe of the Fengal Archipelago. It was a perfect little circle of green on the edge of a vast blue sea. A thin streamer of white smoke trailed from the volcano, dissipating five hundred lazy miles downwind into a faint shimmer over the water.

"So that's where it all started," Timo said. "It's pretty, all right." He shook his head. "And nobody down there knows that's what their planet is famous for."

"And almost nobody out there in the Gass knows anything *else* about Calema. Which is really very sad because . . . it's a whole world. To them, to the Leebs, it's THE whole world. And it *is* enough. It's complete. It's beautiful."

Timo observed a few seconds of tactful silence. He had learned that anything that seemed like a counterpoint here would be enough to set Mack off for an hour-long diatribe about . . . well, he still couldn't really say what Mack was on about. He liked Mack— he was a smart guy and interesting to talk to, but this . . . this mania, this . . . it was some notion of "purity," as nearly as he could tell. Timo had sniffed it out in many of his agents, too. In this little patch of the Eternal Game, having your people go native was an ever-present danger, especially with the regenning. But for some of them, that was precisely what had brought them to this line of work in the first place, and to the prospect of a lifetime posting "in planet." A dream. An ideal. "The Ungassed Planet." Good grief.

They drank up the wine, and Timo left. He said he was going to bed, but Mack knew there was still a major meeting at the Human offices. Cooking up something with the Trokees probably, or the Gerts. Brab gave the Glag sign for "Don't mind me" and went to sleep on the table, drawing the broad folds of his sleeve over his head. Unu resumed the DP precisely where she had left off. Mack took notes on his reader as he listened, sending updates to files on a dozen articles he was writing in the ongoing "Caleman Library," his life's work.

Much later, once Unu had left, he stood alone at the window for a long, silent while. There was a storm in the Dead Clouds of Brogora, and the twinkling of the lightning flashes was almost hypnotic. Tomorrow he would see to the Inquiry. He had some ideas of his own. And then the incident with the Wizards' Guild of Falthing needed looking into. Tomorrow would be another big day—meaning long and with a lot of unpleasantness and bureaucratic bother.

But the blue-and-green planet at his feet, rolling slowly along its path through the cosmos, was beautiful and free, and, for the moment, at peace. Mack felt an odd rising sensation in his chest. He grunted and shook his head. The next instant the feeling, whatever it was, was gone.

It was love.

Chapter 3 • THE SOCIETY OF LESSER KNOWLEDGE

Preamble to the Preface of Dabbian History, Volume Twelve:
The Barbarian Wars
From the Caleman Library, the collected works of McAdoo Haywood Giraomiuchaeyae 1331.

THE SIGNIFICANCE TO *the Dab League of the Second Barbarian War is still—even now, thirty years after the fact—lost on the other nations of Calema. To them it is a matter of some derision. It is proof of the inferiority of Dabbian culture, and of the entire social structure of the Little Kingdoms, that they came so close to annihilation.*

It was certainly inauspiciously begun. The voyages of exploration of the previous century brought fabulous riches to the Dab League's neighbors. Fengal began by discovering the Honey Islands. Then North Gadgerus stumbled on the Outer Islands with their gold and natives too peaceful to resist their own enslavement. South Gadgerus ventured across the Tepid Sea to find the greatest prize of all: The Medicine Islands. Even Shalk eventually stumbled onto Black Whale Island to give them a "prize" of their own.

Dab came late to the exploration game. Their tentative forays eastward turned up only a few fishing beds off the northeast coast. It wasn't until Captain Brow's expedition was blown off-course five hundred miles due east that they discovered Thankallthegods Island—In truth a continent larger than Gadgerus.

Thankallthegods didn't have the gold, silver, or spices they had been seeking, but it did have a mild climate, plentiful game, and vast stretches of undulating hills suitable for raising sheep and cultivating barley. The aboriginal people they found proved to be, in Brow's words "too high-spirited for enslavement and too thick-headed for trade." But they seemed also to be too few to pose a threat. The great Dabbian Migration began.

The commoners seemed particularly ready to abandon "Dabby" and their wretched plots of land and lowly status. Parts of the eastern Little Kingdoms of Wilder, Chalkstump, and Threemish became dangerously low of inhabitants. The immigrants fanned out along the broad floodplain of the Undecided River. With so much rich land there for the taking, there seemed no need for civic organization. Any dispute could be settled by someone moving further upstream.

Then the Barbarian attacks began. These were really just occasions of opportunistic thievery, but they quickly turned violent when the Dabbians resisted. Once the Barbarians discovered what poor fighters the newcomers were, new bands came pouring down from the hills to get their share of the easy plunder.

The so-called First Barbarian War was little more than a protracted retreat to the sea. The Barbarians, whom the Dabbians had at first derided as "hairy brutes too contrary-minded to agree on slaps or yanks"[11] *proved avid imitators of the newcomers' ways. By the time the last, overcrowded ships left the shores of Thankallthegods, the Barbarians had begun fashioning simple bows and arrows of their own.*

---

11   A children's game for deciding who goes first.

The re-introduction of the migrants to Dab created yet more social upheaval. The taste of self-reliance provided by frontier living had raised the ambitions of the former peasants. They traveled from estate to estate seeking better terms—and got them. All the old calculations of levies and taxes were out the window. The Dabbian Emperor (really a figurehead appointed or deposed by the seven Dabbian kings) hit upon the idea of assessing the Emperor's tax according to the number of peasants in each kingdom. The kings immediately began granting titles to every peasant who had a bit more property or could speak Dabbian a bit more properly than his neighbors. By the time the Emperor rescinded the tax law, the Titles Race had made nearly a third of the population nobility.

Then in the year 565 GD[12] bizarre vessels appeared on the Eastern Sea. They had the general shape of a Dabbian "shiver" (a common sailing ship) but with the hull constructed of lashed-together sticks and sails made of poorly tanned animal skins. And with Barbarians spilling over the gunwales.

The Barbarians, handicapped though they were with primitive weapons and an ignorance of all seamanship, had in their favor great numbers and a cheerful disregard for discomfort, pain, or death. They fell on the fishing villages of the Dabbian east coast in waves, plundering and terrorizing the population. It was the Second Barbarian War.

This is where the story diverges from the many other tales of invasion and pillaging that litter Caleman history. Rather than calling on their powerful neighbors for help and signing away the royal treasury and an island or two, they called on the tinsmiths.

---

12   Gassian Discovery.

Now Dab has many tin mines and a long folk tradition of the iconic tinsmith—a clever, sometimes mischievous fellow who, on the spot, can mold and chisel and grind a simple lump of tin into whatever useful object the good country folk need. The desperate kings called on the tinsmiths to make something—something new, something clever, something unheard-of—to beat back the Barbarians.

They created the sighted trebuchet, calibrating each device at its location and giving them distance markers and a simple line-of-sight range-finding system. Along the way some unknown tinsmith invented algebra for the aiming process. They standardized the stone sizes. Now as the ungainly Barbarian ships toiled in, nearly every stone was finding its mark. The defense of Scurrytown, in which a single trebuchet on a hill above the city sank a fleet of ten, made believers of the whole country. Every Dabbian boy wanted to be a tinsmith.

Other inventions followed—many ill-conceived, even disastrous. But a new mindset had seized the country: "Victory through mischief!" (Their word for technology.) They equipped their fighters with stinger flingers, nettle bombs, and treacle gum tubes. Then came the rake, a sort of monstrous crossbow, followed quickly by the dreaded jar-spear. This was a rake bolt equipped at the head with a jar of Toop oil, trailing a burning wick.

Once the Barbarians saw their stick-ships going up in flames, their stomach for plunder was over. Their ships disappeared back over the eastern horizon.

True, the eastern coastal towns were decimated, and Quark Island remained (and still remains) in Barbarian hands, but their country was safe and whole again. And Dabby had a new type of hero.

*"**Oh yes, I** can feel the difference now. It's almost like floating on air!"* Dothram Lumbush gave a little squeeze to the soft leather of the seat beside her and turned her bright eyes up to young Lefton, standing on the carriage step and bending slightly to peer in.

"No, Dottie. That's just the padding on the seat. It's always been that way."

"Well, I think it's very nice." She was seated just to the far side of the bench. There was a quite usable portion of bench beside her, where her dimpled hand was still lightly patting the leather.

"Are you ready to see the real mischief?" Lefton's wide grin was a little alarming.

Dottie giggled. "That just depends. I . . . Lefton! LEFTON!"

Lefton had begun pumping his legs, setting the carriage madly rocking. "Isn't it marvelous!" he said.

"STOP!" The word came out in a protracted, rising shriek that pulsated with the movement of the carriage.

Lefton stopped. In the hushed moment that followed, one could distinctly hear horses stamping in the nearby stables, a family of geese squawking and flapping away, out of the courtyard, and from the distant open window of the big house, the piping voice of Count Spood, "A third octave Baggo![13] Did you see it?"

Spood was in the study with the Duke. On the table before them sat an outlandish but strangely beautiful contraption. It was a sort of open box with the top consisting of a narrow wooden rail that swooped back in forth in a graceful zigzag, starting from nothing at one corner and ending in the far corner at a height of about three feet. The rail was a continuous, hollow sound

---

13   The notes of the Leeban chromatic scale are named after the twelve Retired Gods.

chamber, and all along the way, narrowly spaced, were strings of different colors. Atop the rail were hundreds of tiny tuning pegs. Now as the Count spoke, various strings all along the way picked up the harmonics and visibly vibrated, creating a rich hum that precisely echoed every tone of his voice.

"And did you notice the rapid excursions into the plus five octave?" he babbled, waving his hand above the lowest stretch of rail like a conjurer. "That's beyond the capacity of most Leebs to even hear! Definitely not . . ."

"It was Dottie," said the Duke, closing the subject with the finality only the lord of a great and ancient house can muster. Vexation rumpled his broad chin as he raised his head and hesitated, anticipating further sounds of distress. "I knew she wasn't in the kitchen! Well, I'd better have a look."

Torvum Arumbeed, 11th Duke of Haflum, flung the door open and crossed the lawn in great thumping strides, with Spood loping in his wake, losing ground. Although inches taller, the Count was apparently built of less robustly engineered parts than the Duke.

A young man's head popped out of the carriage door. Like much of the yeomanry around Hafswide, he had shocking orange hair. This hair sprang from his head in a riot of loops and coils, barely tamed at the moment into a very improper pigtail. The head popped back into the carriage.

"It's no good, Lefton. I know you're in there."

A few moments later Lefton spilled from the carriage to the ground without touching the step. When he straightened up he had a fat disk of shiny tin in his hand. "I was just getting the clicker, Your Grace."

"It's done, is it? Just in time! Let me see." The Duke took the device and turned it over and around several times. "Hmm. Hmm. I suppose this . . ." The device had a small crank in the middle of one side. He gave it a few turns, producing a very satisfying ascending whir. And then the disk began clicking, at a firm and even rate of twice per second.

"Splendid! I think you've got just the right pace." The Duke began to march, lost in thought, making a small, "chucking" noise every few steps. His eyes were on the metal disk. His path was a rough oblong around the carriage. As he was traversing the far side, with Spood and Lefton trailing at a respectful distance, the girl slipped out of the carriage and hurried away to the big house. A large figure in an apron appeared in the kitchen door with her arms crossed and a glower on her face. His Lordship might be easily distracted but Matron Deebee knew all the foolishness the girls of the estate might be up to.

"You see, Count," the Duke began without turning around, "This device maintains a steady, even cadence, such as a drummer does for a band of soldiers." The Duke's face lit up. "I shall call it 'the Self-Regulating Drummer!' You know, this might have an application in your music, Count." He held it out. Spood took it after a moment's hesitation.

"I suppose. Although a minus first octave Miri is not useful in many compositions."

"The tone can be changed, Your Lordship," Lefton volunteered.

"I suppose that would be useful then." Spood proffered the disk to Lefton at an awkward arm's length. The fact was that he found the clicking, with no visible Leeban agency, rather ominous.

"Of course, it isn't really for *music*," said the Duke a little crossly. "Young Lefton here has perfectly captured the proper pace of a Mazillum Trotter. Mark my words, this will revolutionize travel!"

"I'm not sure I follow."

"The concept is simple. It all relates to time. Now suppose the king has summoned you to call upon him at noon on such-and-such a day. How can you be sure how long it will take you to cover the intervening distance? With . . ." he snatched the device from Lefton's hand and held it up dramatically beside his face. ". . . the Self-Regulating Drummer, the moment you set out, you can be assured of precisely when you will arrive!"

"I make it a point to get there early."

"Dash it all, man, of course! The point of the matter is . . ."

A rumbling clearing of the throat stopped the Duke in mid-thought. The three men turned around.

"Yes, what is it, Sand?" The Duke's dignity and reserve had instantly returned to him. A good butler ought to have that effect.

"Your Grace, the Marchioness has arrived."

"Oh. Oh, my."

"And there are presently a dozen others taking refreshment in The Hall of Pageants."

"The what?"

"He means the Long Hall, Your Grace," Lefton volunteered.

"Quite right. Just as I ordered." The Duke squared his shoulders and tugged at his jacket so that it rested smoothly over his ample girth. "Come, Lord Spood. Let us meet the other guests."

They were almost to the house, Sand discreetly behind them, when the Duke stopped suddenly. "Oh, but you haven't even looked at the carriage! It's quite the thing! Young Lefton has created an entirely new form of suspension. Revolutionary!"

Lefton remained in the courtyard alone, the Self-Regulating Drummer clicking away in his hands. "A different tone," he murmured, already formulating a design.

THE DUKE OF Haflum was the host and chief benefactor of the Hafswide chapter of the Society of Lesser Knowledge. The name still irked him. The founding chapter in Deruffillum had settled on that name some ten years ago and showed no indication of considering a change. They thought it was a pretty straightforward way of indicating what they were about—useful knowledge, practical, not the sort of old legends and genealogies and courtly manners they were stuffing young people's heads with these days down at the University of Deruffillum or the University of Breedrup or (grandest and most tradition-bound of all) the University of Homerduk.

The Wizards' Guild was the only transnational organization in the world,[14] and the universities were their creation. It had been a natural progression. For centuries every king—and at one time Calema had had a king for every island and every large valley and almost every crossroads town—every king had to have a wizard in his court. It was a status thing, like having a contingent of Brogoran bodyguards. The wizard knew the correct interpretation of

---

14   Still unaware that they live on a planet, Calemans don't feel any special need of a name for it. They live, of course, in "the world," which is everything there is—well, except for the stuff in the sky, which you can't do anything about.

the dance of the moons and the flocking of birds. He knew potions and charms, and a great many useful poisons. He practiced leap-sight and mind-delving and occult persuasion. All these practices remained tightly guarded mysteries. A wizard was no one to be trifled with.

The Wars of Consolidation[15] eliminated lots of kings but none of the wizards. In fact, in those troubled times, they multiplied, making themselves indispensable to every minor nobleman who could afford it. The Guild was created as the way of parceling up the rapidly changing territory, and of limiting the occasions of poisoning each other to only the most necessary cases. Once they had a guild, the cumbersome system of apprenticeship and apprentice exchange could be jettisoned in favor of "universal training" in a few large cities.

And so, "universities." Now that they had visible symbols of the majesty and brilliance of the Guild, it was necessary that these be maintained in the appropriate style. Collecting dues from the member wizards never really worked out. Everyone, as it turned out, was in exceptional circumstances. All the time. Where was the money to come from?

And here the Guild worked their greatest magic of all: they created a beautiful idea. It was more of a dream, an ideal, a goal so lofty one could only claim to approach it, never to have attained it. And they gave the dream a term: *The Great Knowledge.* So you've taught your son to collect the rents and command the servants

---

15   Two to three centuries ago. In these modern days there was a single king for almost every continent. The uneasy split between North and South Gadgerus had yet to be resolved. And of course, the backward Dabbians hadn't got around to their War of Consolidation at all.

and ride his horse without falling? What will he do when he comes together with his fellow nobles and he *doesn't know what they're talking about*? They'll all happily be discussing philosophy and art and classic literature and who knows what else. And quick as a wink they'll see—your Junior doesn't have *The Great Knowledge.* Oh, mortification!

The Guild's universities sold The Great Knowledge by the bucketful. The old apprenticeship program for wizarding became a separate, advanced program for only the select few. Now they could look over all the noble youth of the land and recruit only those who were the brightest and most enterprising and who *could keep a secret* to be the next generation of wizards.

And so when the best minds of Dab got together to try to build on this new thing that had come up during the Great War—this thing of creating new devices, making old devices better, *experimenting* instead of just believing what the ancient masters said—they needed a word for it. "Tinsmithing" hardly covered it anymore. They were finding they could do this experimenting in all sort of pursuits, not just making weapons. This was so practical, so immediate, so un-philosophical, so unlike what the wizards were teaching, what else could it be but "The Lesser Knowledge?"

THE LONG HALL seemed deserted when the Duke and Count hurried in. It took Arumbeed a moment to locate his guests who, instead of admiring the tapestries or pillaging Matron Deebee's refreshments along the Long Table, were all congregated in a tight knot at the far end of the hall. As the Duke made his approach, the voices of his guests became audible, so that, contrary to good form, he overheard a great deal too much conversation before he was able to be a part of it.

"But surely Your Ladyship is not suggesting that this *island* copper is suitable for making good Dabbian bronze."

"I heard they use only slaves in the mines."

"And they keep the poor wretches perpetually inflamed with (a stage whisper) Foxfoot!"

"What utter bosh!" This was spoken by an imperious contralto voice. A voice that seemed accustomed to being the final word in any discussion, and accustomed to being heard and obeyed. The Duke of Haflum was brought up short in his tracks. "They give them Muzzy petals to keep them all docile."

"But My Lady, how can they work?"

"Very badly, I can assure you. Many of them were missing hands or feet."

By this time the Duke had regained his senses and reached the circle. Some of the gentlemen stepped aside with a deferential nod and a murmured, "Your Grace." He found himself suddenly face to face with the Marchioness.

"What? You've actually *been* to Stony Island?"

This was not the speech he had prepared.

This was his first meeting with Her Ladyship Hathet Damberell, Marchioness of Frolirillum. She was reported to be a woman of quite singular interests. Upon the death of the Marquis, rather than remarrying or devoting herself to genteel works of charity, as good form would dictate, she had invested the better part of her fortune in a small fleet of merchant ships and set about establishing a web of business relationships that now encompassed four of the civilized continents as well as most of the new islands. Rumor had it she was fabulously wealthy.

Ordinarily such freakish behavior would have placed her well outside the Duke's circle of acceptable acquaintances, fortune or no. But then Lady Hathet professed an interest in The Lesser Knowledge. More than that, she personally supported a workshop up in Frolirillum that was reported to be doing *nothing but* experimentation. Every day. All the Lesser Knowledge bigwigs in Deruffillum spoke well of her. And now she had requested to attend this meeting—*his* meeting. He couldn't imagine why, but then, it was beyond him why this woman would do anything she did.

"Your Grace," she said gravely, and executed a sweeping curtsy in the grand style of a century past, nearly bowling over a hapless baronet on the port side. When her eyes were once again raised to his, he thought he saw a gleam of amusement there. That was troubling.

Old habit carried him through the moment. "Your Ladyship," he said with a hurried bow. "Welcome to Hafswide Castle."

"Is it true this is the very place they first used the Hafswide thresher? A marvelous invention!"

The Duke's inquiry on the comfort of her travels died before it was spoken. He gaped instead. Thresher? He had *seen* the contraption. Noisy and dusty as he recalled. What the devil did a gentleman care about a thresher?

"I saw one last summer and tried to get my men to make one, but something was off. Simply fell to pieces! I'll just have to have another look while I'm here, I suppose." And all the men standing around laughed as if she had told a whopping good tale. Was this seemly? Should he apologize for their boisterous behavior?

The truly puzzling thing was she looked like a lady—that is, like a respectable matron of a certain age of the upper nobility of Dab ought to look. Too tall perhaps, and she refused to slouch like most women with such a handicap would do. Not overweight, but "wide-beamed" as the sailors say. Strong features—high brow, firm chin, wide-set eyes—and a ready smile. There she was, smiling at him again!

"Some refreshment, My Lady?" he asked, and turned quickly. "Gentlemen! Please, help yourselves. We'll be wanting to get to the demonstrations soon."

The chief activity of the Society of Lesser Knowledge lay with the demonstrations. Sometimes the members have to put up with a bore, especially if he were of the upper nobility, who simply wanted to give a speech, but it was understood that we were here to *see* something.

Torvum allowed himself a touch of pride with the notion that he arranged these evenings with just a bit of . . . he didn't want to call it *flair*. That would not be appropriate for the gravity of his position. But a certain tasteful *style* then. Each demonstration ought to leave an impression.

And so he had the young Viscount Parig Nain out on the front sweep with his "flame ejector." Nain was always keen on weaponry. This was basically a Zimmer spire on a stick that, if everything went right, would eject a bright blue column of flaming Toop oil for a distance of several feet. Parig's devices were always crowd-pleasers; Torvum had given permission to the children of the staff to stand a respectful distance away on the lawn to watch.

It came off well, which is to say nothing valuable was set on fire. The triggering mechanism—a stub of smoldering spongewood snapped forward to the back of tube—worked about half the time. And his flame-proofing for the inside of the tube actually lasted for three ejections before the tube itself erupted in a great orange ball of flame—at which point the children applauded, and the adults retreated to the inside of the house.

The Marchioness seemed quite amused with Count Spood and his Emanation Box. Like everyone, she couldn't resist the urge to sing into it and see the strings dance to the tune. Spood was happy to explain: it was all to do with the special mix of Cariv fur and slimp fiber in the strings. Very sympathetic to emanations.

"And what do you use it for?"

The Count's eyes lit up with the feverish glow of the Truly Committed. "Bird calls, My Lady! Did you know that the male Spood Nuthatch has five distinct mating calls, depending, apparently, on his perception of himself? Or that Spood's Argue actually inverts the calls of other species in order to confuse and frighten them away?"

"I did not know that."

"No one did! But with this device one can *plainly see* every nuance of a bird's song. I've scored them all, you know." He paused significantly. Receiving nothing but a blank look from his interlocutor, he modulated his enthusiasm. "That means I committed them to paper. Of course, I had to create an entirely new system of musical notation to do so, but that was a simple matter."

"Mm-hm."

Spood elaborated on the subject of bird calls. The Marchioness, staring into the ever-transforming Emanation Box and listening to Spood's monotonous[16] voice, was falling into a mild hypnotic state.

The Duke came to her rescue. "I'm about to show the carriage," he said. "It's in the back court."

The Marchioness shook her head and blinked. "Yes, yes of course."

There were other, lesser demonstrations going on in the smaller halls. They were making their way along a particularly dimly lit and poorly decorated hallway (strange, thought the Duke, that he should notice this just now), when Lady Damberell came to a sudden stop. "Whatever is that smell?" she asked. It was a powerful, musky, piney smell, not unpleasant.

"Oh, now let's not . . ." the Duke began, but it was too late.

"Hello," the Marchioness said, poking her head in a door. "And what are we demonstrating here?"

The man she was addressing was stirring a pan resting on a heated stone in the middle of a long table strewn with various plants. He was leaning over so far that he seemed to be stirring the pan with his own wispy beard. Moment by moment he lifted the spoon to examine the precise state of the brown liquid.

"It's almost there," he whispered. The few gentlemen in the room laughed nervously and exchanged glances.

The Duke of Haflum assumed his full height. "My Lady," he said stiffly, "May I introduce . . . Mr. Chumber Sackman." It

---

16   How sadly ironic.

pained him to make this sort of introduction. So bare. So incomplete. This man, whom the conventions of hospitality and gracious living were now forcing him to introduce to Her Ladyship, this man had no title.

The Society had been firm on this point. "We are concerned purely with knowledge, not with titles. Every man's accomplishments will make a place for him." All very grand. Those wide-buckled dandies in Deruffillum, I'll wager, never had the owner of the village livery stable standing in their drawing room and talking to their guests.

"Ah," said Chumber, and quickly tipped the contents of the pan onto a broad wooden tray, spreading the liquid thinly and evenly with the spoon.

The Marchioness stepped forward for a closer look. "It is clear now," she said.

"Perfectly clear," the commoner intoned significantly. "Seeds . . ."

"Oh, dear," said the Duke.

"Seeds! The greatest mystery of this world. The mystery of life, of transformation from dead stuff to living. We see it all around us and so we are dull to it. But it is a true miracle, My Lady. Every seed—the Gripweed seed, the humble barley seed—even when it is a dry shell and dead as . . . as this plank, it has the key of Life!"

He paused as if to allow everyone a moment of silent reflection.

"Seeds," said Lady Damberell helpfully.

"This substance is made from an extract of Sarum beans. I am still cataloging the properties." He tapped the clarified liquid, which now seemed to be hardened. Without further ceremony he flipped the wooden plate over and what seemed to be a pane of clear glass clattered to the table.

"Careful!" said the Duke.

"Not to worry, Your Grace. It won't break. I don't know that it *can* break. I haven't finished my analysis."

Analysis. It was a new-fangled Society of Lesser Knowledge word. It seemed a little preposterous coming from the lips of this dumpy, fumbling, thoroughly common tradesman. The Duke stifled a chuckle. "Well, now, imagine. Glass that doesn't break! This might actually prove to be useful, my good man."

Chumber was holding the sheet up to the lamplight, looking for imperfections. He turned to the Duke with the sheet still in front of him, rendering his head for the moment distorted into something like a frog's head. "It is *all* useful," he said with a modest assertion of dignity. "If you can just get to the heart of the matter."

"Your Grace, here you are!" It was Dottie at the door. As the Duke turned to her, his lordly manner came back to him. You could see it in the set of his chin. Dottie quickly curtsied, careening lightly off the right doorpost, and then, seeing Her Ladyship, she went down again and, encountering the left doorpost, ended by floundering backward and somewhat falling into the arms of a passing Sir. "I'm sorry, Sir," she trilled.

"That's all right, Dottie. Awfully narrow hallway here anyway." Dottie was a great favorite with the gentlemen at these gatherings. "Hello, Your Grace, Your Ladyship. I hear they're giving the carriage a spin out back."

"That's what I . . . Wait, I had a tray." With one finger at her pursed lips Dottie pivoted and looked doubtfully up and down the hall.

"Back in the Rose Room, I think. I'll help you look," said the Sir, trailing after Dottie as her quick feet carried her away from the Duke's displeasure.

"Shall we go?" The Duke offered his arm. Once they were out of the house, the Duke offered a quiet apology. "He means well. He does turn up with unusual plants from time to time. But poor Chumber is really quite—shall we say, eccentric—when he gets on the subject of his seeds. Something of a crackpot really. But harmless."

"I found it interesting."

"It's very kind of you to say so."

Lefton had the matched set of four bays hitched to the carriage. The outside lamps were turned up their brightest, despite the fact that rosy sunlight was still filtering in through the trees in the Duke's park. The carriage's brass embellishments fairly glowed.

"She's awfully long," said a voice from the crowd.

"Turns like a dream!" Lefton called from his place on the box beside the coachman. "Watch!"

There were murmurs of appreciation from the more knowledgeable of the onlookers as Grabble the coachman coaxed the big bays into taking a sharp angle right, and the carriage pivoted to follow. He brought the carriage smartly around in a complete circle and set off at a trot along the wide back sweep.

The Duke and his lady guest were let through to the front rank of the viewers. "We've prepared quite a demonstration!" he said, barely repressing the urge to explain more.

"Look out!" somebody said. Others joined in a chorus of warnings. Logs had been embedded in the sweep at irregular distances, and the course of the carriage was going to take the wheels directly over these obstacles. In response, Grabble flicked the reins to bring the horses to a faster trot.

The groaning of the crowd came to a crescendo as the wheel hit the first log. The carriage tipped up slightly on that side and came back down to a level and steady keel without slackening its pace. The same happened as every obstacle was encountered. The crowd burst into cheers and shouts of amazement. They had been prepared to see Grabble and Lefton bounced from the box and for the carriage to swing and shudder like a ship in a storm. Grabble brought the carriage smartly around the turnabout at the end of the house and came parading back to the audience.

"What kind of chains are you using?" someone shouted.

"No chains at all!" Lefton answered. "It's lightly tempered memory steel!"

Some men had already gone to all fours to get a look under the carriage. "Those curvy bars there? The carriage is suspended on steel bars? It ought to jolt like the dickens!"

"Memory steel!" Lefton repeated. "Just watch. Watch how they work." He swung down from the box to the passenger step and then set the carriage to bouncing, just as he had done with Dottie. The gentlemen peering at the underside of the carriage voiced their approval.

A rather foppish-looking fellow, complete with the walking stick and enormous tri-corner hat that were the latest rage down in Deruffillum, was trying to get Lefton's attention. He had been mincing around the carriage but couldn't bring himself to get on his knees and soil his fine, iridescently green breeches.

"Oh, young man, young man!" he called, waving a lace handkerchief. He had that upper-crust Shalkin accent which every right-thinking Dabbian man considered prissy and every woman swooned over and thought was ever-so-sophisticated. At last he got too close to Lefton to be ignored.

"Young man—oh, this is just thrilling—young man, where did this metal, this 'memory steel,' come from?"

"There's a blacksmith down Stafswide way who came up with it. Trying to make an unbreakable sword, but this was what he came up with."

"How dreadfully clever."

The twilight was deepening. The Marchioness bid the Duke farewell and pledged to come to other meetings when she could. The gentlemen visitors began to thin out, congratulating the Duke on another roaring success of a Society of Lesser Knowledge meeting. A gentleman, a successful merchant who lived abroad and "dabbled a little in Lesser Knowledge" and came to these meetings when he could, approached the Duke once he was alone. Was it true he had also made a "clicking device?" He thought he had heard something about it.

"Oh, that's the Self-Regulating Drummer. Just a silly notion, I suppose. Something for a man who cares that his horses trot along at the proper pace. I think he left it inside the carriage."

When the merchant climbed in the carriage, he found it already occupied. The fop from Shalk was there, as well as some minor noble from the far side of Dab. The fop was holding the Self-Regulating Drummer, which was clicking merrily away.

"Hello, Meggy, Stum. It's just us then? Oh, well. Mind if I have a look?"

Meggy handed it over. "Here you go, Reeg."

Reeg turned it over a few times. "Nice. Very nice."

"Young Lefton is a fine craftsman."

"He should go far." Meggy sighed and stood up. "Gentlemen, it is getting late."

MEGGY TOLLUM, WHO in his Human life went by Markus 210 Kleinhoffer Choraboru[17] 1331, had a long carriage ride—in his bumpy old un-springy carriage—back to Deruffillum. Soon his driver had them trundling along the old river road, the longer and less-used route. Meggy put his head out the window and saw deep darkness all around, save for the flickering glow of the headlamps. He sat back in the seat and kicked off his fabulously buckled shoes. By now the supercilious simper he had been sporting the whole evening at the Duke's had faded away. He was completely serious. He closed his eyes and composed his thoughts.

The code for accessing his link and calling in a report was four numbers, an object, four numbers, a word. He quieted his mind and thought clearly about each number and thing in its turn. After a brief pause he had his response, the tiniest of vibrations. It would not have been noticeable at all, except that it was coming from the back of his skull. He was On.

"The report on the meeting of the Society of Lesser Knowledge of Hafswide. Today." He was whispering quite faintly, in Shalkin-accented Human. He recited with dry exactness the entire guest

---

17 A Tumba name.

list and then cataloged the demonstrations, also naming who was present at each, and who asked questions. Then came a long accounting of who was seen talking with whom.

At the end he came to the Duke's new carriage. "This Lefton Steep has found a local blacksmith capable of making spring steel. I will follow up with a visit to Stafswide soon. And it appears that young Steep has already designed two very useful springs: the leaf spring for the carriage and the spiral wound spring for his 'Self-Regulating Drummer.' This 'Drummer' is in fact a perfect prototype for a spring-wound timepiece. A great leap forward indeed, for all manner of scientific work.

"Unfortunately it was only I and two of my fellow spies who were there to appreciate his achievement. End Report. Good night, Timo."

Chapter 4 • CHUMBER'S SHACK

The Sulphur Swamp was deep in the Night Forest, upwind, on most days, of Hafswide and everything else that suggested civilization. It was Chumber Sackman's favorite place in the world. After so many years of tromping around in its muck and undergrowth, he had lost a good deal of his sense of smell. Sometimes he would just look around and marvel at how he seemed to have the whole place to himself.

The Sulphur Swamp had its own heating system, a network of hot springs that gurgled up a steady supply of hot water in an assortment of fragrances, leaving much of the swamp perpetually shrouded in a slightly yellow-tinged fog. The plant life of Dabby loved it, reveled in it. Here were hundreds of species unknown to the rest of the planet. It was Chumber's life mission to catalog them all.

Chumber's semi-waterproof boots had given up the struggle for the day; his wool socks were now soaked and rolled down around his ankles. It was a familiar sensation and didn't especially bother him. He was having a good day. Three potential new plant varieties already! He would have to get back to his laboratory before he could be certain, of course.

Hey now, this droopy-stalked weed with the milky excretions looked a lot like a Tumbledown Shoot, but these leaves had a serrated edge to them. He snapped one off to get a better look. It wasn't until he had to bring it extra close to his eyes that he realized the fog must be rising. Was it that late? Better get back to the lab before darkness fell.

He pulled up the whole plant and stuffed it into his already-fat sack. As he turned, something poked a hole through his boot. His foot came out of the boot when he lifted it, as if the boot had been nailed to the squishy muck below the few inches of water in which he was standing. He reached down and felt. There was the root, poking into the side of his boot. It was just a tiny thing, but he couldn't seem to snap it off. He took his stubby knife and sawed on it. When he lifted the knife up, the bright edge was gone, as if he had been grinding it on a stone.

Ironroot! Could it be? He had seen it in some old collections, but nobody knew where it came from. It was harder than iron, actually, and it was only because of its usually gnarled shape that people called it a "root." It was a beast to work with, but if you happened to have a piece in the right shape for your purpose, it would wear forever.

He reached down with both hands now and burrowed into the mud, feeling along the root, following it as it snaked a path back to an island choked and overflowing with briars and vines. The root seemed to be getting softer here as well as larger. He knelt in the water and mud and heaved on the root, fetching up a tangle of other growth with it. Now at last he saw it, a jet-black, veiny rope among the pale fingerlings of the other roots.

A few more tugs, and he was forcing his head and shoulders through the outer wall of briars. He came to the host plant, a low clump of purplish leaves with stalks poking through. And on the stalks were a few withered flowers and lots of bulbous pods with . . . seeds!

The Ironroot seeds were pale, almost white, and slightly cleft into two rounded lobes, like the Mishymash Beans he had eaten as a child. He gathered two handfuls of them. He scratched his hands and face on the briars poking deeper into the patch. When he couldn't see any more through the gloom and gathering fog, he staggered to his feet. He could barely see to recover his lost boot from the water.

It was a good thing he knew the Sulphur Swamp like he did. For the last bit he was really just feeling his way along the winding path to the laboratory.

Well, "laboratory," to him. The few others who ever chanced to see it inevitably called it a shack. He lit a lamp and then another and then a couple of Greasewood shims for good measure. This was an Occasion. He had a rough worktable made of salvaged pier planks. The Ironroot beans he put in a bowl to keep them from rolling off the table.

The beans, despite their humble appearance, proved as hard as, well, Ironroot. His knife couldn't cut them, his hammer just sent them caroming off the walls. By wedging one into a crack in the table and whacking it with a piece of flint he got a small shower of sparks. The beans seemed impervious to water or alcohol. Something, of course, had to be able to soften these up. They were no good as seeds if their mysterious insides couldn't be reached. Some substance in the viscous black ooze that stood in for dirt in the Sulphur Swamp must be the key to penetrating this shell.

Chumber had furnished his lab with the chipped and cracked dishes of his wife's discarded tea set. Now he set out a row of saucers and placed one bean in the center of each.

On shelves lining one wall he had his "potions," precious glass bottles of every size and shape and color, filled with his own concoctions. He took down half a dozen bottles and carefully placed a drop from each on the lined-up beans. No reaction. He washed and dried the beans and thought some more.

This time he used bottles marked with a skull. The fifth one down began to hiss and smoke. He checked the label of the bottle. "Shalla Poison." He had distilled it himself from Shalla berries; good for cleaning bricks. After a minute or so, an opaque brown liquid began to leach out and puddle around the bean. Smoke was coming out of the liquid. He could feel heat as well. He got up and opened the window flaps.

By the time he got back to his stool, the liquid had vaporized entirely, leaving a shriveled husk where the bean had been, surrounded by a lumpy residue of brown dust. He blew on it, the dust swirled away, and he saw flashes of something bright and green. He blew again. This time he heard a very high hum, so high that he thought at first it was coming from inside his head. The brown dust flew away, and he saw small green dots scattered across the saucer.

He fished a pair of tweezers out of his workbox and gently brought one of the green dots up to his eye. It was a crystal, bright and fine and sharply defined as any gemstone. He blew on it and heard the high humming again. He could feel a faint vibration through the tweezers.

Jewels from seeds! If only he could produce them in a larger size! He hunted up his largest serving dish and poured the remaining beans in. His hand trembling only a little, he poured on the whole bottle of Shalla poison.

He stepped back. An eerie whistling seemed to emanate from the air around him . . . no, wait. That was a Screamer Bat passing over the roof. A minute crawled by. Was it doing anything? He picked up a lamp and held it close. Now he could just see a tendril of smoke creeping over the side of the dish and coiling to the floor. All right. There was the hissing.

The Shalla poison was starting to hurt his eyes. He stepped outside, leaving the door open. The hissing inside was getting a little alarming. He pumped the door to help the air move through. The creaking of the bronze hinges joined in with the night sounds of the Sulphur Swamp, and the flashes of lamplight from the doorway made a peculiar stop-action show of the fog rolling through his little clearing.

"You're not going to blow up your shack again, are you?" The voice came from the deep darkness under the trees.

Chumber stopped with the door swung open. "I don't think so," he called into the darkness. "But it smells kind of bad right now."

A figure emerged through the fog. "I'll just stand over here then."

"Hi, Giggerum. What brings you out here in the middle of the night?" Giggerum Sudge was a cobbler in Hafswide and Chumber's best friend. Mr. Sudge made it a policy to steer clear of Lesser Knowledge and Great Knowledge alike, lumping both activities under the ominous title of "meddlin'." He was awfully proud of Chumber though, mixing with the gentle folk up at the castle.

"The roan is foaling. Gladsome sent me out to get you." Gladsome was Chumber's wife.

"Tonight? That's early."

"Yup. She was thinking it could be a tricky birth." The roan mare had been a big investment for the livery business, one of those fancy-stepping horses from Shalk. Chumber's boys took care of most of the regular business these days, but a hard foaling . . .

"Give me a minute." Chumber peered inside. No more hissing, but the smoke was still pretty thick. He pulled a handkerchief from his pocket and covered his mouth. He ran in and lingered for just a moment over the still-smoking dish. Just a bowlful of lumpy dust at the moment. He snuffed out the two lamps. One Greasewood shim had already burned down to a stub. He picked up the other and stepped out.

The light from the shim wasn't much more than a firebug glimmer in the pressing darkness of the swamp. But Chumber and Giggerum knew the way home from here.

Fifteen minutes later a breeze came up and blew the last of the smoke from the shack. It sent up a small cloud of dust from the dish on the table. The room started to hum.

UNU'S OFFICE ON the Gassplat didn't look like an office to anyone except her or, theoretically, to any other Corgurid who might ever visit. It was little more than a narrow box of a room with a platform on which she assumed the tuck-legged Practical Thinking

Position of her species. The large, office-sized reader in her hand was the only equipment present, and even that she put to little use, preferring to perform most operations in her head.

She was analyzing the data on current Gadgerene-Shalkin trading patterns when a flashing red dot appeared in the corner of the reader. She gave it a tap. "NOTICE OF UNUSUAL PLANET ACTIVITY" the caption said, and then "Dab, Deruff Kingdom" followed by a set of coordinates. Below it was a live satellite image of the area. It was nighttime in that part of the world, but the image seemed to show a brilliant yellow light coming from space and focusing on a tiny patch of ground. No, on second thought, the light was coming from the ground itself. A volcano? There hadn't been any signs.

Various words appeared, superimposed on the image: "Temperature characteristics," "Nearby features–geological," "Nearby features – Leeban." The words "Chemical Composition" appeared as well, but remained flashing. She tapped it the moment the flashing stopped. The reader became a densely detailed swirl of lines and colors, with columns of text below.

One particular broad band of color told her the story in an instant. She drew in her breath sharply—as close as Corgurids ever came to screaming in panic. So great was her consternation she had to read the complete text twice more before she could allow herself to believe it.

"It can't be here," she whispered. "Not on this planet. Not even in this sector." Her fingers fluttered across the reader as if on their own. Mack appeared. He turned to look at her, with some surprise.

"This must be something big," he said. His smile disappeared when he saw her face.

THE CELESTIAL OBSERVATORY on the roof of the University of Strammang was normally a peaceful place. It was a place for quiet, thoughtful work, carried out in near-darkness. There were no telescopes at this time, only a scattering of dimly lit enclosed booths where the wizards and wizards-in-training could repair to consult charts or make calculations while keeping the illumination from affecting the vision of the observers.

It was around midnight, and Chancellor Undertower was just emerging from the stairwell and panting heavily from the climb.

"Um, mind your . . ." one of the younger observers began. The thump and mild expletive that followed told him his warning was too late. This was an ancient building, and the passageways seemed to have been made for a much smaller race of people. The outline of the Chancellor appeared against the stars, one hand on its forehead.

"All right then, where's Derving?" The Chancellor said crossly. "Derving? Is that you?"

"He's over there, sir." Someone was pointing to the northeast corner of the roof. "Everybody's over there."

Undertower straightened his robe and arranged his face into the scowl that had quelled a hundred faculty committee rebellions. He was getting too old for this kind of foolishness. He marched toward the grouping of men in the corner, letting his shoes thump with baleful significance on the tiles beneath.

"Derving, what's this nonsense about a prophecy? If this is some underclassman prank, I'll . . ."

No one had taken the slightest notice of him. They were still looking away to the northeast. Rising above their heads was a pulsating shaft of orange light that rose far into the sky. The Chancellor took up a place at the end of the row.

One of the young scholars was peering through a skyscriber, a sort of sextant. "It's risen four degrees since I got here," he announced quietly.

"How long?" the Chancellor asked the man next to him, speaking in respectfully hushed tones now.

"About fifteen minutes. Oh, hello, Gerund."

"Derving."

"They're saying it's Drebbell's Ladder."

"I suppose it *could* pass as a 'ladder of fire, reaching to heaven.'"

"What else could it be?" said a quavering old voice from among the watchers.

"It's the sign," someone else said.

"Five degrees," said the lad with the skyscriber.

"Thank you, Shamgath."

"What should we do?"

"Drebbell didn't say."

"A ladder of fire."

"The end of the world."

"Well then," said the Chancellor, and stopped when he saw every man turn to face him. They were waiting for him. They were afraid. They were waiting for the wisdom and gravity of a great wizard. It was one of those moments that plumb the depths of the soul.

"Well then. If it *is* the end of the world, we'll want to get the paperwork right."

Chapter 5 • THE BIG HOLE

CHUMBER AND GIGGERUM had just reached the Cart Road and turned toward Hafswide when, as Giggerum would put it later, "the sun come up in the middle of the night." In an instant they were standing in a cheery yellow light as bright as mid-morning. Fifty feet away, a stumpweasel was standing in the middle of the road, blinking at them, caught in mid-slink. The men turned and saw a tower of yellow flame that disappeared into the sky.

"Why can't we hear it?" Giggerum wondered out loud.

"Sound travels slower than light," Chumber said, happy to have, for the moment, something in the realm of the Lesser Knowledge to talk about. "Wait." He began counting under his breath.

The sound hit. They had been expecting something like continuous thunder, but this was more of a dull roar, like a waterfall.

"So how far away is it?" Giggerum asked.

"Three-and-a-half miles." Their eyes met. Chumber nodded solemnly.

"What manner of meddlin' have you been up to then, Chumber?"

"Just seeds, like always. They are powerful things. I need to go see this."

"Are you crazy? We'll be cooked! I can feel the heat from here!"

"You go on home then, Giggerum. I can't ask you to come with me. This is . . . a phenomenon. Serious Lesser Knowledge stuff. It's my duty to go observe it if I can." He took a step or two in the direction of the flame tower.

Giggerum stepped with him. "You'd be observing your stove from the inside if somebody didn't stop you! Well, I suppose I'm a good enough friend to hold onto your shirt if you go to pitch yourself into a phemonon. I'll do the observing with you, Chumber Sackman, and don't try to stop me."

"Thank you, Giggerum." Chumber hesitated. It seemed an occasion for a few fine words, like His Grace the Duke spun in such abundance at the Solemnities.

Giggerum just scowled. "Let's get going then," he said.

The flame tower collapsed and disappeared before they made it halfway back, producing a great, rippling clap of thunder before plunging them into darkness. It was slow going from there. Chumber went in front, feeling his way along the familiar path, with Giggerum keeping a firm grip on his shirttail.

Once they got close, they had all the light they needed. A ring of burning trees perhaps half a mile in radius served as a gigantic bullseye for the site. The flames didn't seem to be expanding; the Sulphur Swamp had powerful reserves of dampness to bring to this fight. But inside the ring was a charred, smoking desolation.

The hissing sound they had been hearing for the past ten minutes was soon explained: at the center of the fire ring a dense cloud of steam was billowing out of the ground. Giggerum pulled back on Chumber's shirttail. "Are you crazy?" he said. "Can't you feel the heat?"

The heat from the steam was indeed oppressive. "Oh, right. I guess so," Chumber said. 'Just a minute." He looked around and spotted a rivulet of char-blackened water winding a tortuous path toward the steam cloud. He pulled a couple of rags from his pack and lumbered (movement is difficult with a terrified cobbler attached to your shirt) to the water. He soaked the rags in the water and handed one to Giggerum. The other he tied around his face, leaving just a narrow slit for his eyes between the rag and his hat.

The two of them edged closer to the steam cloud by slow degrees. "I don't believe this is your place after all," Giggerum said, the words coming in short bursts with lots of panting in between. "This is all down in some valley."

"This is it. The flame must have eaten out the ground underneath so it all dropped down a bit. Look, here's the Twisty Gum Tree where the path breaks off. Where it used to break off." He laid his hand on the sheared-off trunk of a tree in a once-familiar shape. It was crusty black, riven with fissures and leaning crazily away from the steam hole.

"Yeah, but, that would put your shack over on the other side." He pointed.

"No, look at the curve. It's making a perfect circle. And I'd guess about . . . two hundred feet across. That puts my laboratory right in the middle."

"Well, all the dancing gods. I've heard some tall tales about magic beans . . ."

"Oh, Giggerum there's no . . ." At that moment the trunk of the Twisty Gum Tree snapped off, and Chumber staggered and nearly fell. Giggerum caught him under the arms and began dragging him away from the steam hole. Chumber got his feet under him and started staggering away from the hole too.

Once past the fire line, which was already dying down from the mist dropping out of the steam cloud, they found their way to a muddy slough and threw themselves in. The water here was warm and smelled of rotten eggs, but at least it was wet. They dragged themselves onto the muddy bank and panted for a good long while.

"Giggerum, I've got a big favor to ask."

"If you want me to keep this a secret, I don't think it's going to work. You could've seen that all the way to Deruffillum."

"Further than that, I think. I just mean, don't tell anybody it was at my shack."

"Now Chumber, if you're worried somebody's going to complain about the damage, well shoot, it's just the Sulphur Swamp."

"It's not that. I'm worried somebody might want to figure out how to do it themselves."

"You think so? Is the world really that crazy?"

"It just might be."

THE VILLAGE OF Hafswide exists chiefly because an ancient Duke of Haflum didn't want the Cart Road to cut through his park. This was many generations ago, when actually planning which way a road went was a newfangled idea and possibly a threat to the natural order. So the Cart Road took a sharp right turn in the middle of a rolling sheep meadow close to the Duke's estate, and somebody put up an inn. They figured, correctly, that future cart drivers would be put out just enough by the unnecessary detour that they would want to call it a day and knock back a tankard or two of good Dabbian ale while complaining about it.

So the Big Swide Inn ("swide" meaning "pull over" in Old Deruff) came first. The village straggled along afterward, filling in with extra services for travelers and for the Duke's tenants, as housing for the Duke's tradesmen and as a place for the yeoman-farmers of Haflum to exchange their extra barley and wool and eggs for fancier things.

This morning the door to the Inn could hardly stop swinging. Everybody in town wanted to air their theory about last night's Big Light. There was a good deal of talk about "signs." But Dabbians not having very developed beliefs about the end of the world, it didn't appreciably raise the anxiety level in this room. On the contrary, there was a distinctly holiday air to the occasion. Several of the bolder talkers wanted to get up an expedition right away to go and investigate.

"Don't be crazy!" said an old codger in the corner. "It's up in the mountains a hundred miles away at least!"

"Gods, if it was making such a racket here, think of the poor people over in Gabberlum!"

"What's the matter with you folks? Don't you have eyes in your heads? It wasn't more than twenty miles from here!"

"It was approximately six miles east-southeast of my estate." That was Count Spood, speaking in his usual prim tones and stirring his cup of brown tea. When the room fell silent, he looked up in surprise.

"You've been there, then!"

"He's a good sight braver than he looks!"

"Of course, I haven't *been* there," Spood continued, a little affronted at the idea. "It was a matter of simple geometry."

There was a quick exchange of quizzical looks around the room. "All right, Your Honor, I'll bite," said a farmer with a wry grin on his face. "How did your Geeom Tree tell you how far away the fire was?"

"No, no, gentlemen, this is not an attempt at wordplay. *Geometry*. While the fire was going, I noted the angle of the blaze, paced off one thousand yards on the Cart Road, and noted the angle again, which had been altered by five-and-a-half degrees. Well, there you have it."

Argum the innkeeper broke into the puzzled silence that followed. "So, Sir Spood, I'm guessing you walked along the road a bit and watched the fire and you *figure* it's about six miles away. Well all *right* then." He nodded agreeably and most of the room nodded with him. It was often his business to make argumentative folk believe they were in agreement.

"In a manner of speaking. I used figures in order to reach . . ."

"And a fine head for figures you have!" To this Argum raised his cup of thistle tea, and a great many cups and glasses and tankards were drained in the general toast that followed. Argum set himself to refilling them.

"Well, when do you propose to lead us to the spot?" asked the wry-faced farmer.

"What? Me? Why would I want to do such a thing?"

Over the rumble of derision that followed, the voice of Parig Nain rang out. "Come now, Sir Spood," he decried. "Aren't we both men of the Lesser Knowledge? Isn't this 'tower of flame' a rare and astonishing phenomenon that fairly cries out for investigation by men such as ourselves?"

The rest of the men in the room were deeply moved by such oratory, having no trouble at all in reading their own fine persons into the phrase "men such as ourselves." In short order the whole room had decided to set off at once.

"Hey there, Chumber, aren't you coming with us?" said Viscount Nain.

"Ah, well, you know, there's a new foal at the stable . . ."

"You have your boys for that! Come now, I've heard you know the Sulphur Swamp like your own herb garden. Your village needs you, man!" And so it was decided.

THAT IS A very big hole." This analysis was delivered by the jocular farmer as he rocked on his heels at the precipice of a crater having vertical walls and a precisely round perimeter. His companions had made nearly the same observation several times already, but . . . it was *such* a big hole. It needed saying several times.

The crater was indeed about two hundred feet across, and appeared to be at least that deep, although that was hard to say with the pool of water at the bottom. Who knew how deep that water was? A network of rivulets felt their way across the wasteland perimeter to it, making a steady, thin cascade of water that plunged over the edge on all sides, sending up a fine mist that became a shifting cloud bank down below.

Parig was on his stomach and stretched perilously far out over the void. He had a knife in his hand, which he was attempting to drive into the wall of the crater. His efforts were producing a rather musical tinkling sound that flung cascades of echoes around the vast chamber. "It's glass!" he exclaimed. "Extraordinarily thick, clear glass. The whole thing." He swept his arm in a grand circle by way of illustration. Count Spood dropped to his knees and grabbed the man's jacket to keep him from tumbling in.

"Oh, yes. I'm much obliged to you," said the Viscount absentmindedly. "What sort of heat do you suppose it takes to turn dirt into glass?"

No one ventured a guess. The party that had been so boisterous in the forest was a little dumbstruck here on this blasted plain. Most of them had set themselves to the task of walking the whole perimeter of the crater. They were getting pretty thinly scattered. Here it was just Spood and Parig and a couple of villagers. And a very quiet Chumber Sackman, who kept looking out toward the ring of forest around them as much as looking at the big hole.

"I've heard tales of these things," one of the villagers ventured. "Way out there on Black Whale Island. But they're mountains there. 'Fire mountains' they call them. They smoke all the time and they spit up melted rock once in a while."

"Melted rock! You'd believe anything, Glarum."

"No, it's true," said Spood. "I've seen them." He frowned and peered down at the misty pool below. "They weren't very much like this, though."

Chumber spoke up at last. "Do you know what they look like when they start?"

Parig Nain laughed. "No one's ever seen one *start*. They're mountains. They're just *there*."

The villager called Glarum was thinking very hard. "Well then," he said, "If no one's ever seen one start, no one knows what it's *supposed* to look like. Right?" He looked back and forth at the two Sirs, neither of which cared to offer a rebuttal.

The other villager got up the courage to make his first venture into the strange world of Lesser Knowledge. "But this one's going down, not up," he pointed out.

The two Sirs thought about it and nodded gravely in true Lesser Knowledge fashion. "There's that," said Spood.

This was as far as the Lesser Knowledge talk went that day. Except that, as they were leaving the blasted area, Spood observed sadly that a prime bit of the natural habitat of Spood's Crested Tit-pink had been destroyed.

There was an incident shortly after they re-entered the forest. A farmer taking up the rear of the well-dispersed line shouted out, "Ho there! What village are you from then?"

Chumber turned around. "What is it, Nonesuch? Who are you talking to?"

"That man over there. Well, you can't see him now." Nonesuch and Chumber were joined by Viscount Nain, and all three stood peering into the gloom of the Sulphur Swamp forest.

"Perhaps you saw a bear,"[18] Nain said.

---

18   Of course he didn't actually say "bear." A bear is an earth animal, just like the horses back in chapter two. What he saw was a Caleman animal very much like a bear. The horses weren't really horses either. Let's face it, if I stop to explain the precise physiology of every animal and plant along the way, this story would just grind to a halt. So if I say "bear," you just go ahead and picture an earth bear, and you won't be far wrong.

"No bears in these woods," Chumber said impatiently. "What did he look like?"

"Tall. He was just standing there, watching us."

"All right then, how was he dressed?" Nain still sounded skeptical.

"I'll just go see," Chumber said, and stepped off the path and started making his way through the thick underbrush.

"I didn't see his clothes, just his head."

Chumber made plenty of noise getting through the brush and under the branches and vines. He wasn't worried about bears, but it was best to scare away any stumpweasels before you met them. They could run up your trouser leg if they were frightened.

He came to a small open space. There was even a shaft of sunlight slanting in, rather busy with bugs and the fine miasma that passed for air in the Sulphur Swamp. No people. The floor of leaves and twigs might have been a little trampled down. Something had been here once. He bent to take a closer look. He caught his breath.

As a boy, Chumber had played with friends in a limestone cave down by the river. It wasn't much of a cave, but it did have one large room that was far enough from the opening to be always shrouded in deep gloom. There they had played "statues," their own version of hide-and-seek in which all the hiders simply stood still, wherever they were, keeping quiet as they could.

It was that rare game at which Chumber was actually pretty good. They said he had great hearing, but he knew that wasn't it. He didn't really hear them; he felt them. It was a mysterious feeling; he never told his friends about it because it would have sounded a little crazy and, well, he had enough trouble as it was. But the feeling was really a negative one: over there, just past arm's length to the left, was a patch of *not space*. The space wasn't there, and so he knew there was a body instead.

Now the feeling came back to him, strong. There was a patch of *not space* right in front of him. Impossible, of course; it was right where the sunlight played on the ground. But it was that same old, familiar feeling. He could reach right out and touch somebody if he wanted to. Right there. *You're it.*

He stood up straight. Nain and Nonesuch were still standing over there on the path. "Well?" Nain said.

"Nothing! Nobody here!" He reminded himself to smile. And then, for no reason at all, he took one large step to the right before leaving the little clearing. Whatever it was he couldn't see, he sure didn't want to bump into it.

Chapter 6 • BUU

MACK LIKED NORMAL. The greatest disruption in his life, the Tertiary Committee, rolled around every two Standard Planet years. He had faced up to this prospect pretty bravely, he thought, when he took on the Planet Clerk's job. There would be arguments, intrigue, unpleasantness. There would even be tactical nastiness directed at him personally, whenever he had to decide against some powerful interest.

He had accepted that 12.5% of his life would be taken up by sordid politics, in the knowledge that the other 87.5% would sail along to the serene hum of bureaucratic normality. Reports. Research. Arcane scientific panels. Distinguished visitors. And at all seasons there would be time in the day for his life's work, his magnum opus, his gift to history, The Caleman Library.

But things were not normal. In the past two days, at least thirty Unsanctioned Visits had been registered on the logs. The present state of cloaking technology made it absurdly easy for a species to sneak in a quick, off-the-books mission to the surface, but ordinarily the Station Chiefs showed some restraint. They knew that every U.V. was going to generate an official inquest from Mack's office, and those things could drag on for weeks.

But then, Mack hadn't started any inquests at all these past two days. He had been in nearly constant meetings with his superiors.

A Planet Clerk, when his planet is in trouble, discovers he has an apparently infinite number of superiors. The trouble could be summed up in one word.

Buu.

In addressing the complexities of faster-than-light travel, the species of the Gass had dozens of major technological approaches currently in use. Even after thousands of years of free exchange, and pilfering, of ideas, deep-space craft still came in a fantastic assortment of designs. But when it came to old-fashioned rocketry for short-range travel and maneuvering, you just couldn't beat buu gas. No matter how funny the shape of the craft, they all had the familiar buu jets, big and small, poking out on all sides.

It was all weight-to-thrust. A little tank of buu gas no bigger than your fist was enough to push the whole Gassplat to an orbit a mile higher. It burned clean and left no trail of particulate or radiation. It hadn't been improved on in ten thousand years.

By now the analyses were all in. That volcano-like eruption down on the surface was undeniably a buu burn. Calema had buu! Soaps and candles were all very nice, but a planet with buu gas could write its own ticket.

Well, somebody would write its ticket.

For that matter, no one had ever heard of buu gas on a planet before. There were only seven or eight companies mining buu at the moment, and they were all operating on remote asteroids under especially inhospitable conditions—hot interstellar plasma clouds and blue supergiant star systems—places any sensible person flew around, if they could. Those little green crystals that disintegrated into buu gas in the presence of any atmosphere were supposed to be the result of especially mysterious, unreproducible, early-big-bang events.

The great buu rush was on. The big companies already had their exploration teams racing in from around the galaxy. However the Gass parceled it out, they wanted a piece of this action.

Mack's office was an irregularly shaped space squeezed between his living quarters and a life-support module. He had no less than six large Readers arrayed around him, giving him moment-by-moment updates of what Ninthwave® was calling, alternately, the "Calema Crisis" or the "Buu Rush." He was tapping notes into a seventh Reader in preparation for a briefing of the Sub-Committee of Economic Buffering when the visitor note appeared in the corner of all his screens. A non-species-specific voice announced, in Diplomatic Babata, that Timotei 101 Sjogren Thyarohhaefii 1331 was at the door.

Mack finished the sentence he was writing and tapped in the code for opening the door. All his Readers went blank (the Ministry's definition of "classified" was extremely broad) and the door's latch clicked.

"This is an official visit," Timo announced, and stepped in. It was understood that every official space on a Gassplat was under constant monitoring—visual, auditory, olfactory, vital signs, and several other means of communication known to exist in the galaxy.

"Well?"

"I am here to inquire, on behalf of the Human Interest, where the Special Assembly will be held."

"The Directorate still hasn't decided if there will be a Special Assembly. Too many galactilogical experts have built their reputation on theories that don't allow buu to be on a normal planet." He paused, a pained look on his face. "And by 'normal,' I mean ..."

"Yes, yes, I know," Timo said hurriedly. "Class C." "C" was for Corgurid. Timo knew Mack's discomfort was over the Diplomatic Code's thick section on Correct Usage of Terms. The article on the word "normal" was especially sticky going.

Word on the plats was the Protected Planets Directorate was soon to hold a Special Assembly on the subject of Calema. Various interests were already drawing up their briefs—which were not brief at all. There were fortunes to be made beyond all dreams of avarice; this was no time for reticence. Some members of the Directorate had already gone into hiding to escape all their new best friends.

Timo squeezed into an odd nook close by Mack's table and sat on a shelf. He hadn't been in Mack's office many times. He couldn't help looking around and marveling at the drabness, the sheer anonymity of the place. Poor old Mack just didn't know his way around the System. "They're going to have to partition though, aren't they?" he asked.

The correct term for the meeting the Directorate was soon to have was, "Special Assembly on the Articles of Partition." It was the grandest, most solemn, most protocol-riddled event the Gass was capable of producing. These things could go on for years.

The whole idea of "protected status" was that the planet would be left alone by outsiders until it was ready to deal with them as social and technological equals. Not real equals, of course, but at least close enough to pretend. But now there was buu. Calema was the ripest of ripe plums for the picking. Of course the Gass had to step in. Six hundred years of benign and discreet scientific observation were over. It was time to divide the spoils.

"I don't see any way . . ." Mack began.

When a couple of seconds went by with the sentence left unfinished, Timo's gaze returned to the Planet Clerk. Mack's hands were folded on the table before him. His head was bent. It looked almost like he was praying. It was hard to tell, but his eyes might even have been closed. His face was drawn tight, as if he were waiting for a stab of pain to subside.

"Hey, I'm sorry, Mack. I didn't think . . . This must be kind of sad for you."

"Not just for me. For millions of people. For everyone."

"Right, you mean the Leebs. I guess it'll be quite a shock for them all right. But, you know, the PPM has a . . . a program for this. I'm sure in a few years . . ."

"Never. Never." Again the bent head and the pained look.

"Are you all right?"

"Of course not. You shouldn't be, either. Partition, Timo."

"Well, but at least they'll be in the Gass, you know. They should *love* that! I mean, think of all the amazing things they're going to learn. And they'll have the whole galaxy to find out about, and explore!"

"Have you ever heard of Maoodooam?"

"Well sure!" Timo said, brightening at the memory. "I had a little Moaaveeo[19] on my bed like every other kid. I loved that thing."

---

19   A boy Maoodooam, the title character of the children's classic, "Moaaveeo and the Hoppity Village."

"I was there. Maoodooam. It was my first assignment in the Ministry, to monitor the Sababan administration according to the Partitioned Planet Code."

"Oh, I see. Yeah, I've heard the Sababans are pretty ruthless."

"It was a model administration. They bent over backwards. In two years there, I wrote only 131 citations!" Mack paused significantly.

"Umm, wow," Timo said.

Timo knew the bare facts of the matter. On Maoodooam the issue hadn't been natural resources, it had been a simple matter of location. Maoodooam had the misfortune of being right on the dividing line between two especially antagonistic "Galactic Empires." So before these two went to war over it, the Gass brokered a deal to split the habitable territories of Maoodooam into two spheres of influence, with massive Gassian oversight, of course.

The Maoodooama were a herd species: large, slow, gentle creatures with marvelously dark, expressive eyes and that ever-so-marketable wavy golden fur. Before partition their society had been an intricate web of interlocking extended families taking in the whole population of the continent. Every child could recite their place in the Great Ascendance. They had lived simply and communally, gathering under great tents—cleverly woven out of the infinite supply of grass—if the weather was bad but preferring to sleep in the open. Their seasonal migrations had provided each herd with a pleasant rhythm of reunions and partings with the others.

"I was there two Standard Years," Mack continued. "Two years of steady decline."

"I thought the Gass provided lots of material assistance for these things."

"Exactly. Mountains of material. Whole cities of warehouses. All the Maoodooama were working regular jobs—made-up jobs, of course, because what could they supply that the galaxy wants? To work regular jobs, they had to live in cities. In houses. Houses filled with amazing, magical things that did their work for them. Provided for needs they had never known they had."

"What about 'Preservation'?" Timo asked. "Isn't that like, half of what the Ministry is there for?"

"That's the theory. The 'Two Pillars: Preservation and Integration.' We were so high-minded. The code—the Partitioned Planet Code—has more than ten thousand articles on the Preservation side. Beautiful articles, by the way. I was on one of the committees. The happiest days of my life." A faint smile and a faraway look began to steal over Mack's features.

"Well?" Timo said.

"None of it worked. The difference was too great. As soon as their world was touched by the Gass, it started to unravel. No, it dissolved. Like in that commercial. You know, for the Flossian supersolvent."

"Right! Where the tar pit turns to water, and all the animals come out singing, 'Oh-do-ree-do-day! We . . .'"

"Please don't. Don't sing that."

"Sorry."

"The difference was too great. It wasn't just that everything they had known and loved was proved wrong. It was proved *ridiculous*. They were ashamed."

"Ashamed of the Great Ascendance?" Timo looked crestfallen.

"You're thinking of the children's sim[20]."

"Well, it's a great song."

"The real thing is more of a chant. But nobody does it anymore. Unless it's for the tourists."

"No! What *do* they believe in then?"

"They believe in Ninthwave®. When they aren't working their make-believe jobs, they're sitting in their houses and watching other people's lives. Which are so much more interesting than the lives of their friends and brothers and sisters and cousins. *That's* Maoodoama culture now."

Timo's Reader hummed. He looked at it and frowned and put it back in his pocket. Then he pulled it out and looked at it again. He seemed perplexed.

"More news?" Mack asked.

"No. I . . . I have to go." He thought for a moment. "But Calema won't be like that. Because they're further along, right? They'll be able to handle it."

"Yes, they'll 'handle' it. They'll handle it in the worst possible way. If the noble Maoodooamans couldn't handle the shock of partition, where does that leave the greedy, lazy, treacherous, superstitious Leebs? Everything they have will be lost. It will disappear in a generation. Everything we've done will be lost."

"Maybe they'll surprise us."

"They're hardly better than Humans."

---

20   A sim is a kind of intense, interactive movie, delivered directly to the brain. Most species have laws limiting the degree of realism. For humans the restrictions are among the tightest in the Gass, so naturally the illicit sim industry is obscenely profitable.

Timo was still reflecting on that remark when his Reader hummed again. "I have to go," he said, getting up slowly. "Maybe . . . I don't know. Never mind."

A few moments after Timo had gone, Mack's dormant Readers came back to life.

He had a dot. It was Unu. "Oh no. Am I late for another meeting?"

"Not by much. And it isn't official. The Calema Preservationist Society just wants a holograph chat."

"There's a Preservationist Society?"

"It's all over Ninthwave®—a campaign from the Calema Soap people. A billion people have signed up already. Everybody wants to know about the planet on the detergent box. You're kind of a celebrity."

Mack took a moment and attempted to absorb this information. He couldn't. "There's a Preservationist Society?"

"Actually I'm calling because there is activity in Sareemport." This was a major city on the South Gadgerus coast. "A large fleet is setting out. It looks military."

"How large?" As he asked, he tapped the link to the satellite footage.

"Fifty-nine vessels so far. There are more in the process of being launched, and still others en route on the Kamer River."

"And they are headed east," Mack said. They were both silent for a moment. The question—the Big Question—was so obvious it hardly seemed necessary to say it out loud.

"We won't know for sure until they get around Shalk," Mack continued.

"And by then . . ."

"By then it will be too late." Too late to save Dab. The ponderous bureaucratic machinery of partition would take months—years maybe, if somebody wanted to gum up the works. By then the Gadgerenes, and whatever off-world power was secretly arming and advising them, would have made Gadgerus an imperial power once again, and Dab, and all its Buu gas, their private preserve. And that would be the status quo they would be locking into place with partition.

"This is . . . a disaster." Mack ran his hand through his already-disheveled hair. On the reader, Unu's face remained a composed, professional blank. She was awaiting instructions. He was probably embarrassing her with this moment of emotion and indecision. Corgurids place a high value on philosophical detachment.

Sooner or later this girl would probably take over for him as Planet Clerk. Probably sooner, come to think of it. His heart wouldn't be in it once the partition went into effect. Not that that was a requirement. Sometimes it was better if a Planet Clerk did *not* have his heart in it; many a Clerk had run afoul of Gassian policy because of a too-strong emotional attachment to his planet. He was supposed to apply Gass policy with an absolutely even hand, let the chips fall where they may.

Unu was still waiting. Yes, after all, this was a job for a Corgurid, not a Human. Corgurids were so blasted *content*. No one had said anything to him, but he had always suspected his appointment had been something of a test case. *Let's give the Human a chance.* Because Humans, everybody knows, are restless and changeable. Whatever they have, they want something else. "Fringers." That was the undiplomatic term. Those Humans. Fifteen hundred years in the all-encompassing Gassian embrace and still not bought in. Always out on the edges of civilization, looking for . . . something. Or something *else*. Just not reliable.

All right then, he was only Human. Kind of late in the game to be making a career change, but he was single. No close relatives. Nobody would care if he just disappeared into the Gass' wide margin of frontier. He would probably have to do surface work again. He would have to learn to deal with animals—the unauthorized, unpredictable kind. His shoulders gave a spasmodic twitch. He could do it. His jaw began to take on an uncharacteristic firmness. Hell yes, he could do it. His *forebears* (it was a romantic old Human word that for him conjured up visions of covered wagons and noisy firearms) had faced worse. And succeeded. And *conquered*.

"It might not happen, sir."

"What? What?"

"Partition. I am sorry, sir, but if I might be so bold as to interject a personal observation?"

"Huh? No. I mean . . . Okay, be bold."

"Thank you. It may not come to partition, sir. Calema may be preserved after all."

"I don't see how. And even if that miracle should happen, there's this." He waved a hand at the reader. He meant the Gadgerene invasion fleet, but he realized it probably looked stupid. It probably looked like he meant *her*.

"Miracles are a matter of perspective."

He recognized this as one of the inscrutable truisms of Corgurid religion. He never knew what to say with this sort of thing.

"What I mean to say, sir, is simply that none of us here on the plat want partition. We're all doing what we can."

"Of course. Umm. Thank you, Unu. Now, what was this meeting?"

"The Calema Preservationist Society."

"What do they want?"

"They just want to talk with you. You're famous now."

"Yes, but what do they *want*?"

ONCE AGAIN HIS working day went deep into the night[21]. Back in his quarters, he was restless and unfocused. He couldn't even drum up any interest in his current Library project, a treatment of the Gadgerene quadra- and octagods. He rang the Earthplat.

"This is Earth Station Calema, and I am . . . Oh, hello, Mack."

"Hi, Sarah. I'd like to talk with Timo."

"Just a minute. Hmm." She was reading something. "He isn't in. He . . . was recalled to Earth for consultations."

"That's interesting." He paused to let her elaborate. The normally talkative Sarah kept her mouth closed and smiled the bland, universally non-threatening, non-defensive, non-committal

---

21   "Night" was an arbitrary convention on an orbiting platform. Most of the people whose work required them to deal with others were on "first" shift. That was about it for outward cues. Working on a plat was a good option for a species with a non-standard sleep schedule. The Mlamowarrers work in ten-minute shifts, lightly sprinkled through the Standard Day. Not team players.

Face-of-the-Human-Race smile she had been taught back at Human Interplanetary Intelligence Academy.

"Is there anyone else you would like to talk with then?"

"I guess not." He wanted to mention that he KNEW no outbound transports had left the Earthplat the last two days, and that nobody of Timo's pay grade would be sent such a distance anyway, but he fought back the urge. He said something polite, and she said something polite, and they signed off.

He stood at his great windows looking down on the planet. The line between day and night very nearly divided the view into two, and Dab had just passed into the darkness. He stared hard but could make out no detail. Somewhere in that blackness was the mysterious spot throwing the galaxy into an uproar.

"Stay out of trouble, Timo," he whispered. "It's a different world now."

Chapter 7 • A ROOM AT THE INN

"*THE GOOD THING* about being stationed in Dab," Meggy liked to tell his fellow Humans, "the *only* good thing really, is the beer." He had a tankard of Diddlyum's Milkmaid in his grip now, and the great room of the Big Swide Inn was already beginning to take on a friendly, fuzzy glow. The local tradespeople were just coming to grips with the realization that fancy-talking City folk could be downright foolish with their silver. This would be his second night to put up at the Big Swide, and already there seemed to be an understanding that his table was specially under the jurisdiction of Goldie, Argum's broad-beamed cousin. The fuzzy glow was definitely to her advantage.

He had spent the day trooping around the Big Hole—now the official local name for the spot—and listening in on and occasionally contributing to the absurd speculation of his fellow Lesser Knowledge dilettantes. A fallen star, a new form of lightning, an especially deep pocket of swamp gas, dragons—he listened with proper supercilious wonder to all theories. He never heard anything that could explain a local source of buu gas, though.

His head began to buzz. He sat up straight and shook himself. No, there it was again. He sighed and slowly got to his feet. It wasn't the beer after all.

Back in his room, it took him a few tries to get the answering code right. It was Timo on the other end of the link. Timo speaking Shalkin—which is actually the same as Dabbian but with longer words and with the old grammar intact—and apparently drunker than Meggy was.

"Slow down, I can't understand you."

"I feel amazing! I can jump up and touch the tree branches! See?"

"No, I can't see. Settle down, Timo, you're air-drunk. Sit down. It'll pass in an hour or so."

Some planets had this effect on Humans, at least on Humans who have spent a good long time breathing sterile spacecraft air and feeling only artificial gravity. It's as if your senses explode. Suddenly everything looks brighter and sounds louder. The air even tastes better. And for Humans, Calema seemed to have this effect to a dangerous degree.

"I can't sit down—the ground is too bouncy. I think I'll just run up and down the road a bit."

"Don't do that. Listen to me, Timo. You have to be quiet. You don't want to be noticed." Meggy was sitting on the floor of his room, behind the bed, keeping his voice low. With an air-drunk, the best thing was to speak loudly and simply in a calm voice, like a kindergarten teacher. Here in a room over the inn's kitchen, he was reduced to a hissing whisper. And the quieter he spoke, the more exuberant Timo's responses became. He pulled the coverlet off the bed and draped it over himself like a tent. "Where are you?"

"On a road outside Strammang. Strammang!" With the sharp-edged Middle Shalkin accent, the word had a melodramatic ring to it, as if he should be flinging a cape off his shoulders as he said it. "Strammang! Strammang!" He giggled.

"For all the gods' sake, be quiet, Timo! Get off the road. Find a place to be alone."

"Who wants to be alone on a night like thish! Like thiz."

Over the link, the sensation of Timo thumping his head with the heel of his hand made Meggy's own head ring. "Cut it out! You don't want to hurt the bug."

"I don't think izz working rye. It tickles."

"That's just the air. Sit down for a while. Take shallow breaths."

The "bug" they were talking about was the language insert. Everybody in the spy service (Human Interplanetary Intelligence—"HIPI" in officialese, "Hippie" to those in the ranks) had a slot in their brain just behind the temple to accommodate it. It looked like a fuzzy caterpillar. It could be programmed with multiple languages, in an order of preference, and with local coloring. A newly programmed bug was disorienting; people tended to switch languages in mid-sentence. If Timo had just been fixed up with a new bug, he was doing extraordinarily well. The wait time for field agents was usually a week. But why in the world had they dumped him here now? Timo the up-and-coming administrator? The plat guy?

"Are you someplace safe now? Someplace nobody can hear you?"

"Uhh, hold your horses." (Giggle, snort.) "Horses!" Sound of breaking branches. Sound of swearing. Sound of falling. "Okay. Thizz good. I'll just stay here a while."

"Timo, why did they send you? I mean, what is your mission? And why are you calling me?"

"Oh. The mission. The mission. I'm going to catch a boat in Strammang and come to Deruffillum. See, I'm laying a trace."

"Yes, I'm familiar with laying a trace." With potentially hordes of spies looking out for you, it didn't do to just pop up as if you had, well, dropped out of the sky. There needed to be a plausible story and a trail of some sort. "That's a good trace." The kindergarten teacher again.

"It sure is. So it should take about two days to cross over to Deruffillum. You can meet me then at the Deruffillum Society of Lesser Knowledge. You're ... we're ... I'm your distant cousin."

"Right. Right."

"I'm a baron's son from Middle Shalk with an interest in Lesser Knowledge."

"I see. I'll meet you in Deruffillum then in two days. I suppose I'm to bring you here to Hafswide then?"

"What? Right. That's the plan."

"All right." An uneasy pause. "But Timo, what are you going to *do* here?"

"I will assess the situation ..." This was spoken quite grandly and there was obviously supposed to be a follow-up clause to the statement. Silence. "Yes. That reminds me. Some of our people are working on the theory that this wasn't a natural phenomenonenon."

"What do you mean?"

"Nobody's ever sniffed buu gas on Calema in the six hundred years we've been here. The planet was given a going-over by scientists from more than a hundred species. Nothing. In fact, very little mineral wealth of the useful sort at all. Murds[22], does my head hurt."

---

22   A Dabbian foot fungus. A swear word only among old ladies of highly proper upbringing. Profanity is a tricky business for foreigners.

"That's a good sign. So . . . what? Somebody *made* buu gas?"

"The Wizards' Guild has a huge store of folk medicines and potions. Maybe somebody got a recipe wrong."

"In the middle of the Sulphur Swamp?"

"It's a theory. But listen, you know some of the locals. Is there anybody . . ."

"No wizards around here. They're big-city people."

"Was there anybody living in the swamp?"

"It's a pretty foul place. Well, I know one old crackpot who goes there sometimes. But . . . Let me think. No, I just saw him this morning. He didn't get blown up."

"Well, talk to him anyway. Maybe he saw somebody."

MEGGY AND TIMO talked a while longer, but this was the point at which their eavesdropper left the conversation.

Argum Seez, the proprietor of the Big Swide Inn, removed his earpiece and stood up from the spindly table that served as his desk. He would have begun pacing, but his "office" also served as the inn's pantry and there wasn't room for more than one step in any direction. So he stood, and thought.

His species' intelligence service was thorough enough that none of his listening equipment was visible. Even the earpiece just looked like an odd sort of bottle-stopper, and even more so once he tamped it back into the top of a bottle. Argum had every room of the inn equipped with the best sound and radio-frequency and trans-dimensional frequency monitoring devices in the known galaxy. He had heard everything of both sides of this conversation. Now he knew he had to act, and quickly.

Only one moon was up, and the village of Hafswide slumbered on, wrapped in deepest shadows. The room above the baker's shop had a glow of lantern light in one window, throwing a ghostly crisscross pattern on the building across the street. In the shadows below it a darker shadow passed by. At the corner it stopped a long time, looking in all directions, before slipping across the street and turning in the direction of Chumber Sackman's house.

Chapter 8 · **STRAMMANG HARBOR**

DISCREET OBSERVATION. AS a Snapper (a sort of graduate assistant) back at Human Interplanetary Intelligence Academy (Hippie U), Timo had been something of a star at D.O. His record at the D.O. Long Simulation, a legendary 24-hour holographic sensory bombardment, still stands. They had him teach the class after that.

But an early morning stroll through Strammang . . . He was a kid in a candy shop, an ingénue at her first ball, a country bumpkin at the fair. He bought a barley roll. He bought it with a coin! How medieval was that! It had been baked ten minutes earlier, from flour ground yesterday, from this year's barley crop. He bit into it and it seemed to him he could smell the field of heavy-headed Dabbian barley glowing in the sun and hear the metronomic *slick-slick-slick* of the scythes as the cutters, fanned out in their long diagonal, measured off the field in the ancient way—long-step, short-step, long-step, short-step.

"Get out of the road, you great, hulking idiot!" The cart driver's gorgy—a hump-backed, spindly legged creature like a donkey but with less charm—actually took Timo's sleeve in its teeth and gave him a yank toward the gutter. He slipped and dropped his satchel. A boy laughed. This was not Discreet Observation.

Great hulking idiot? A storefront had a strip of bubbly glass for a window. He paused to take in his reflection. Well, his clothes were disheveled from a short night's sleep on a pile of leaves, but he had been assured they were quite the fashion. He might be— yes, he thought he could pass himself off as a ne'er-do-well young rake wending his way home after a night's revelry. He tipped his high-crowned hat at a cocky angle, slowed his pace, and added a bit of a swagger. There. Now the people he passed just glanced and looked away with a knowing smile.

This was called, "The Momentary Story," and it was number 8 of "Nine Principles of the Cover." Unlike all the other recent graduates of Hippie U., Timo didn't call it "*The* Nine Principles of the Cover." This was something of a sore point with him because he had written the blasted thing and had never intended that anyone consider it a comprehensive treatment of the subject. It was just a paper he had tossed off as an extra-credit project his second year. But it was so *neat*. So *systematic*. It became the subject of a short course, then part of the core curriculum. Timo had barely escaped a professorship at the Academy.

He smelled something wonderful. An adolescent girl was tending a brazier with rows of fat sausages spitting and sizzling. He glanced around but there wasn't any sign saying what they were or how much she was asking.

"Those smell amazing!" he said. The girl looked up at him and her eyes got large. She started to say something and then gulped it back, lowering her eyes and making a sideways half-curtsy. She was blushing madly.

"I'm sorry," he said. "I didn't mean to . . . well . . ." He didn't know what he had done wrong. It could have been anything.

"They're only sausages, you know," she mumbled. "I'm sure a gentleman like yourself could find . . ." She was looking everywhere but at him.

"They're just the thing! And I'm famished. Tell you what, I'll take two."

"Really?" Now she turned her face on him with something like a look of wonder.

At last he understood, or thought he did. Here he was unusually tall and broad-shouldered and, by Leeban standards, with very masculine features. He was dressed like a lord and his (to him) outlandish costume was perfectly tailored and really quite flattering. He was a hunk. If they had had comic books, their superheroes would have looked about like him. No wonder people were trying not to stare.

Well, good grief. How was he supposed to blend in? How could he operate like this? Now Meggy's comment made sense: *But Timo, what are you going to* do *here?* Javitz had seemed so urgent, desperate even. "We need everyone we can muster, Sjogren. There's no time for the usual protocols. We need to know what this is *now*." As a mission statement, it did seem unusually broad.

He heard a clanging bell. That would be the sign of a ship weighing anchor. So the harbor must be that direction. He turned right at the next corner, but none of these streets were straight. It meandered a while and emptied into another street that didn't seem to be heading his way either. He stood at the corner and looked in all directions, and remembered he was carrying a couple of sausages.

They were spectacular. Once again his senses seemed to top out. The spices were sweet and peppery, exotic. Probably from Fengal. Maybe the Spice Islands. There was so much to try!

"You're an eager one this early in the morning, love." The woman slouching in the doorway was wearing a knowing smile. And not a lot else. "But get a load of you! I'm guessing a stallion like you isn't quite done for the night, eh?" She leered at him and gave a toss of her head toward the inside of the . . . dwelling.

He must have been grinning at her. Or who knows? Maybe the sausages were the signal. His briefings hadn't covered this sort of thing. "Thank you for the kind invitation, Madame," he began, and stopped abruptly. That was just what had popped out. His basic vocabulary and inflection seemed to have been programmed for only the most formal settings. It would take real effort on his part to speak any other way.

"What? No, the Madame's in . . ." she jerked a thumb toward the interior and then her face dissolved into a look of sour suspicion. "Hey, are you making fun of me?"

"I assure you I have the utmost respect for the quality of your services." *Oh stop, stop, STOP!*

"Get off with you! We don't need your high-and-mighty talk around here!"

"I wish you a good day then." The tip of his hat happened before he knew what his hands were up to. At least his feet seemed under his command. He turned on his heel and got himself around the corner before something round and metallic—possibly a spittoon—clattered past him on the cobblestones.

He wandered these back streets for a while longer before a distinctive smell lured him over to a broad, well-populated street.

There it was—the fish market. The harbor shouldn't be far away. From here he just followed the slope down.

The ships were a couple of hundred feet out, tethered in ranks to ancient, barnacle-encrusted pilings. Here at the docks a chaotic assortment of smaller craft was jostling for a spot to tie up. There was a lot of shouting and jeering and shoving off of each other's boats with oars. There was a great deal of shouting here on the dock, too. It took him a while to make sense of it. Some people were hawking wares to be found in the boats below. Others, made up in gaudy uniforms with more braid and ribbons than any admiral could possibly have earned, seemed to be shouting about particular ships out there in the harbor.

Emmy Noster to Brightbay in an hour!

Chinger's Dream to Nabbley about noon!

The Great Matoo to Sareemport, last boat out!

So this was how it was done. These cargo ships, once they had taken care of the main business and were about to weigh anchor, filled their few available cabins with what passengers they could find on the spot. There were no signs, no posted prices, and the bargaining was fast and rough. The ropers (the men in the quasi-military get-up) were on a tight deadline. They barked out their offers and counter-offers in a clipped, jargon-heavy slang, literally turning their back on any customer who seemed to be wasting their time.

Timo strolled along the dock, listening for any mention of Deruffillum. It took a while. Even though Deruffillum was the nearest foreign port to Strammang, it was not a large trading partner.

Grumming's Lance to Deruffillum in an hour!

The roper was a fat man in a too-tight blue-and-gold costume. He was sucking in a deep breath before making his callout, and each call ended in a gurgle of phlegm. He seemed desperate enough.

"Hello, my good man. I'd like passage to Deruffillum."

"The extremely fine cabin is spoke for, Your Lordship."

"That's all right. I'll take what you have."

The man looked up at him with something like alarm. "We can't . . . I suppose I could put you on the waiting list, My Lord."

Waiting list? Timo looked around. No one seemed to be standing by, waiting for a cabin. And the man had no list in his hand. "Oh, very well," he said, remembering to assume the aggrieved haughtiness of a Middle Shalk noble this time. "Put me on your silly little list." He looked away as if this was all quite beneath him.

"Uhh, I can't. The list is full."

"What?" The man flinched as Timo turned on him. He seemed confused and almost frightened, but his chin was taking on a harder set.

"That's right, Your Lordship, we're all full up. Painfully sorry."

A dozen cutting remarks came quickly to mind. His bug was just loaded with the vocabulary of offended honor. But what was the use? The man didn't want his business.

Grumming's Lance to Deruffillum in an hour!

Blast! He had hardly turned his back on the man!

His luck was the same with two more ropers for Deruffillum-bound ships. They seemed eager and respectful at first, but it all turned to suspicion and then outright hostility as they talked. He sat down to think about it. Maybe he wasn't playing the part right. Maybe there was some signal he just wasn't getting. Or giving. Bargaining rituals were so specialized, even within the same species. Once again he was up against the limits of his training.

He was getting hot. It was already past noon and many of the ships had already sailed. He needed to move quickly.

He tried full-on belligerence with the next roper, starting right in by demanding the extremely fine cabin and tossing out a ridiculously low offer. It worked. At least the man was talking with him. They seemed to be on the verge of striking a deal, but then this man clammed up too. He hemmed and hawed. He thought of new difficulties. At last he claimed it was impossible.

There were taverns along the waterfront; the closest one had an awning of a sort and a scattering of tables in the shade. It looked inviting. Once Timo had passed out of the afternoon glare, he noticed something about the clientele: the men at the tables were all like him. That is, their clothes were all the same rich, brightly colored material, snug-fitting and furnished with the outrageous cuffs and collars that announced, "This man does no work with his hands." All the men standing about were also well-dressed, but in a less showy style. As he watched, another of these more sensibly attired men came in from the sunshine, bowed to an old fellow at a table, and bent to whisper some confidentiality. The old man nodded with satisfaction and pressed a lace handkerchief to his lips. The younger man picked up a pair of bags and turned to go.

So. That was the fault in his presentation. He was much too grand a personage to even be seen speaking with the likes of a roper. If he was carrying his own bag, something was wrong; he was up to no good. He needed a servant. Probably a couple, if the ratio here of standers and sitters was any indication. He drank a beer, which was also wonderful, and considered his options.

A couple of small, darker-skinned men passed by, chattering in an exotic tongue his bug couldn't even place. Had to be from Melligar—the island of a thousand languages. They dodged around the larger bodies as they went, and no one paid them any mind. They seemed invisible to the locals, part of the waterfront, like the seagulls. Timo dashed down the remnants of his beer, plopped his tankard on the table of a pair of grandees too shocked to take the appropriate offense, and set off to follow the Melligari.

Their ship—if you could call it that—was a good way off from the rest, nearly to the breakwater. It was a Melligar Pile. Timo dropped his bag and thought good and hard, standing alone on this nearly deserted stretch of dock. He could just wait until tomorrow and take a *real* ship.

Picture a great, round house built by a dozen men without any teamwork at all. In fact, they're working against each other and each one is furiously building on his part as any random piece of material comes to him, the object being to achieve the greatest height before the whole thing collapses. Now picture this towering madhouse rocking back and forth in response to the minute, otherwise imperceptible swells rippling gently across Strammang Harbor. With every stroke of this pendulum timbers creak, shutters flap, and every joint gets further from true.

"She is the Princess of the Eternal Isle."

"I beg your pardon," Timo said to the ragged Melligaro standing beside him and staring raptly across the harbor.

"Hers name. My great-grandfather build her."

"That's incredible."

"Hokay, he *help* build her."

"Are you sure? I mean, can it really be that old?" The sailor seemed a pretty ancient mariner himself, although with the whip-hard muscles of his arms and the deeply tanned leather of his face, "preserved" might have been a better term than "old."

"She's young. Pile never sink."

"All right. Fine. I'm looking for a ship to Deruffillum. As quick as possible."

"Okay Deruffillum. You want to passenger, yes?"

"Yes."

"Ten stamps Shalkin. No good talking about it. That is price."

"For the extremely fine cabin?" The price was laughably low compared with the rates he had been hearing all day.

"All cabins extremely fine." The man's face was aglow with sincerity and pride.

Timo reached for his purse. "Are you sailing soon?" he asked.

The man shrugged. "Today."[23]

They rowed him out in a dragonbug—an outrigger that was more canoe than boat. But it skimmed across the harbor at a surprising clip while the rowers, who seemed to be idly dabbing their paddles in the water at random moments, carried on a lively argument in what seemed to be at least three languages.

He clambered up a slender rope ladder to reach the deck. Now,

---

23   With three not-so-large moons in different orbits, the tides of Calema are quite variable and frequent enough that a Pile probably couldn't make it clear of the harbor in the space of one high tide anyway.

Timo was a well-traveled man. He had been on hundreds of space-craft, most of them not built with Humans in mind, many of them with strange gravity or no gravity at all. But he had never been on an actual sea-going ship. He was pretty sure though, that they were not supposed to act like this Melligar Pile.

Now that he could stand at the rail and look down at the water, he was pretty sure the rocking wasn't caused by waves at all. The ship, as far as he could tell, was doing it on its own. He backed up to a wall and crouched down to get his eyes level with the gunwale. The buildings of Strammang slowly sank out of sight. He waited. Half a minute later they eased back into view. Extraordinary.

A passing crewman stopped to stare. "Hey you, sir. You not sick are you?"

"What? No, I'm fine. I'm just . . . What is making the ship rock like this?"

"Rock?"

Timo rocked his forearm to demonstrate.

"Oh, the nodding! Yes, many waves yesterday."

Timo thought about it and then found the roper—whose name, the man averred with utmost solemnity, was "Roper"—and had his berth changed to one on the deck level. It wasn't a bad room: tiny of course, and between the walls, ceiling, and floor, not a single ninety-degree angle. But no bugs, snakes, or major species of vermin.

The sound of running feet and many voices brought him back onto the deck. He quickly ducked and then rolled to safety behind some bales of Fengal linen. Every man had something like a Zimmer spire on his shoulder. But these were Melligar tree spires, each at least fifty feet long, and as the men jogged along the deck, the far tips of the spires whipped up and down so rapidly they were barely visible. You might have walked right into one except for the warning given by the droning whir of their movement.

It was a wonder how the crewmen kept from sweeping each other right over the railing. They were planting the spires into deep sockets which jutted out at all angles from positions all over the ship. Many of these were up on the "village," as the Melligari called the jumbled tower of the ship. They scrambled up the outside of the buildings, still chattering away to each other. In short order, the ship was a monstrous pincushion gently rocking at the far end of Strammang harbor, a safe distance away from the normal ships—the ugly girl at the ball.

There was shouting and pointing at the stern—or it might have been the bow. Now that he was on one, Timo perceived that a Pile was slightly oblong rather than perfectly round. Another launch was approaching. In short order two young men in elegant attire came clambering over the railing. One of them was fair skinned and fair haired, the other rather darker. Their clothing was "elegant" chiefly by the manner in which they wore it; every movement was polished and yet carefree. It was a knack the ruling classes cultivated on many planets, to be so secure in one's superiority that commanding came unconsciously, just as obeying came unconsciously to the lower orders surrounding them. The Melligari felt it. They stopped talking to each other. They bowed and gestured in an exaggerated manner that was almost pantomime. A whole troop of them came one by one over the railing carrying baggage.

The young men's clothing was in the same outlandish cut as Timo's but all in black, with just a few dramatic flashes of silver metal. Timo felt something rubbing against him. He looked down and found that he had begun rubbing the broad buckle of his sash with the sleeve of his coat. What was this? Even he, another species (and a greatly advanced one, he was quick to tell himself) was feeling the urge to smarten up in the presence of these gentlemen.

And that could only mean that these were wizards—drawn from the ranks of the aristocracy and mysteriously above even them. Wizards inhabited a social plane ineffably apart from mere mortals. Timo had read all about it but had chocked up the mysterious powers of the Wizards' Guild to the backwardness and gullibility of the pre-scientific Leebs. Now he wasn't so sure.

The Melligari at the stern (or it might have been the bow) were scurrying about with ropes and pulleys and a sort of platform woven of heavy reeds. They tossed it over the side. After a minute or so of men arranging the lines and straining to haul them in, another man in black appeared outside the railing of the ship. He rose into view like a god, erect and serene, by all appearances levitating upward simply because he willed it. He stepped over the railing without looking down. Oh, well, of course. A short staircase had been whisked into position a moment before.

This man also was dressed in black and silver, but his outfit was supplemented with a billowing black cape and a silver-knobbed black cane. His features were worthy of carving in granite; his hair was a flowing silver mane. And it wasn't even windy.

All the Melligari bowed, each in his own way. Their culture had no tradition of bowing; they were making this up as they went. The wizard slowly turned his gaze to take in the ship and all its inhabitants. He did not seem pleased.

"I wish to speak with the captain of this vessel," he pronounced.

The sailors glanced nervously at each other. "I think I am a captain," one of them volunteered. "And Signomer, aren't you a captain too?"

"Maybe." Signomer made this confession reluctantly. "And don't forget Cargomer and Weatherit. They're up top today."

"No, no, no. I mean the Captain. The main man. The boss."

"Yes. Yes." The sailors all smiled and nodded.

"I've heard they don't really have a captain," said the lighter of the impeccable young men in black. "The responsibilities are all scattered about somehow. It's terribly complicated."

"Extraordinary." The elder wizard's gaze wandered further afield and spotted Timo among the bales of cargo. For the first time, something like a knowing smile played across his face. Did he perceive somehow that he wasn't Leeban? How deep did this wizardry business go? Timo's Neemnot friends had some amazing stories.

"You, sir," the wizard called out to him. "I see you are a gentleman of some refinement. Where shall we find accommodations? The extremely fine cabins should be satisfactory."

"I'll see what I can find." And so Timo, their predecessor onboard by all of fifteen minutes, became the wizards' accepted go-between with the Melligari. It seemed so natural.

The elder wizard was Gerund Undertower, Chancellor of Strammang University. The two younger men were named Derving Vale and Shamgath Pergak. Timo had a passing impression that Shamgath was in some disfavor, something to do with a miscommunication with the roper of the ship they should have been taking.

But wizards don't air grievances in front of ordinary folk. Wizards don't have difficulties. They are the effortless masters of all situations. In a very few minutes they were ensconced in a surprisingly spacious cabin in the front of the ship and drinking proper Shalkin black tea, with Timo their guest and with two Melligari standing respectfully by. They were discussing the rigors of sea voyages past, with Timo happily padding out his resume as a Shalkin noble to keep up. It felt so natural.

Timo's cup—fine Gadgerene porcelain—was on the table. A ripple radiated out from the center of the liquid's surface. As Timo bent to examine the phenomenon, Shamgath craned his neck to peer out of one of the window slits. "It appears we have set off," he announced.

They all went on deck. A crewman was just ascending the "village" over the wizards' cabin. He came to a spire and felt around its base until he found a small groove. He put one finger inside and slowly pulled back on it. A great, leaf-like fan unfolded from the sides of the spire. It was a delicate thing, dusty green and thin as a butterfly's wing. Fully extended, it ran from about one-third up from the base and out to the very end, widening very gradually and forming a rounded tip about six feet wide. Signomer, strolling along the deck, pointed and called out a command to the crewman—or it might have been a greeting; the whole launching affair seemed to be proceeding at a leisurely pace. The crewman climbed higher and started the same proceeding on another spire.

In a minute's time about one out of four of the spires was "fanned." This apparently was the Melligari method of accounting for the direction of the wind—fanning open only the spires set at a certain angle. Already the Pile was easing out of the harbor in a wide, gentle arc. Their wake was a mere shimmer on the surface. This would not be a rapid voyage. But at least the rocking had stopped.

Chapter 9 • **A MOONSLIGHT STROLL**

TIMO'S CABIN SEEMED to be on the path of a major thoroughfare to the top of the Village. He opened his eyes the next morning to the faintest glimmering of morning light. Why was he awake? *Thump, thump, thump, creak!* Ah yes, that sound. The sound of people running along his roof and leaping to the next level. The steering of the vessel was still a mystery to him, but it seemed to involve constant adjustment to the spires. He went out to have a look.

The sea was quiet and green and covered with a fine, pre-dawn haze. They seemed to have the ocean to themselves, except for the occasional whale. These were long and black and rolled smoothly by as they spouted, hardly breaking the surface. Timo stood at the rail and tried to gauge the speed of the Pile. He chose a bit of foam on the water's surface and watched it slip along toward the stern at an easy walking pace. So . . . not fast at all.

A boy of perhaps ten years of age landed on Timo's roof, pattered to the corner and swung himself down from the eaves. He noticed Timo standing at the rail and paused to consider this wondrous sight.

"Why don't they just put in ladders?" Timo mused out loud.

"What 'ladders'?" the boy asked.

"Good heavens, you speak Shalkin. Extraordinary." Timo remained leaning on the rail. The boy's stance suggested that he might fly away at any sign of danger.

"I hear many tongues," the boy said. "What 'ladders'?"

"A series of vertically arranged steps or rungs," Timo recited, before stopping himself. He was going to have to learn not to just read off his internal dictionary. "You know. A thing made for climbing." He pantomimed climbing a ladder.

The boy laughed. "A cack!" he said. "Cacks for girls! Cack-ladder-ladder-cack."

"You learn fast. What's your name?"

"No name yet."

"Hmm. I see. You don't have a position—a job—on the ship yet." The boy thought about it and nodded. "But what do other people call you?"

"Boy."

"Yes of course. What I mean is . . ." Timo paused and then sighed. "Well then, what is Melligari for 'boy'?"

"Stob."

"Really? Stub? All right then. I guess I'll just have to call you 'Stub.' My name is Lord Timden Batherum of Tipstitch." In the circumstances he found he couldn't pronounce the title without throwing a little mock dignity into it. He added a sweeping bow. The boy laughed heartily and scampered away.

The wizards were the only other passengers on the ship. Timo found himself in their company a great deal. In a strange way, they seemed to need him. The Melligari were eager to provide their three black-clad guests with the best the ship could offer and maintained a vigil of sorts outside their cabin. But communication between the crew and their passengers was stilted and rudimentary at best and as often as not ended with the Melligari smiling and nodding in panicked fashion and backing out of the room saying, "Yes indeed! Yes indeed!" after which a new batch of attendants would arrive and the miscommunication would begin again.

Wizards, Timo found, were social animals. They craved conversation, but it must be only the most brilliant sort. Witticisms, allusions, bons mots, ripostes, asides, quotations—they could keep it up all day. Timo was dazzled. They hardly noticed when he lapsed into a bashful silence. Or perhaps it was simply exquisite politeness that kept them pretending that he was keeping up. In any event, they didn't want him to go.

Late the second evening, Timo bade them goodnight and left for his own quarters. It was a clear night. Two nearly full moons were up and the sea was calm. He strolled the deck, feeling his mind clear a bit with each circuit of the ship.

By the third time around he was almost himself. Right. He was undercover. Human! And he was on a poorly defined emergency mission with planet-wide stakes. The faint whisper of care that had lingered on the edge of his consciousness all day, like a forgotten item from a shopping list, was rapidly coalescing into a knot of fear in his stomach. My God—had he let something slip? He had been so eager to please! To impress, if he could. What had got hold of him?

He had never believed in magic. With all the reports that had featured the Wizards' Guild—and now that he thought about it, almost every international development did—he had filtered the information in his own mind to dispose of the more fantastic elements. He had chalked it up to the limitations of working in the local languages. Amusing, really.

Now he knew better. These men had exerted a power over him. What was the word? A spell. Bizarre! Unthinkable! But what had he actually said to them?

They had talked about their own mission. Not all at once, of course. Not as if it really mattered. Oh so casually, it had slipped in and out of the conversation. "That matter to attend to over in Dab." "Goings-on at the University? Quite a stir in the Portents Department, wouldn't you say?" "I've been brushing up on my 'Visions of Drebbell the Farseeing.' Frightfully thick going for my taste." "But that's how it is with the end of the world. Always a little murky." "We're just popping over to sort it out."

They were going to Hafswide too! He felt dizzy from the realization. If he had said anything . . . anything . . . But he couldn't think of anything dangerous he might have brought up. Mostly he had agreed. Mostly he had asked wide-eyed questions, and laughed at their jokes, and marveled out loud at their knowledge. He must have looked the fool, but . . . maybe he had at least looked a *native* fool. Maybe his cover was still safe, even if his pride wasn't.

He was so deep in thought he almost ran into a figure standing at the railing. "Hello, Lord Timden," the figure said with perfect equanimity. It was Derving, obviously pleased to see him. Timo felt a warm rush of gratification. *Stop that! It's just a spell! Fight it, man!*

"I couldn't sleep," Timo answered as gruffly as he could.

"Hard to sleep on a night like this," Derving agreed. "Just look at those stars. So bright. They must have a lot to talk about tonight."[24]

Timo followed his gaze, which seemed to be directed to a grouping of stars to the northeast which he believed was known as "The Whale and Eel" in Shalkin mythology. "I don't know much about starwork," he confessed.

"An educated man such as yourself! That's a shame. But I suppose your many business affairs don't leave you much time for contemplating the business of the gods."

"Well, no," Timo answered, a beat too late. He had forgotten this part of his cover story. What was the rest? He was the youngest son of a Middle Shalkin baron. He lost a good deal of his father's money with his ne'er-do-well ways, while dabbling in Lesser Knowledge. He was going to meet a distant cousin in Deruffillum before going on to Hafswide.

"But now Drebbell's Ladder has appeared!" Derving spun to face him. "Did you see it?"

"I ... was asleep at the time. Sorry."

"I saw it from the roof of the University. We all came running. A magnificent sight! A sign from the heavens in our time!"

Derving was gripping the rail and staring toward the east as if reliving the experience. He didn't seem as tall as he had been. His

---

24   According to the Caleman form of astrology, the stars are passing overhead in a sort of ages-long promenade, mostly gossiping among themselves and not too concerned with life down on Calema. Now and then they get into a spat, and this is where most of our troubles come from. The wizards have a vast compendium of star lore explaining all known history and a great deal more besides.

collar was askew and his expression was intense, almost fierce. Timo had a sudden realization. *I'm not under the spell anymore. However they do it, maybe they can't keep it up if they're distracted or carried away with emotion.*

"The three of you are going to Dab to verify this . . . sign?"

"What verification does it need? We all saw it! But yes, we are going there to investigate. Perhaps when we see the actual spot, we'll know better how to interpret the sign."

Now that his mind was clearing, Timo could begin to think critically about what he had heard in the conversation of these three over the course of the day. There had been tiny slivers of clues tucked away in what they had said and left unsaid, the way they had sat and moved, their expressions when no one was supposed to be looking. The wizards were not in such perfect harmony as they wanted people to believe.

"Chancellor Undertower knows what it means, of course."

"How could he, when he hardly believes in the prophecies at all?"

"But surely he is a powerful wizard!"

"A powerful academic!"

Bingo. It was the way Derving spat out the word "academic." Scorn, contempt, heaps of irony. This was the underlying tension Timo should have picked up on. Derving was the True Believer of the bunch. The Wizards' Guild—of course!—had the same fault line running through it as with any other long-standing movement or party or religion: the elites don't actually Believe. Gerund had the polish, the charm, the intellectual flourish to navigate the treacherous waters of the Guild's highest leadership. He believed fervently in the organization. He just didn't believe in the Magic.

Now what about the third member? The exotic-looking one. Timo thought he had noticed a hint of extra reserve on the part of the other two when they spoke with him. Just a slight discount to everything he had to say. Doubt. Wariness, even.

"What about Mr. Pergak? He at least must find it a great honor to be included in this mission."

"Sham? Yes, I suppose. Not many of his kind in the Guild."

"His kind?"

"Fengali. Didn't you know?"

"Ah yes, yes, of course." Timo hadn't noticed much of anything in the presence of the wizards, but now, his mind clear, he pictured Shamgath and saw the obvious signs: the darker skin, the trim build, the rakish good looks. Fengal men had a reputation the world over as suave and passionate lovers.

Life was easy in the Fengal Islands. The crops—three harvests a year—practically grew themselves. The trees from which they built their houses were impervious to rot. Fish were abundant and varied and so easy to catch, it was hard to tell if a Fengali fisherman, at any given time, was working or taking a siesta. It was a stable, peaceful, cheerful society. The Empress (the succession of the royal house had been matriarchal for centuries) had to gently remind her subjects from time to time to pay their taxes. They had been known to be lax about that. But it wasn't anything personal; they were lax about nearly everything.

So wizarding had never really taken root in the Fengal Islands. There was plenty of local superstition, but not much demand for the more spectacular occult effects wizards made their living on. These people didn't feel the need for a supernatural edge. In the islands, the natural was just fine.

"How did a Fengali come to be . . . at the University?"

"Oh, he's a wizard all right. Rather a good one, considering." *Yes, there's that condescension.* "It's a gift after all, Lord Timden. A higher calling. It could happen to anyone, from any nation."

"This is interesting. People just notice they have these powers? Does the Guild go looking for them? Is there a test?"

The wizard smiled mysteriously. "We just know, Lord Timden. We just know."

"What do you know about this . . . sign?"

"Are you beginning to believe too? Can you fit the prophecies in with your 'Lesser Knowledge'?" Derving took a step toward him and put his hand on his shoulder. "What do *you* say about it?" His gaze seemed to be searching Timo's soul.

"I don't know. I—I didn't see it."

"You must have some theory about it. These days everyone seems to feel free to speculate on such matters. What do *you* say?"

Now the hand was touching his chest. Timo took a step backward. He felt a little light-headed. He looked up and saw a third moon in the sky. For the life of him, he couldn't remember the name of that moon. "What were we talking about?"

Derving turned away from him and leaned heavily on the railing. He looked tired. "This and that. And the end of the world. I wish you a good night, Lord Timden."

TIMO FILED A report that night. They were to pass on to Meggy that he would meet him in three days, not two. But it wasn't a total loss, he told himself. He had gained lots of useful intelligence about this group of wizards coming to Hafswide. Timo also inquired, in a subtle, roundabout way that could be taken as ironic, about any reports of mind control from the wizards of Calema.

Derving filed a report that night too. He used a keyboard that looked like a useless old pouch, with cracked leather and a broken drawstring. He slipped it over one hand. A moment later his prosthetic eye picked up the prompt. His fingers in the pouch began to move in intricate patterns and lines of text scrolled rapidly across his sight.

"We have a fellow passenger on this vessel, an unusually tall Shalkin, the younger son of a baron, by the name of Timden Batherum of Tipstitch. Please confirm this identity. I believe he is an off-world spy, and not a very good one. He betrays a much too scientific outlook and lacks any of the local superstitions. He is quite susceptible to Allure, but unlike Leebs, he seems impervious to Adjuration. Gert or Human would be my guess, judging by his awkward movements. Please advise."

Just before morning the answer came: "All Baron Batherum's sons, legitimate and illegitimate, are now accounted for. Your Shalkin is an undocumented spy, not among our allies. No previous record. Continue to observe. Do not terminate unless necessary. Sabotage his efforts if this can be done discreetly."

Chapter 10 • A SWARM OF BUNGS

Excerpt from "A Brief History of Caleman Technological Development" Volume 5.

THERE IS STILL a great deal of conjecture as to the cause of the relatively slow pace of technological development. I have already dismissed several of the more far-fetched theories in earlier volumes. The theories that remain all have a good deal of evidence and sound reasoning behind them. I believe that all of the following factors have contributed in a significant way.

First, the "Six Civilized Continents" (to use the terminology of the natives) are rather widely distanced from each other. The cross-cultural exchange that has served to accelerate development on so many planets has been nearly non-existent on Calema until just a few centuries ago. Some continents experienced epochs of hundreds of years in which there were no wars, no threats inside or out, no natural disasters—in short, no compelling reason for development of any sort.

Next, for most of the last thousand years, since sea travel between the continents became normalized, the culture of South Gadgerus has been accepted as the true measure of civilization. While Gadgerus has a rich artistic heritage and the finest buildings and monuments on the planet, it has also proved monumentally resistant to change of *any sort. The worship of the Sareem (the Gadgerene Emperor), the deep stratification of society, the Book of Days[25]—really every aspect of Gadgerene life informs the population that perfection was achieved countless millennia ago. Fulfilling one's assigned role in the prescribed manner—that is success, and the only true happiness.*

And as if the sheer distance between the continents were not enough of a barrier, there are the bungs . . .

The following morning was fine and fair, with a following breeze shoving the old *Princess of the Eternal Isle* along almost at a real sailing ship's pace. Now there were smaller, grayish whales dotting the surface of the water. They all seemed to be cruising with them to the east. Timo had ambled along nearly the full length of the deck before he realized the crew seemed to be missing. He spotted them—or at least a large group of them—seated along the uppermost roof of the Village. They were speaking to each other in low voices and pointing a lot. Timo peered at the hazy horizon but couldn't make out a thing.

In half an hour or so he spied a boat going the same direction as they were. Then he saw another one and then four more. He walked around to the other side of the Pile, and there were seven more vessels scattered along the horizon. They didn't look dangerous to him. Two of them were plainly fishing boats. None of them looked military.

---

25   The Book of Days, ca 4,000 years old, provides the Gadgerenes with a detailed, mystical analysis of the meaning and purpose of every day in the year. Gadgerenes don't actually plan anything—they consult the Book. Every literary work of Gadgerus, and this includes the instruction manual for the maintenance of the Kamerduk sewer system, is understood to be a further elaboration of the Book, and as such, must be written in the same turgid poetic style.

He heard the patter of small bare feet and turned to see Stub swinging himself down to the deck. "Good morning, Stub. So, it appears we aren't the only ship in the sea after all."

Stub's face remained grave. "Very bad. Very bad thing, more ships."

"What? Do you think they are pirates?"

"No! I think they are . . . bonged." He pronounced it "bong-ged." At Timo's blank look, he tried again. "They are *sizibong*." He hit the flat of his palm with his fist.

Timo's bug finally finished riffling through its dictionary. "Oh, *bungs*." He scanned the water again. His bug had provided an image of something like a very large, bulbous crocodile, with a massive head. Timo blinked and gave his head a shake. In the image, the creature's head was a broad vee, like an anvil, and it had a goofy smile. It was in fact Kokoloko, a cuddly dragon on a Ninthwave® children's program. This couldn't be right. *No, you dolt*, his bug insisted. A *bung*! Now the fat crocodile in the image was racing up from the depths of the ocean. It was aiming its ugly anvil head at a ship.

"Murds!" Timo gasped. "We've got bungs!"

"There!" Stub pointed over the railing at one of the fishing boats. Its sails were slack, as if it were making a poor attempt at changing course. As they watched, it turned abruptly toward them and the mast whipped backward. The ship wallowed as if in a violent storm.

Timo leaned over the rail to peer at the water nearby. There were a couple of whales next to the ship, but no bungs. "No *here*," Stub said. "No here yet. We middle."

Timo's mind was reeling as his bug's files of information on Caleman sea creatures poured into his consciousness. What had possessed these people to venture onto the sea at all?

Bungs are a species of fish that have evolved in a peculiar way to take advantage of the large populations of whales in the Caleman oceans. Caleman whales are not especially large or dangerous. They tend to travel in vast, widely-dispersed pods, scattering quickly at any sign of attack. Bungs are larger, faster, stupider, and a great deal more vicious than their prey. They like to slaughter a lot of whales at once, creating large "red pools" out on the high seas. These are actually an important feature of Caleman marine ecology.

A swarm of Bungs will mark off a circle many miles wide and proceed to "herd" the whales toward the center, using their broad heads as rams. It takes hours. When the right concentration of whales is reached, the feeding frenzy begins.

Now to Bungs, boats look a lot like whales. Any ship finding itself in a Bung circle is in for a very rough ride. Ships don't respond as quickly as whales do. They don't scurry away toward the center of the circle. It makes the Bungs angry.

Now the ships on the left were close enough that Timo could hear the sporadic thumps, like distant cannon fire. The ships were trying to turn left and break out of the ring. Every few seconds the prow of a ship would be violently shoved back toward the center of the ring. A large merchant vessel took an especially hard hit and the sound of splintering wood wafted across the water. One of the fishing boats veered away for the relative calm of the inner circle. The two groups of ships to either side of the Melligari Pile were both slowly careening toward them like drunken sailors.

"Can they break out of the circle?"

Stub shrugged. "Maybe. Fast enough. Strong enough. Lucky."

"Are we fast enough?"

Stub laughed and shook his head.

"So what you're telling me . . ." A resounding thump from beneath their feet broke Timo's concentration entirely. The deck rose and fell. Timo flung himself headlong and grabbed the railing with both hands. Stub, aside from a slight flexing at the knees, showed no reaction at all.

"You all right?" Stub asked.

Timo, on his knees and still clinging to the railing, took a moment to reflect. A crewman ambling by gave him a puzzled look. "Sure, I'm fine." He stood up, looked across the water and gave a start. The ships that had been pacing them on their right-hand side had disappeared. Stub pointed. The ships were nearly in front of them now, just about to disappear behind the bow. Stub made little horizontal circles with his finger.

"I see. We are spinning. But wait, this is good! This must be why Piles are made this funny way, to withstand an attack from bungs! They don't tip over; they just rock and spin a bit. How very clever! Marvelous! We are safe after all!"

"No. Not safe. Other ships." At Timo's inquiring stare Stub provided a dramatization, banging his fists together and making apocalyptic crashing noises.

"Oh."

Now the crew began shouting again and pointing, this time to the east. A half-dozen ships were ranged before them, all damaged to some degree. The one that was still mobile was attempting to limp back to the relative safety of the center. One was sinking. Two others had been driven together, forming a "T" that was now spinning slowly toward them.

The crew of the Pile scrambled to close up the fans on the spires. They left a handful open on either side to afford some maneuverability. They drifted by the two joined ships with a hundred yards or so to spare. Now it was the sinking ship they needed to avoid.

"Can we help them?" Timo was pointing. "Can we pick up the survivors?"

"That would be ill-advised, Lord Timden. For the present all the ships must try to avoid each other." It was Gerund. The other wizards were with him, looking as serene and commanding as ever. A couple of crew members stopped what they were doing to stand by. Gerund stood at the railing and made a majestic survey of the destruction around them.

He'll have a plan. Everything is going to be all right. Timo blinked and shook his head. "Don't be stupid," he murmured to himself.

The Chancellor finished his observations, calmly stepped back from the railing, and nodded. The crewmen standing by sighed with relief and grinned at each other.

"Er, now that isn't going to be a problem, is it?" Gerund said, indicating with a wave of his hand a tremendous black ship approaching from the stern. The crewmen shouted and scampered up the Village. The Pile tilted ever so slightly and began a leisurely arc to the left.

"That appears to be doing the trick." Gerund glanced aloft and raised his mellifluous voice. "Well done, gentlemen! Well . . ."

A thunderous CRACK interrupted the Chancellor's speech. The entire party that had been standing at their ease on the deck suddenly found themselves pitched into the air. A moment later they collided with the walls of the Village, with those on the inside serving to soften the impact for those following. Then they were flung back and scattered across the deck like so many dice.

Timo rolled into the railing. As he was facing out, he was treated to a 360° panoramic view of the entire bung circle. He viewed this memorable sight several times in the seconds that ensued, as the Pile spun like a top. There went a line of a dozen or more ships in various stages of distress. There went the two ships with one embedded in the other. There went the black ship still aimed past them and sailing at a good clip. There went the black ship bearing down upon them at a good clip. There went the black ship with sails filling the sky and bearing down . . .

The black ship had a sharply raked hull that rode up over the Pile's stern with ease. The figurehead on the prow, a lustrously painted dragon, drove through the first several compartments on the Village's second story. Timo and all the men around him levitated for a moment at the impact. They dropped to the deck and began to roll downhill to the stern.

Bales of Fengal linen were rolling past and bodies were dropping off the Village like hailstones. A hefty sailor thumped to the deck just in front of Timo and pitched into him. Their collision redirected Timo into a wall. He grabbed a beam and hung on. A boy even younger than Stub fell to the deck and grabbed hold of Timo's sleeve as he passed. Their eyes met. The boy smiled and nodded as if to say, "Thanks." He scrambled to his feet, still holding onto the lace around Timo's cuff. He looked up and shouted at someone on the Village. The next moment a bale of linen caught him in the chest. The lace ripped from Timo's sleeve. The boy tumbled over the railing.

"Man overboard!" Timo shouted. It is doubtful that anyone heard, for everyone else on the ship seemed to be shouting as well just at the moment. Timo leaped up and looked over the railing, setting his feet and clenching the rail, as the deck was still sloping precipitously to the stern. The boy was floating face-down in the water. All around him whales were frothing the surface in blind panic.

Timo clambered over the railing and jumped. On the way down he remembered that the bungs would begin their feeding frenzy momentarily. He remembered that he still had on his elegant jacket, the one with all the padding and buckles. And his shoes. He remembered that he had never attempted to swim in his newly reshaped body.

He plunged into the water, which was shockingly cold. He kicked off his shoes and swam for the surface. Just as he was emerging, a gray whale breached over him. He rolled along the underside of the whale for her full length, like a beer can under a bus. The next time he found himself above water, he was a good fifty feet away from the Pile. He wriggled out of his jacket and started swimming.

Growing up, Timo had always been told he was a bad swimmer. Of course, growing up on a Trokee-majority planet where most of his friends had those shovel-like, slightly webbed hands and feet, it was hard to know for sure. He was, in fact, pretty good for a

Human. For a Leeb, he was epically good. Some of the older Melligari stopped their shouting and running to watch.[26]

Swimming with whales is not as fun as it sounds. He was getting tossed around a lot. He couldn't see where he was going. An extra-large whale, a black, scooped under him like a snowplow and carried him a good distance. Fortunately it was the right direction. The whale's snout was broad and flat and it gave him a chance to stand up and have a look around. He spotted the boy, and as the whale slipped back below the surface Timo dove cleanly away. By this time a large contingent of those on the Pile and on the black ship were watching the Timo show with something approaching religious awe.

He swam the last few feet to the boy and looped his arm around the boy's chest and under his arms. The boy seemed very light. There was no time to check his condition. The whales were even more panicked now, and it was everything he could do to fend them off and stay above the surface. There seemed to be a patch of clear water opening up and forming a broad avenue leading to the Pile's stern. He set off into it. He heard shouting above him. The Melligari were standing at the rail and shouting and pointing at a spot to the rear of the Pile. *That must be where they plan to pick us up.* He was making for it in good time now that the water was calm.

Bungs are a bright silver-green. Their eel-like motion can make them seem to "flash" as the light catches their scales. Timo saw a

---

26   For Melligari, maritime disasters are a way of life. A ship driven over the gunwales by bungs and stuck prow-first in the Village? "Hoohawah," they would say, with a one-shouldered shrug. Meaning, approximately, "Yeah, yeah, we know the drill." Some of these men had sailed the Dragon Sea, west of Melligar. Bungs, at least, stay in the water.

mysterious flash well below the waves. A moment later the flash was much nearer the surface. It was probably just as well he didn't know what was coming.

The bung's head caught him at an angle, lessening the impact and "flinging" them somewhat rather than simply smashing them flat. Timo and the boy went airborne. They launched in a great plume of spray, tumbling in an eccentric rotation, maaaan – boy – maaaan – boy, as Timo's grip held them together. The arc of their flight carried them higher than the railing of the Pile and the crowd of rapt onlookers standing there. They hit the water and sank from sight.

The roper called out some orders. Two men ran up the deck (still fairly angled, although the crew had already starting to shift ballast down below) and cast out a net with three slender ropes attached. It settled beyond the spot where Timo and the boy had splashed down. They waited. Their eyes met. The older of the two nodded, and they gently began pulling on the ropes. The ropes drew tight. "Aaah," went the crowd.

Their catch was a man, a boy, a couple of small squid-like creatures and many good-sized fish. They hoisted the load onto the tilted deck and let the lot of them roll along together until they came to rest against a couple of barrels. Some crewmen loosened the net and then chased around scooping up armloads of fish before they could flop overboard. Another sailor picked up the boy and carried him to the railing. He laid him over the railing so that his little body balanced at the midriff and drooped on either side. The man gently picked up the body and dropped it across the railing again. On the third such maneuver the boy spewed up a large quantity of seawater. The man stood the boy on his feet and spoke to him rather roughly, giving him a little shake with each word. The boy opened his eyes and answered. Everyone once again said, "Aaah." The wizards clapped, as did the members of the black ship's crew, some of whom had already clambered down to the Pile.

Meanwhile two Melligari were standing over Timo and pointing this way and that, debating how best to pick him up and drop *him* across the railing. The logistics of the thing were a bit dodgy, this fellow being so large and long. Timo suddenly pitched onto his side and threw up a bucket of water. The two Melligari shrugged and stepped back.

There was a disturbance in the crowd. Two grim-faced Brogorans, strapping, fair-haired young fellows in quasi-military getup that left a great deal of well-toned muscle in view, were shouldering their way through.

Timo opened his eyes and saw, very close by: netting on wet planks, bare feet, and a squid patiently undulating his way to freedom. The squid rolled his sad eye upward, as if giving a warning. Timo rolled over and looked up at the most beautiful woman he had ever seen.

Chapter 11 • THE EMPRESS DALADA

HER DRESS WAS white and golden. Her skin was a deep bronze; her hair was black and heavy and plaited with gold cords. She was saying something he couldn't make out. In Melligari. The crewmen were bowing ecstatically and one by one dashing away to do her bidding. She turned and flashed in the sun. No, that was the gold. It wasn't her clothes that were golden after all; she was draped and decked and encircled in actual gold.

She was tall—as tall as Gerund, who was standing close by, open-mouthed and for once not the master of the scene. She looked up at the black ship and pointed and called out something that was obviously a command. This was in another language, a mellifluous and flowing and elegant language. Fengal. She looked down and graced him with a benign smile. He was inspired. He tried to get to his feet. He must have been a little woozy still. He ended up flailing about and knocking his head on a barrel before finding himself on his back again.

She issued orders in a third language, this one harsh and crammed with aspirants and sibilants. The two hulking Brogorans stepped forward and raised him to his feet. As his legs seemed to be rather playfully making up their own instructions at the moment, the Brogorans were obliged to hold him up in an approximately vertical orientation.

"I am filled with admiration, sir, for your courage, strength, and skill." She spoke Shalkin with a lovely trace of Fengal accent. "I am left to wonder if you are a demigod come to this world on some divine mission."

The word "mission" threw him for a moment. He glanced at the sky, trying to jog his memory. *Yes, a mission. I have a mission! Wait, don't tell me. It has something to do with . . . rockets.* He glanced around. *But I'm on a ship! Hey, is that the ocean?*

To those gathered 'round, his glance to the sky and then to the people seemed a confirmation: he was consulting with his fellow gods to determine if these mortals were worthy to be entrusted with the sublime mystery of his mission.

"I am sorry that I have been so presumptuous. I crave your forgiveness." The woman curtsied deeply. The hem of the gorgeous white dress formed a perfect semicircle behind her on the deck, picking up a good deal of seawater and fish scales in the process.

I hope she has another dress. "Oh, that's all right," he finally managed to say. He meant to wave his hand dismissively, but the gesture put him off balance and he ended up with a sort of circular flapping motion instead. The people gasped. Clearly the guilt was being expunged before their very eyes—firsthand, so to speak, with no need of temple or altar or priest. They edged discreetly backward. You don't want to get hit with scraps of flying guilt. "I mean, well, sure, I forgive you." He had to speak slowly. The buzzing in his head made his own voice strange to him. *Wait, that's Shalkin I'm speaking.* It was starting to come back to him.

"I am Dalada, Empress of All the Fengal Isles. If it pleases you, I humbly invite your presence on my ship."

At this precise moment the bung feeding frenzy began. Whales and fish and bungs frothed the surface of the sea all around them, and the Pile began to vibrate and pitch. The buzzing was worse now. He couldn't hear what anyone was saying. Down where the black ship lay over the gunwales, waves were sweeping over the deck. They were red. Men began to float out of the sky. Timo had collapsed to his knees. His head rolled back. Men were floating out of the sky hanging onto clouds. It was beautiful. There was music.

To the Brogorans, Timo seemed to be trying to shake himself free. They gently let go of his arms. Timo just managed to clap one time, a dazed, beatific smile on his face. *Good show everybody!*

SOMEONE LAID A hand on his shoulder. He opened his eyes. The ceiling above him was gracefully arched wood. The bed beneath him slowly lifted and subsided. His eyes followed the curve of the ceiling to where it joined the wall. The wall there was colored glass, panes of pale green and blue and pink, cool and serene. He closed his eyes.

Now the hand shook his shoulder. "Time to wake up, O Magnificent One." It was a man's voice, cheerful and with a musical accent. "Ah! There you are!"

The man was dark-skinned and wearing a gaily colored, loose-fitting shirt. Fengal. The man's hand was warm on his skin, and Timo realized with a start that his own shoulder was bare. He took a look. He was just about all bare. Only his slight linen briefs—white with the family crest in lavender needlework—kept him from being in the altogether.

The man laughed. "Your clothes were wet, O Exalted One. And somewhat the worse for wear. But I assure you, Her Majesty has not looked on your unclothed form. Peligath took your measurements while you were asleep. Ah, there she is now." A Fengal woman was entering the cabin with a suit of clothes draped over one arm.

The bed Timo was lying on was very soft; it took him a few moments of thrashing around before he successfully vacated it. "Where are my own clothes?" he demanded.

"What we could recover of them," Peligath said with a hint of a smirk, "has been cleaned and is now drying in the rigging. But please, look—you have these."

"She is an excellent tailor, O Glorious One."

"Look, I am not a god."

"Ah, right, of course not."

"We understand."

The two Fengali nodded confidentially to each other. Peligath laid out the suit of clothes on the bed and picked up the shirt, which was mint green with piping in brilliant blue. "Oh yes, Torger," she said to the man, "it will bring out his eyes perfectly." She held it ready.

Timo allowed himself to be dressed. The clothes did fit perfectly and were much less binding than his Shalkin ensemble. Even in his stocking feet, Timo felt taller and handsomer. A check of the looking glass gave him pause. He did indeed look every inch the dashing hero. He also looked vaguely . . . seductive?

The mirror was rather cloudy. He hunched down to get a better look at his face. "Is that makeup?"

Peligath laughed. "I told you he would be shocked," she said to Torger. "These Shalkins are such prudes!" "He just put a touch around the eyes," she whispered to Timo. "You really have very good structure."

Torger, who had busied himself setting the table, came over for another look. The two Fengali stood very close and gazed at his face in a professional way, saying "hmm," and "mm-hmm," from time to time. Timo was at a complete loss.

"Oh," said Torger, at last taking notice of Timo's astonished look. "You are wondering about *us*. We are . . . *shiaspa*." He frowned. "Shalkin is such a clumsy language."

"Something like 'married,'" Peligath said.

Torger shook his head. "No, it's . . . well, all right. Something like 'married.'"

Timo's bug churned away and turned up nothing. They hadn't given him any Fengal. He had read somewhere that while Fengal social arrangements were nominally the same as everyone else's, they allowed themselves a good deal of latitude.

"Right," Timo said. "Are there a lot of married or . . . *shiaspa* couples on this ship?"

"The *Paninanina* is a large ship," Peligath said. "The voyages can be very long."

"The . . . is this a royal ship?"

Peligath smiled and took a step closer as if sharing a delicious secret. "You will be meeting the Empress tonight!" she said.

"You've made quite an impression on Her Majesty," Torger

added. "She's ordered tubefish!" The two Fengali had to chuckle at this and followed up with a few comments in Fengal, which struck Timo as being possibly ribald in nature. They were looking at him. He was getting uncomfortable.

"Your shoes!" Peligath exclaimed, suddenly serious. "I know just the thing!" She was nearly running by the time she got to the door. Torger returned to setting the table.

It was a spacious room—extravagantly so for accommodations aboard a ship—paneled throughout in honey-colored wood. The furnishings were few and elegantly simple—nothing like the baroque Shalkin style. There were fresh flowers on the table. Hatches were propped open along either side, and at the far end of the room a row of glass windows admitted a flood of slanting light. Timo stepped over and looked out. This cabin spanned the stern of the ship. Judging by the wake below, they were flying eastward at an astonishing clip, yet the ship scarcely registered the movement.

"A bit faster than a Melligar Pile," Torger observed. "You'll be happy to know we were going to Deruffillum too."

"What about the boy I was trying to save?"

"Good as new. He wanted to stay with you, but of course, he belongs to the Pile."

That seemed a funny way to put it. Timo shook his head. So many things he didn't know. "Before I passed out, I . . . but maybe I was dreaming. I thought I saw men falling from the clouds. Or something like that."

"Those were puffer pods they were carrying. You know. To stuff the hold wherever there is a break in the ship. They blow up when they get wet. Another reason Piles never sink."

The sun was already low in the sky. "How long was I . . . asleep?" Timo asked.

"Most of the day. Her Majesty was beginning to get worried."

"Are these her quarters?" Torger nodded.

"Am I . . . free to go?"

Torger laughed again. It was an easy, affable laugh. Unlike his wizard-trained compatriot Shamgath, this Fengal man seemed as cheerful and open-hearted as a puppy. "You're on a ship!" he exclaimed. "Walk as far as you want! I will find you when it is time for dinner. Oh, but wait a moment." He went to a cabinet and pulled at a wide, flat drawer on the bottom, which slid open noiselessly. Within was a double row of men's slippers. Torger cocked his head to glimpse Timo's feet and then counted off so many from the end and extracted a pair of gray slippers in a felt-like material. They fit perfectly.

On the deck there were more Fengal men than women, but also a sprinkling of Brogorans. Only the Brogorans had recognizable uniforms. The Fengal men, at least those tending to ropes or clambering in the rigging, were dressed in gaily colored tunics and breeches that ended just above the knee. They all seemed marvelously fit. Everyone bowed or curtsied as he passed. And the women stared with a frankness that he was beginning to find rather alarming.

Gerund Undertower emerged from a cabin, spotted him, and turned back to give the message to his cabin mates. "Lord Timden! I am pleased to find you in good health. Fengal tailoring suits you, it appears."

Derving and Shamgath emerged and gave their felicitations as well, and despite his sternest resolve, Timo felt himself glowing at the wizards' approval. They had been invited aboard the *Pani-nanina* so that they could reach their destination while the Pile was left to make repairs. Gerund had sized up the situation immediately and subtly encouraged their hosts in the notion that it was only natural a demi- or quadragod kept the company of wizards while appearing in the world of mortals.

They took a leisurely promenade around the ship. The Empress, Gerund informed him, was closeted with some ministers on pressing state business. "She is a conscientious sovereign. Astonishing facility with languages, you know. She is trying, as I understand it, to make Fengal something of a power in the world."

Timo sneaked a glance at Shamgath. "Will she succeed?" he asked.

There was a just a flicker of—he might have rolled his eyes, but that would be beneath a wizard's dignity, and so Timo knew he had seen it wrong. "Only the gods know," Shamgath said with just the right twist of ironic mystery to suggest that he had inside knowledge on the subject. Then he sighed. "But Fengal is Fengal."

"What do you mean by that?"

"They don't appreciate the Great Knowledge," Derving said.

"Wizardry in Fengal is of a somewhat different nature," Gerund took up smoothly. "Still . . . in its formative stage, one might say. But Lord Timden, have you had an audience yet with Her Majesty?"

"I just woke up. I hear we're having dinner together this evening."

"Will this take place in her quarters?" Shamgath asked. Timo nodded. "Aaah!" said the wizards in chorus.

"What? Does this mean something?"

"It means you're a very lucky man," Gerund pronounced, while Derving and Shamgath exchanged knowing nods.

"Any Fengal woman of noble birth considers it her prerogative to take lovers," Shamgath explained. "For the Empress, it is nearly compulsory. If she didn't, people would talk."

Derving added, "And now that she and just about everybody on this ship takes you for a demigod—well, what self-respecting Empress could refuse a challenge like that?"

"Wait a minute! Don't I have a say in this?"

"Is something the matter?"

"Are you hurt?"

"You're not . . . He's not "fancy," is he?"

"Oh, dear. I didn't think of that."

"I'm not a demigod and I'm not . . . 'fancy.' It's just . . . That isn't how we do things back in Tipstitch." The three wizards were eyeing him expectantly, with nascent smiles at the ready, waiting for the punchline. "You know, family honor and all that."

"What about your lovers in Tribbledor and Strammang?" Derving asked. "I thought it was all that Middle Shalkin stuffiness you were running away from?"

They had him there. But he couldn't afford to become the acknowledged lover of the Empress of Fengal. He would be expected—perhaps compelled—to stay with her. The mission would be over. He needed desperately to get alone and use his link.

Torger appeared. "Dinner will be ready momentarily . . . My Lord," he said to Timo, still a little aggrieved that this guest would not accept a higher title. He was about to say something else when he caught sight of Shamgath. Their eyes locked. As best as Timo could discern, Torger was amused, as if the sight of a Fengali man in wizard's black was by nature a droll sight, like a dog in a clown costume. Shamgath, with just the slightest shifting of his feet, assumed the classic posture of aristocrats everywhere—aloof, at ease, commanding. Any sculptor would have swooned from inspiration.

This was a situation rife with social dangers. Gerund, naturally, stepped in. "Torger Dimbak, isn't it? I am delighted to meet you! I am Gerund Undertower, Chancellor of Strammang University and an avid enthusiast of Fengal cuisine. I've often wondered— what is that sauce that makes Gool mushrooms turn that amazing sunset orange? Perhaps you can tell me as we go to the Empress' quarters." And arm in arm and chattering away like long-lost pals, the two left, Gerund turning his head just enough to send back a nod indicating that Timo should follow.

Shamgath drew himself back down to his normal height and turned away with a scowl. Timo met Derving's eyes and shrugged. "What can I do?" he said.

"You mean you really don't want to be the Empress' lover? Extraordinary."

"I have my reasons. Is there anything I can say to . . . gracefully decline?" The two began making their way to the Empress' cabin.

Derving's face was a picture of brotherly concern. "Hmm. This is a tough one. You *could* say that your heart is already taken. Let's see . . . You've pledged your troth to the girl from the next estate." He was speaking rapidly as they walked. "The two of you grew up together. Childhood sweethearts. She is your one true love. Yes.

The Empress would be deeply touched. She would be bound to respect that."

"Thank you, Derving! You're a lifesaver!"

Peligath was waiting at the cabin's double doors with a pair of handsome shoes. These had a vague resemblance to the Shalkin high-fashion monstrosities he had been sporting before, but the heel was lower, the buckle smaller, and the fit much, much better. Once Peligath had helped him put them on, she ceremoniously backed away. Timo looked up to see that Derving, Gerund, and Torger had slipped away as well. Everyone on the ship had. The two Brogorans, the tallest of the cohort, who had taken up position outside the Empress' door, seemed to possess anti-magnetic properties. He was alone. They opened the doors.

The Empress Dalada's dress was red. It was not your workaday, primary red such as you might see on a barn in Hafswide or on a prostitute in Strammang. This was a saturated, electric, tropical flower red-orange with a silken smooth sheen. It bent the space around her as she crossed the room. She said something. He said something—he didn't know what. It was hard to hear with that dress in the room.

His earlier impression was immediately confirmed: she was indeed beautiful. Not as tall as he had thought, but then, at their first meeting he had been flat on his back and slightly delirious. She was slender, like most Fengal women. And she had the broad cheekbones, wideset eyes and raven hair to pleasingly round out the tropical paradise dreams of any Leeban man.

But hers was not a delicate beauty. She was not slender in the willowy, flowing way that invites a man to catch her lest she fall.

These shoulders were wide; these hands looked like they had a grip. And when she paused to reset a napkin blown by the opening door, the action was quick and decisive and—one might have said—impatient. She looked up and smiled a radiant smile. She stepped back and looked him over from head to toe, pleased, and wanting him to know that she was pleased.

"I hope you don't mind the suit of clothes in the Fengal style. If I may be so bold as to comment on the appearance of someone such as you, the effect is . . . flattering."

"Thank you. Um, Your Majesty. And thank you for the clothes. I like them very much."

She approached him to one side, looking at his lower extremities now with a critical eye. Without thinking, he executed a quick turn. "A clever compromise," she breathed.

"The shoes?"

"Peligath is a gem." Her eyes made a leisurely traverse back up to his face. "The wizards tell me you are a baron from Middle Shalk."

"Just the third son of a baron. I won't inherit the title, I'm afraid."

"Well . . . You hardly need it."

"It would make my life a good sight easier, I can tell you." He threw a note of pettiness into this. He was glad for the chance to settle back into his cover character, the spoiled aristocrat.

"A man with your powers? What would you want with an easy life?"

Powers. "Really, Your Majesty, you have the wrong idea about me. I'm only Leeban."

She took his hand and turned it over in hers, examining it. Yes, she did have a firm grip. "So it appears," she purred.

Her head was bent. The gold cords woven into her hair were actual gold—twisting strands with hundreds of tiny links. He caught the scent of her. It was something musky and wild. He breathed it in. He wanted her and here she was, right here, touching him. He felt his whole body relax, as if he had stepped out of a cold place and into bright, baking sunshine.

In the corner of the room, a servant shifted his feet. The fellow was looking directly ahead, not at them, but there was a knowing smile on his face. Timo straightened suddenly. *The mission!* Dalada turned her gaze upward. From this close, he could see the flecks of gold in the depths her dark eyes. She seemed only a little surprised. And amused. She did not resist when he withdrew his hand.

"I knew a woman once who set about to collect the memories and known records of all her ancestors." She turned away toward the table, moving slowly, letting the dress translate every small step into a whispering invitation. "One of her great-grandfathers was a mysterious fellow with any number of local legends to his credit. There were people who said he bid all his friends goodbye and climbed to the top of a mountain. A mighty storm came up out of a clear sky and covered the mountain—just that mountain. His body was never found. That was when she knew she was an octagod. It explained a lot of things."

"That's a . . . remarkable story."

"It doesn't seem so very remarkable to me. The gods are a restless lot. I'm sure this is true in Shalk too." She reached the table and turned to look at him. She seemed to be searching his face for secrets. "You may not be who you think you are."

He tried to assume a look of affront. "We keep meticulous records of our ancestors in Tipstitch, Your Majesty. Every family does. It's our most popular hobby. It is highly unlikely there were ever any chances for . . . improprieties."

"It sounds perfectly dreadful. Shall we eat?"

The food was almost too much for Timo's space-dulled senses to handle. Nothing was bad or too spicy. It was simply that each new dish was an experience of flavor and texture too subtle, too complex, too rich for his palate to fully comprehend. It was very distracting. Two servants noiselessly padded in and out of the room, making dishes appear and disappear in response to infinitesimal signals from their sovereign.

The Empress was full of questions. Timo quickly exhausted the resources of his cover story and was left to fabricate with increasingly reckless abandon. By the time the desserts began to accumulate on the table—at which time it was dark outside and the curtains had been drawn across the windows and the lamps lit—he had transformed his boyhood into quite the rollicking tale. And as much as he tried to make himself out as a privileged lay-about, his natural instincts as a man of straightforward purpose and action seemed to keep peeking through.

On her side, the Empress never showed anything but keen interest and admiration at everything she heard. She had a way of sitting back slightly and saying "Hmm!" or "I see," or "Fascinating," and then holding the pose for just a moment, as if the information was being shunted this way and that until reaching its proper place in a vast repository. It might have put him on his guard, but she had such a dreamy, almost co-conspiratorial smile the whole time. He was flattered.

The windows were curtained but the hatches were open along the sides to let through the cool sea breezes. Timo thought he saw a light slowly crossing the view. "Are we passing an island?" he asked.

She turned her head to follow his gaze. "Those should be the Dabbian Hills. We have entered the Maybay. The *Paninanina* has made good time." Another subtle signal set the servants' feet to padding the floor again. "We have an excellent liqueur of kaleef berries, from the Spice Islands. A Fengali secret. A perfect end to any meal."

"Then I would love to try it. Just a little."

It was exquisite. And potent. They drank from small glasses which the servants replenished apparently from the far side of the room. At least he never caught them at it. She opened up about her own life, which she insisted had been terribly dull—nothing but preparation and instruction from an endless procession of tutors brought in from all over the world. And even now her life was all business. So little time for pleasure. It was a touching plaint.

She chattered on in her low, musical voice. Timo, no longer tasked with explaining himself, was getting more and more relaxed. She showed him a little table set against the wall, the top of which was an intricate mosaic of the Fengal Islands. Yes, it was a lovely place. And that shoreline was beautiful. And the view from that mountain was a wonder, no doubt. Mm-hm, it would be nice to see it sometime.

He had her hand in his. Not sure how that happened. But she was indeed beautiful. Now she was close. Had he pulled her to him? He couldn't remember. She was looking up into his eyes. She looked vulnerable, hopeful.

He kissed her. She folded herself within his arms. The kiss continued. Her hands began to explore.

"Don't you think we should . . ." he said, pulling away an inch or two and looking around the room. He was thinking of saying something about the servants, but it appeared he and the Empress had the room to themselves now.

"We should," she said breathlessly, and began unbuttoning his jacket. For a woman in the throes of romantic passion, she was terrifically efficient. The jacket was on the floor and his shirt was halfway off before he understood what she was up to.

"Wait a minute. Just a minute," he said, taking a step backward.

"What is it now?"

"I . . . I . . . can't do this."

"Nonsense. I've never seen a man more ready."

"What I mean is . . . There's a girl. A childhood sweetheart, from the next estate."

"That's a beautiful story, my dear. We all have our first time." The last shirt button was released and he felt his trousers suddenly loosened. This particular suit of clothes, he perceived, had been specially made for rapid access. He retreated to the dining table, holding up his trousers with one hand.

"Her name is Antissa! I swore I'd be faithful!"

"That didn't last long."

He quickly reviewed the tales he had been spinning. "Oh." He now had the table between them. She took two steps left. So did he. She was beginning to look a little cross.

"Come now, Lord Timden. This is silly. Whatever your Shalkin propriety demands, I'm sure that by now you can say you've done your best."

"She is my one true love!"

That seemed to stop her. She stepped back and scrutinized his face, deep in thought, one slender finger playing along her cheek. "Well then," she said slowly. "If it's true love . . ."

"I'm sure you understand, Your Majesty. I hold you in the highest regard."

"But you are not her goodman. She is not your goodwoman."

"Well, no. Not yet."

The Empress laughed. She held it back for a moment, and glanced at him, and burst into laughter again. "This will be a treat," she said. "What a lovely night we shall have!" She pulled out a chair and sat down. She made herself comfortable. "Please, have a seat."

He sat. "So you're not upset," he said.

"Not at all. A calculation is one of my favorite pastimes."

"'Calculation'?"

"You will tell me all about your Antissa. List all her excellent qualities. Wax poetic. Bare your soul, Lord Timden. I want to know exactly what it takes to be your 'one true love.' And then ..." here she leaned forward, well over the table, fixing him in her gaze. "I will provide proof that I am the better woman."

"That's the 'calculation'?"

"It is a very civilized method. The rules are of ancient origin. And then we will make love."

"Well . . . What if . . ."

"I've never lost."

He reconsidered his options. He might be able to stretch out the calculation an hour or more, but she seemed awfully certain of the outcome. Well, she was an empress. This was her ship; not getting her way never crossed her mind. He was essentially her prisoner already.

No, that was a weak excuse. Those dark eyes holding him in his seat were more than beautiful. They were eyes that gathered in and weighed every movement and expression he made. The Empress Dalada had been picking his story apart all night. Never pretending to doubt a word he said, she had silently constructed her own version of him. And although she knew nothing of the Gass or of his mission, she probably wasn't far from the truth. She knew there was no Antissa. She knew he was more than a scapegrace son of a nobleman. She knew he was hiding a much larger secret than either of those things. She was wrong about the demigod thing, but she had him dead to rights on the fact that he really, really wanted her.

He needed help. "Could you excuse me for a moment, Your Majesty?" He nodded to one of the closets on either side of the row of windows. "Necessary rooms" Torger had called them.

She gave a small, knowing smile and nodded. "Don't be long now," she called over her shoulder as he passed.

A tiny hanging lamp, swaying gently with the ship, cast a shifting amber light over the furnishings, which were all beautiful, and delicate, and made to a feminine taste. Under his breath, he recited the code for his link.

Nothing happened.

He tried again. No tingling in the back of his head. He tried the backup link. The recovery link. The diagnostic link. Nothing. For the first time since "Survival Day" back at the Academy, he was absolutely alone in the universe.

That must have been the buzzing in my head just before I fainted on the deck, he decided. *Does the station know? Can they tell my link is out?* He didn't think so. He stooped to look at himself in the mirror. His face had been altered, of course, just before coming down. Who was this handsome gigolo with the smoky eyes, leering back at him? He had to look away.

He heard movement in the room outside. Were the servants back? Would they come for him if he were in here too long? *Hiding in the bathroom.* Good grief. Pretty ignominious for a demigod. Come on, Timo. He squared his shoulders. He checked to make sure these trick pants were fastened up again. He boldly stepped out. One step.

The Empress, still lounging in the chair, had slipped into something more comfortable. The diaphanous garment in question did not so much cover her as cast a faint, scarlet glow over her person. Timo was left standing in mid-stride, as it were, with one foot in the bathroom and one foot in the bedroom. His eyes, untroubled for the moment by any sensible communications from the brain, assigned themselves the task of committing her person to memory.

She seemed not to notice. She casually rearranged her legs and draped an arm over the back of the chair. She slowly turned her glance to him.

He forgot everything. Everything—how he had gotten here, the mission, his name, his species. He was one lucky guy—that was all he knew. And she wanted him too! Well, he was hers, body and soul.

A smile slowly formed on her face. It was no longer the secretive smile that had been flickering on and off there all evening. This was a bold, easy smile. She was pleased. She was content.

He stepped into the room. The hatches were still open to the cool nighttime air. He saw a light outside. A city, actually. A ragged string of lamplights behind a broad stretch of water.

"We're here," he said. To him it sounded far away, like someone else's voice. What was the name of this city?

She moved. She was getting up.

With two bounding steps he dove cleanly through the hatch and into the dark.

Chapter 12 • **ON THE WATERFRONT**

IT WAS A well-known fact that, as Fengal Empresses went, Dalada was exceptionally self-controlled. She had never once been known to say, "Off with her head!" in a fit of jealous rage. She had always said it after careful consideration of the consequences.

Now, with Lord Timden having just dived out the hatch and left her standing alone and ridiculous in her all-but-invisible dress, she allowed herself a moment to take stock of the situation. Her Brogorans were excellent archers. They could easily turn him into a Leeban porcupine before he had swum out of range. But this would involve raising an alarm, and then they, and the rest of the crew, would have a pretty good idea of what had just happened.

She stepped to the hatch. It was a three-moons night at the moment, and it took only a moment to spy him on the water. He was making good time, swimming with long, determined strokes, making for the docks at the harbor. She would have to hurry if she were going to dispatch a boat in time to catch him. And then what would she do with him? She smiled at the possibilities but then shook her head. Ah, well. That would only tarnish her reputation in the end. There would be no disguising the fact that he had left during the night. But no one needed to know how abruptly and early on that had taken place. As for the peculiar mode of his departure? Well, there was no accounting for demigods.

Something was floating away from the ship just below the hatch. She leaned out for a better look. It looked like . . . yes, a pair of trousers. They must have torn away when he hit the water. Fair enough. Lord Timden would be in for a little embarrassment himself tonight.

DERUFFILLUM IS A working town. Even before the sun is putting the first early blush on the hilltops east of town, men are on the docks. Porters are trundling cargo in and out of the warehouses; fishermen are bringing in the night's catch. In the marketplace, the fishwives are setting up stalls and removing the debris of yesterday's commerce, and the night's commerce too—there are always a few drunks sleeping it off in the comparative privacy of the fish bins. Usually they wake up once they're rolled out into the square.

A cackling in the corner hard by Mellian's Public House turned a few heads. "Hey, get a load of you, Big Dub! Looks like you had a glorious night of it!"

"I hope she was worth it!"

A slope-shouldered ox of a man, grimy and with a light dusting of fish scales, staggered to his feet. "Whazzit?" he said. He looked down. He was naked except for a grayish pair of underpants. "Hey!" He searched the ground at his feet. "Hey!"

"Don't look at me," the crab lady said. "What would I do with your filthy clothes?"

"They must've thought you were somebody else," someone said.

"Who could be that desperate? Cackle-cackle-cackle!"

Meanwhile a few blocks away, Timo had discovered a single brass coin in the pocket of his roomy new pants. He held it out to a bread seller. The man hesitated a moment before he took the coin and then reached under the table to pull out a misshapen loaf about the size of his fist.

"This big enough for ya, buddy?"

"That will do nicely, thank you."

The bread seller chuckled. "You're ever so welcome, your honor," he said in a mincing, singsong voice.

Oh. That would be this man's mocking version of a Shalkin accent. Dabbians supposedly shared the Shalk language, but theirs was a harsh, back-of-the-throat version that any well-bred Shalkin pretended not to understand at all.

Timo lowered his chin and thought of a fisherman he had overheard bawling out his crew a few moments before. "Well, all right, then," he belched. That seemed to do. He got the loaf. He flattened his shapeless hauler's cap onto his head and stumped away.

Mornings down at Deruffillum harbor have a bit of a chill to them, even in summer. Timo shivered as he strolled along, eating the bread, heading uptown. The place he was going was on the far side of the city. Up the hill from the docks there were proper shops and fine carriages filling the streets. He stooped to look in a shop window and felt something like a bird fluttering against his back. "Back away there," someone growled.

It was a passing coachman who had just flicked him with his whip. Timo turned quickly but didn't catch the man's eye. The carriage clattered by and people kept walking on with their heads down. No one had noticed a thing.

"How about that," Timo whispered to himself, and smiled. For the first time since he had set foot on the planet, he was *passing*. He set off up the hill at a jaunty pace.

He turned a corner and stopped. Up the street were a couple of Brogorans in the splendid uniforms of the royal house of Fengal. They were standing at a crossroads and eyeing the passersby. Suddenly one of them crossed the road and accosted a tall gentleman in a fine, long-tailed coat and breeches and a towering tri-corner hat. The other Brogoran stepped over and began talking with a fellow carrying a bundle out of a shop. This fellow was also tall.

Timo stepped back around the corner. Dalada hadn't wasted any time. He hurried back a ways toward the docks and then tried another, smaller street going uptown. More Brogorans on patrol. He stooped as much as he could and slunk back toward the harbor. Where could he hide?

The harbor was a busy place now. All the slips and every station on the piers were taken up with fishing vessels or small freighters or tenders from the big ships. Crews of men swarmed the docks, loading and unloading, swinging bundles of stuff onto their backs and tramping away with them. All of them were dressed about like him.

Timo came on down to the main plankway joining the docks and strolled along, looking out to the tenders coming and going on the piers. There. A sleek, high-prowed boat of the same dark wood as the *Paninanina* was just leaving, and working their way through the crowd on the pier were a dozen or so of Dalada's Brogorans. Timo turned and began walking away, forcing himself not to run.

"You there! Big fella!" The voice was coming from the nearest vessel. Timo dared to look up. "Yeah, you! Well? Are you looking for work or not?"

"Yeah, sure! I can haul like anything!" Timo bellowed back.

"We got five, six loads of black tea and clapper nuts up from Fengal to bring in. About a day's work. You going for the hour rate?"

It took Timo a moment to make sense of that. "Yeah. Hour rate."

"Well then." The man was a stumpy fellow with a misshapen nose. He scratched his chin and cast an eye at the golden sun just visible over the tops of the warehouses. "I'm calling it two hours in."

"Ha!" said one of the passing haulers. And the fellow tramping behind him spat and said, "Yer a tight one, Suggo! Less than one hour in, for sure."

"Two hours is my call," Suggo said, folding his arms.

"Done," said Timo.

It wasn't bad work—just walking back and forth from tender to warehouse, carrying large but not especially heavy, coarsely-woven sacks. He kept pace with his fellow workers, who slowed to a gentle stroll as soon as they were out of Suggo's sight. They were a gabby bunch. Grippum had a wife—he used the term "steady woman," which suggested a rather fluid nature to social arrangements here on the waterfront—and a couple of wild boys. Cappy knew how to read. Tark worked the fishing boats when the Slipperies were running the Maybay.

He became "Big Tim," with no debate on the subject. He fabricated a boyhood in a tenant family on a Shalkin estate and a run-in with an overseer, which placed him nicely enough in the general order of things. And explained the accent. When they broke for lunch, the others shared their bread and sausages with him, as well as a bucket of beer from the closest tavern, as a matter of course. That "Big Tim" should show up at the docks late, in a bit of a daze and utterly penniless was as unremarkable an event as a morning mist. He was a hauler, after all. It felt good, this rough camaraderie of strangers. He laughed, and the laugh came out of his belly in waves of deep, bellowing guffaws. He had never laughed like that before.

He kept an eye on the harbor traffic as he worked. Launches of Brogorans kept arriving from Dalada's ship. They set off in pairs, heading up every street into the city. Some of them passed pretty close. They never gave him a glance; he could have been a post on the dock for all they cared.

Big Tim's pay that evening was a handful of heavy brass coins, one for every hour of work. He stood on the dock, clinking the newfound wealth in his pocket and surveying the harbor. Traffic at the docks had thinned out. Dalada's troops had disappeared sometime in the afternoon. Tomorrow he could go uptown, search out the Deruffillum Society of Lesser Knowledge, and Meggy. And Meggy's link. He could get in touch with the Earthplat again. Yes, he really needed to do that, he told himself. But for now, the quiet in his head didn't seem such a bad thing.

"I 'spose yer going to Mellian's?" It was Grippum.

"What?" Timo looked around. It was just the two of them. "Oh. I guess. I can sleep the night there, can I?"

"With as much companionship as you please. They've got food too. The Beer Barrel Chowder is kind of famous in these parts. Come on, I'll show you the way."

At Mellian's, for a few pennies extra you could drink the good stuff, a deep-brown, foamy brew with most of the chewy bits strained out, and an extra kick going down. They called it Anvilhead. His buddies had the idea he needed a lot more of the stuff than they did. He lost count.

There was a fight. Cappy had been playing bugbag—a simple gambling game based on whose stumble bug would emerge from a bag first—and a couple of fellows had the impression Cappy had done the bag shake in an unsporting manner. Accusations turned to threats. Voices were raised. People nearby turned their chairs to get a better look.

"Cappy's too smart for his own good," Grippum grumbled. He and Timo were propped up against the bar. "Looks like he needs us." They weaved their way over to Cappy's table, which was no more than a single plank laid across some sawhorses. Tark was already there. The three of them ranged behind their friend.

"What's this I hear, Cap?" Grippum was all smiles. "Playing the bugs fancy, are you?"

"He was stacking the bag," the fellow across the table said, the words coming in a deep, gravelly slur. He was a broad-shouldered fellow with the deep-creased face and scarred hands of a fisherman. His companion was a younger and taller version of the same theme. "We both saw it." His friend nodded but didn't speak. He was sizing up Timo.

"I know it can look like that, gentermen," Grippum said heartily. "But the thing of it is, young Cappy here's got a nervous condition. Makes his hands shake just awful sometimes. That's why his Ma made us promise to look after him. Ain't that right?" Tark nodded. Timo nodded too.

The older fisherman got up. His companion did the same, but without a lot of enthusiasm. The younger fisherman was about to say something, but the older man leaned his weight on the table so that he loomed over Cappy and sneered, "Bet it was your Ma taught you how to cheat, too."

By this time the room was quiet enough that you could distinctly hear the younger fisherman breathe a long, sorrowful sigh. And then things happened quickly. On the waterfront, an unkind reference to somebody's mother was pretty much the equivalent of a slap across the face with a gauntlet.

Cappy, whose hands had been folded quietly on the plank in front of him, flung his arms out to the side to knock the big man's hands away and send his upper body crashing to the table. The table collapsed. The fisherman grabbed Tark's coat on his way down. The younger fisherman punched Timo in the side of the face. It was a wild swing with little force behind it. As Timo stood with a startled look on his face, Grippum crouched and leaped forward, driving his head into the other man's stomach. The two of them tumbled into the men at the next table, upsetting their table and their drinks. These happened to be fishermen. One of them stood up and shoved Grippum backwards. "Come on, boys,—we can take these haulers!" he said.

"Wait!" Timo shouted. The two newcomers paused, their fists at the ready, looking at this tall stranger with some bafflement.

The younger fisherman got to his feet between them. "What are you guys waiting for?" he said.

His next move always remained something of a mystery to Timo. It seemed to him that he just reached out and grabbed all three men. And then he held them until everybody calmed down and the fight was over. As Grippum described the scene—and he described the scene for years to come, with embellishments as they suited his artistic sense—Timo leaped over the fallen table and fell on the three men like an avenging demon. Before they could blink, he had corralled the head of one of them in the crook of his right arm and grabbed the middle one with that hand, while simultaneously snatching the third one's collar with his left hand.

Then came the famous Whirlwind Spin. He yanked all three men off their feet, stepped back into the open space and spun like a top. As Grippum would tell it: "Their boots went flinging acrosst the room and their socks, too! Their bare feet were whooshing over my head! I counted twenty-one spins.[27] Then Big Tim dropped the fellows to the floor like nets full of gobbers."[28]

In fact, he only spun them three times, and only one boot came off. He really didn't hurt them at all. But the dramatic effect was tremendous. Haulers and fishermen all around the room, paired up and ready to have a go at each other out of a sense of solidarity with their kind, just had to stop and cheer.

And that was it for the fight. Haulers and fishermen alike wanted

---

27   Twenty-one is a number of mystical significance in Dab, that being the number of days the ancient and now retired god Dabberum was on a drunken tear after creating beer. The bizarre and whimsical rumplerock formations of the Dabbian coast, and many other geological oddities, are attributed to this episode.

28   Gobbers—extra-thick jellyfish.

to buy the big fellow a drink. And talk about the Whirlwind Spin. And compare it with the mighty pugilistic deeds of yore.

Timo's room that night was on the house. He nearly had it to himself, too; it was just Cappy and Tark with him. Tark broke out in a fishing chanty he had just picked up. Cappy told him, in a mumbling, drowsy voice, to pipe down. He didn't, and about the fourth time through, Cappy joined in on the chorus. And the fifth time through Timo added his sonorous baritone to the mix. Somebody in the next room said something unintelligible and started beating on the wall. They slowed up the chorus to match the beating, brought the song to a thunderous finish, and then collapsed in gales of laughter.

They collapsed into a bed. Timo ended up with most of it, but Tark and Cappy didn't mind. And Timo didn't mind that somebody's foot was under his head and his arm was draped over somebody's chest. A fine bunch of fellows, these mates of his. This was his last thought before he dropped into the deepest, soundest sleep he had experienced since he was a child.

HE AWOKE WITH a start. The room was dark; there was no window. But outside there was distant shouting of a lazy sort, the clanging of a bell, the splash of water being thrown on paving stones. It must be early morning on the waterfront.

The mission, yes, the mission! Today he would be tested as he had never been tested before. Today he had to rendezvous with Meggy, get to the site of the explosion, find the true source of the buu, and then . . . And then, well, the mission was rather open-ended. Ideally, stake some sort of claim on the buu in the name of the Human interest. And ideally, keep it out of the hands of the Outside Force and their Gadgerene clients once their fleet arrived. To succeed at either one of these goals would be tremendous. He wouldn't just be promoted—he would become a legend. The opportunity for greatness, for lasting, meaningful accomplishment, had found him even in this desolate outpost. Today was his day.

In the dark down at the foot of the bed, some creature emitted an unearthly growl. No wait—that was just Cappy snoring. With great care, Timo extricated his arms and legs from their entanglement with his bedfellows.

Timo had slept with his clothes on. He was ready to go. He stood a moment longer in the dark. He felt the need to say goodbye. It was foolish, he knew. These fellows wouldn't understand what he meant. They wouldn't understand that he was saying goodbye to everything—everything Calema was or could ever have been. It was all about to be swallowed up by an incomprehensibly vast and powerful outside world, a world whose gentlest touch would crush it.

And it really didn't matter if his mission succeeded or failed. There was nothing he could do to stop that.

Chapter 13 • THE ARCHDUKE'S GARDEN

THE DERUFFILLUM SOCIETY of Lesser Knowledge had a house on the grounds of Archduke Glee's palace. The King's palace was ancient and cramped and surrounded by banking houses on the busiest street in Deruffillum. But the Archduke's palace was a grand complex of buildings atop a bluff overlooking the city. You could see it from just about anywhere.

The wrought-iron fence around the Archduke's palace grounds was the longest iron fence in Dab. There were many gates, with a pair of ornately attired guards at each. None of them liked the look of Timo. Or the smell of him. They kept pointing him on down the line, to what they called "The Common Gate," way 'round at the back.

On the far side of the palace the streets were narrower and the homes smaller, although still showing an effort at upkeep. This was where the tradesmen and day laborers of the city lived. Their gate to the palace had a queue of wagons backed down the street, and two pair of seriously dressed and armed guards on either side. A prune-faced clerk was perched at a high counter just inside the gate. Every minute or so, a wagon with a pair of men would pass the guards' inspection and one of them would climb down and hand up a slip of bark to the clerk. Each time the clerk went through his own little ceremony of surprise and distaste, just so these common folk would know what an imposition they were.

This didn't look good. Timo had no idea what was on these slips of bark. He placed himself at a discreet distance and watched. A lot of the men had brown dust on their sleeves and trousers. A construction project? Timo set off into the narrow lanes of the outer town, looking for more dusty men.

On a large, well-rutted street out on the edge of habitation was a warehouse of sorts and a yard with piles of brown roofing slates. Wagons with teams of gorgies were lined along the street, waiting to be filled. Timo ambled by on the far side of the street. Every wagon had a pair of men on the seat. Except for one. "Hey Sagger!" a man on the wagon ahead called back. "Doing it all your-self today?"

"Geow!"[29] Sagger answered. "Zibby didn't show!"

Timo hurried on. He crossed the street and circled back on the other side of the line of wagons. He picked up speed until he was going at a half-trot. "Hey!" he huffed, "You Sagger? Zibby sent me. Said he couldn't make it. Wow!" Now he was leaning on the wagon bench, making it sag his way a bit, and looking around, impressed. "This is some big deal!"

"What's it this time?" Sagger asked.

"He says it's somethin' he ate."

"Somethin' he drank more like it!" called the man in the wagon ahead. He laughed. Sagger chuckled. Timo smiled and shrugged.

---

29   A Dabbian insult meaning, originally, "Go roll in the muck with the billyboes," not-so-subtly suggesting the recipient was unsuccessful with women. Now a jocular greeting among city dwellers.

"Well, get on in! Aren't you a big ol' boy! I bet you can do Zibby's work one-handed!"

It took a good while for the line of wagons to get up to the service gate. It gave him time to get educated on Sagger's home life and his money troubles and his no-good boys. Timo's new buddy didn't ask him much about himself. Apparently he had seen right off this was the strong, not-too-bright type. Sagger flourished a crumpled bit of bark as they approached the gate. The guards waved them through without a glance.

Timo spent the rest of the morning hauling roof slates here and there in a sort of box on his back. "Slow it down a bit, guy. Yer makin' us look bad," was the sum of the instruction he received in his new career. He slowed down. He gawked at the buildings and grounds in appropriate, bottom-rung-worker wonder, and spied out his surroundings. At the lunch break he ambled off into some trees. The Society of Lesser Knowledge house, he knew, was close by the palace on the far side. Today he had to make his rendezvous. He just needed to get close enough to see the visitors coming and going. Then he just needed to catch Meggy's eye.

The Archduke's grounds were famous for having gardens of every sort. And he apparently was on friendly terms with every middling noble in the land, for these gardens were infested with pairs and small groups of the higher classes strolling about. Fortunately there were also patches of natural forest throughout. Timo worked his way along in this cover. He found a deeply shaded spot where he could see the main entrance and most of the courtyard of the Society's house.

It was a mixed group coming and going here—high and low nobility and even some in drab commoner's clothes. Even some women. In the gardens he had passed, the visitors had been at their ease, idling along, admiring the flowers and exchanging aristocratic witticisms. But these people in the courtyard were conversing in earnest. Voices were raised; arms were waved.

There was Meggy! He exited the house in a grand promenade, chattering away with a couple of other noblemen as brilliantly dressed as himself. He nodded and exchanged a word or two with everyone he passed. He seemed popular. But even as he was speaking, Timo could see that his eyes were constantly surveying the courtyard. Good show, Meggy.

Suddenly the babble of conversation petered out. Everyone turned to a spot out of Timo's vision. As if at a signal, all the men bowed their courtliest bow. The women curtsied.

The Archduke appeared, resplendent in a long-tailed jacket with flashing epaulets. He turned and extended a hand to a companion. A woman, dressed in white and gold.

Timo took a quick step backward and thumped into a tree. The Empress! Had she tracked him here? But that was impossible; he was nobody now.

Her Brogorans appeared, four of them. They were dressed now as civilians—that is, in the bright and flattering robes of civilian Fengal men. They still stuck out a mile. They had their weapons mostly hidden and they maintained their guarding positions around their mistress in a loose fashion. But their pale, grim faces and military posture told all the world: Brogorans on duty.

And they were looking everywhere. Timo crouched low behind a bush and watched. The Empress' appearance in the courtyard brought all scientific conversations to a standstill. Queues began to form, all leading to Dalada. Even the Archduke seemed for the moment to be eclipsed. He took it well. He stood a little apart, leaning against a column, arms folded, and looking on with a smile. It was quite a social coup, playing host to an Empress.

The men approached her with some diffidence. These were Lesser Knowledge men, thinkers and tinkerers and recluses, most of them—unpracticed at the courtly bow, incapable of a single saucy witticism. But Dalada gave every indication of being fascinated with them all. She laughed. She leaned in to listen. She laid a delicate hand on one fellow's shoulder and his knees nearly buckled. They were all in her power now.

Even . . . *Meggy! I thought you had more sense than that. Have a little pride, man!* Timo couldn't stand to watch any more. He turned and slipped away.

There was a sizable stand of trees at one end of the grounds, with lush vegetation all around. It seemed a strangely wild place. The narrow pathway leading in was barely visible, almost an afterthought. Ah, yes. The Archduke's famous Garden of the World. Here were plants from all the civilized continents. He had spared no expense. And he had sought out expert advice. Every climatic region of Calema was faithfully represented.

Timo had the place to himself. The Lesser Knowledge folk were all at the Archduke's fete, and the idle nobility prowling the Archduke's grounds preferred the more commodious gardens. After all, the ladies' fashionable skirts wouldn't even fit in here.

He threaded his way through a Melligarian spire grove and paused for some sunshine on an outcropping of glistening black slabs representing the Hermit Mountains of Brogora. And this must be an oasis in the Great Gadgerene Desert. He gathered a pocketful of leathery gum-figs and walked on, tearing into one with his teeth. It was tough and made his eyes water with its pungent sweet-and-sour bite, but it was food. The massive oaks of the Shalkin High Forest were like the pillars of a cathedral. It was cool and quiet here, but a little too open to stay for long. The next habitat, a riotous tangle of palms and ferns and flower streamers representing the outer Fengal islands, was probably a safer place.

Evening was coming on[30]. Timo eyed the rosy haze in the west and sighed. Tomorrow, hopefully, the Society of Lesser Knowledge house would be free of empresses. In the meantime, this jungle would do as well as anywhere for a place to bed down for the night. He burrowed into a thicket of lilycoils and found a spot where, with a little maneuvering, he could just lie down and arrange the various members of his body among the stalks. Uncomfortable but an excellent hiding spot. He closed his eyes and immediately fell into exhausted slumber.

Steps. Someone was walking on the path. Timo carefully— and a little stiffly—turned his head to peek out under the leaves. Only a little moonslight was filtering through the growth overhead. The steps came closer. They stopped. Timo held his breath. The guard or soldier or whatever he was stood completely still. Timo couldn't hold his breath much longer.

The guard jumped. Timo cried out. The guard cried out too. It was more of an "oof" than a fighting cry. And instead of pouncing

---

30 Calema turns about every twenty-one Earth hours.

on the intruder in the bushes, the guard landed heavily back on the path. Timo could see the man's shoes now. They were shapeless and roomy "potato shoes" made of gorgy leather, the same as Timo had on his own feet at the moment. As Timo puzzled over this, the shoes shuffled a bit and the man leaped again, this time perhaps an inch off the ground.

"Ha!" the man said. And then, "Oh! Oh!" He took off at an unsteady trot, headed deeper into the Fengal thicket.

Timo extricated himself from the lilycoils. He stood on the path and let his eyes adjust to the gloom. It was a clear, cool night. The strip of sky visible overhead was well sprinkled with stars. A muffled "putt," like a burp from a small animal, sounded behind him. He turned and saw a spark sailing upward out of the undergrowth. It reached a height just over his head and hovered there. A puff of wind caught it and it danced away, down the path.

Timo followed, trying to get a closer look but not daring to touch it. Against the blackness of the thicket, it seemed to make a small bubble of golden light in midair. If the breeze gave it a sudden bounce, it seemed to flare just a bit more. It drifted closer. He cupped his hand behind it. Now he could see the gossamer thread from which it was suspended. He slowly moved two fingers up either side of the thread. They brushed against something soft—a round puffball of some sort, only slightly more substantial than the air around it. The spark leaped upward out of his reach.

Another spark was tracing a lazy river-course down from the treetops. This one he caught. It didn't burn. It didn't seem to have any weight at all. As it lay on his hand, the glow began to fade. He he could see the outline of a seed, like a tiny teardrop. He opened his hand and blew on it. It flared so brightly his eyes were dazzled for a moment. When next he could focus on it, it was high over his head.

"Aren't they lovely."

Timo turned. No, this man couldn't be a guard. It was plain even without seeing his clothes or his face. Just the outline of the man—short and wide, rocked back on his heels, his hands in his pockets and his head tipped back, looking up at the treetops instead of at him—you could tell at a glance he was as harmless as a Leeb could be.

Timo looked up, following the other's gaze. Three more sparks were caught in a sort of slow whirlpool not far over his own head. "They're amazing," he breathed, turning slowly to follow their progress. "Sparky Flowers. I've read about them, of course, but I had no idea they were so . . ."

"So bright?"

"So yellow. Plant luminescence is on the green side generally, at least on . . ." He stopped himself before saying "*on Class C planets.*" How could he have dropped his guard so completely? He had even lapsed into his aristocratic Middle Shalk accent. This man had to see, even in that poor light, that he was in the rough clothes of a Dabbian laborer. There was simply no explaining himself now.

"I hadn't thought of that," the stranger said, still looking up, not giving Timo a second glance. "But sure, sure, all the glowy things in the Sulphur Swamp are green or blue. Hadn't thought of that. What do you suppose? Is it all that sunshine in Fengal that makes 'em glow yellow? 'Course all the plants in this section are so strange. There's a funny pepper plant right there by where you're standing. It's all curlicues, every little branch, like they can't decide which direction to grow. Here, let me show you."

The man reached inside his coat and drew out a ball of light. He held it up by a string and gave it a gentle shake. The whole thicket went ablaze with the light. Now Timo could see the stranger's earnest oval face and unsuccessful beard. He was dressed in tradesman's clothing, neat and respectable. Timo felt terribly exposed in all this light.

"Won't there be guards here on the Archduke's grounds?" he asked.

"Oh, sure." And still the man hadn't really looked at him. His eyes were fixed at a point on the ground near Timo's feet. He crouched, still holding the light aloft, and moved closer. "There you are!" he sang out, a proud papa calling his child. "Oh," he said, suddenly straightening up. "You're right. They may think there's a fire." He cupped the ball of light in his hand and it faded to a gentle candlelight glow. He knelt on the ground beside a shaggy-looking plant. "Aren't they amazing, all these . . . these . . ." He made squiggles in the air with a finger of his free hand.

"Tendrils."

"That's the word." The man peered up at him. "Have we met? Sorry, I'm not good with faces."

"Probably not. I'm from Tipstitch in Shalk. I'm . . . Tim."

"Chumber. From up Hafswide way." The man gave a quick nod of his head and a blink, the no-frills greeting among social equals.

Timo did the same and then knelt on the ground beside him. "Pretty funny-looking all right. "Can you eat these?" He pointed at a slender pepper peeking through the mass of tendrils.

"Not till they're good and orange. Too spicy for me, though. Oh, are you hungry? I have some barley bread in my bag."

"I reckon I could have a bite. But what is this bag you're holding the Sparky Flower seeds in?"

Chumber showed him as they strolled back to the little clearing tucked cleverly away in the Fengali jungle. He had made a little bag of Sparky Flower silk. It was nearly invisible, but with the bag resting in his palm and the glowing of the seeds retarded by contact with his skin, you could just see the outlines of the bag.

"You know a lot about plants, sir," Timo observed. And that was all it took. The next two hours were an enthusiastic overview of Dabbian horticulture, with a hearty dose of Chumber's scientific and metaphysical speculation, and a guided tour of the Sulphur Swamp.

The man was a wonder of naiveté and genius. There was no end to his curiosity. Along the way, Timo mentioned that he had heard from a Fengali that the Sparky Flowers created something of a nuisance around the forest villages. In the season, bat moths had a habit of getting tangled in the silk and zigzagging all over the place like maniacal shooting stars.

"I'd like to see that!" Chumber enthused. And then his eyes got even wider. "But of course, that's why they glow! You know how moths are with candles. So the moths are attracted to the seeds and carry them away to new places!"

"Hmm, I hadn't thought of that. But how do the seeds know about the bat moths?"

"That's the very question I've been putting to the Society here! How do the seeds know? It is a deep mystery, sir. I think about it often. I ask everyone at our Society. I don't think anyone knows. Not really. There is so much that seems to me to be fanciful. I mean no disrespect. Is there anyone in the Societies of Shalk who is investigating these things, sir?"

"I think you are further along on these matters than any of us."

At this compliment Chumber's grin turned his oval face into a nearly perfect circle. "I just like to look into things," he said, blushing.

They were sitting on a log nicely placed to make a natural bench. From a nearby branch, the Sparky Flower bag cast a cheerful glow around the clearing. They had finished off Chumber's barley bread and his jug of beer, and Chumber was slouched over on one elbow, his gaze dreamy.

"I heard there was a big explosion up your way just the other night," Timo ventured. "I'm thinking it was Swamp Worms." Out of the corner of his eye, he could see Chumber's face taking on a different sort of smile, the eyebrows up, the lips pursed. Yes, this was the smile of a man who Knew Something.

"Come on now,—there's no such thing as Swamp Worms," Chumber said, holding on to the last word, a sure signal he had more on his mind. "Fire-spitting worms! A children's story!"

"You've never seen fire coming out of the ground?"

"Well of course, that's just a Slobbervine. Cover it up with dirt, and it starts to fester. Makes the ground swell up. Then one little spark . . ."

"That *is* remarkable. To think that a few vines could make that great explosion everyone is talking about."

"That wasn't Slobbervines. No sir."

"Oh?"

Wait. Wait. Timo knew better than to ask again. The best informant is one who doesn't think you are particularly interested. Who wants to impress.

"It was seeds, sir! Seeds!"

"Exploding seeds? That's extraordinary."

Chumber told him everything. This took a good deal of the remaining night, as he couldn't help but include a generous helping of his own Lesser Knowledge analysis with every significant fact.

When he got to the green dots, Timo began to feel a little light-headed. He had never paid much attention to the hard sciences growing up, but every youngster in the Gass worlds is abidingly impressed when first posed the question: "What is the most valuable substance in the galaxy?" Everyone remembers that image of brilliantly green buu crystals embedded in black kanchanchanc-itite. What little boy (or otherwise defined gender representing the traditionally more intrepid segment of the species) hasn't dreamed of being a buu explorer? The ancient dream of sudden, fabulous, glorious wealth. Who hasn't felt that?

He was now in possession of the biggest scientific secret Human Interplanetary Intelligence had uncovered in its 1500 year existence. An organic source of buu! This was it! This was his mission! Ahh! And him with his link broken!

"But Chumber," he said musingly, as if the thought had just come to him, "what are you doing here? Why aren't you in the Sulphur Swamp looking for more ironroot seeds?"

"Advice of a friend. He suggested I remove myself from Hafs-wide until the ruckus dies down."

"But you're the only one who knows . . ."

"Ah, sir, not everyone is as dedicated to the pure Lesser Knowledge as we are. Someone might want to use these crystals to do harm. Even . . ." His voice dropped to a wheezy whisper, "To make war."

"How dreadful. But don't you want the Lesser Knowledge to be advanced? You could be famous!"

"If you had seen the destruction those few crystals caused, you would not be so eager for this 'advancement'! Can you picture what would happen if men had this power? What kind of place the world would become?"

"Yes. I think I can." Timo glanced sideways. Chumber was hunched forward and staring forlornly into the dark beyond the clearing, as if he could see the approaching disaster already. Such a nice man. Such a harmless, well-meaning man, to be the fulcrum upon which the whole history of Calema is teetering. Doomed to be a symbol—to everyone either the greatest hero or the greatest villain of all time—when all he ever wanted was to *know.*

How can I spare him from that? How can anyone put things back the way they were and let Calema once again trundle along its way in happy ignorance? I'm just a spy. Not even a very good one, it turns out. There's nothing in my bag of tricks to save him. Or any of them.

"You're a good man, Chumber."

This was enough to startle the liveryman of Hafswide from his thoughts. "Hm. Hm. Well." He gave a nervous chuckle. "Most folks are, I suspect," he said. "But you, Tim, why haven't I seen you in any Lesser Knowledge meetings? You know so much."

'I've just come over from Shalk to see my cousin Meggy. A distant cousin. I don't know anybody else here."

"Tollum! I know him! Well, he doesn't know me, but he's a good man. Very keen on the Lesser Knowledge, even though he ... well ... he doesn't actually know how to *do* anything."

'Yes, that's my cousin. He doesn't believe a gentleman ought to be able to do any practical sort of work."

"Ah, a matter of principle. That explains it. You're staying with him, then?"

"Yes. That is, I haven't met up with him yet. My . . . ship just arrived."

"And you had to see the Sparky Flowers first, of course! But Tollum lives somewhere in the middle of the city, by the King's palace, doesn't he? You have a fair bit of a walk yet tonight."

"I suppose so."

"By all the friendly gods, this won't do! Why, there's plenty of room with us! I'm staying with my nephews in Upperslip Village just over there."

'I wouldn't want to impose."

"Well now, that's nonsense. We Lesser Knowledge men help each other out. You'll come spend what's left of this night with me, and that's all there is to it." He stood up and reached to retrieve the Sparky Flower bag from its branch. "Oh," he said, holding the pose for a moment. "About the Ironroot seeds ..."

"Your secret is safe with me."

Chapter 14 • **WHAT CHANCELLORS DO**

"I HAVE A message from Javitz. It's just coming in."

"What's that?" Timo had been twisted sideways in the carriage seat trying to straighten the straps of his pantaloons, which were buried somewhere beneath a velveteen jacket and layers of flounced shirt. He was missing his roomy dockworker's clothes already.

Meggy Tollum, seated opposite, squinted slightly, as if at a twinge of pain. "Yes sir. I will pass it on verbatim. Station Chief Javitz says, 'YOU'VE BUMBLED AWAY THREE DAYS! THREE DAYS!' Excuse me, I didn't catch that, sir. Right. 'YOU'VE TAKEN AWAY OUR BEST ASSET AT THE SCENE,' I think he means me," Meggy inserted, " 'WHO KNOWS WHAT COMPLICATIONS HAVE COME UP DUE TO YOUR INCOMPETENCE.'" Meggy listened some more, nodding and saying "yes" and "I understand" from time to time.

He signed off and sighed. "We don't have much time. We have more intelligence on the Gadgerene fleet now. 279 vessels in all. Their course is taking them well wide of Shalk. They're definitely headed for Dab. They could be in the Maybay in as soon as a week."

"Do we have any of our people in that fleet?"

"No, and none of our allies are in there either, at least as far as we know."

"They're lying."

"Maybe not. You've missed a lot of news with your link broken. What the O.F. has pulled off . . ."

"The 'O.F.'?"

"Sorry. The Outside Force. Not a very original name, I know."

"Actually," Timo looked out the carriage window as he mused, squinting into the morning sun flashing through the trees. "Actually, it's a measure of how good they are, that we can't be any more descriptive than that. Gods, they kept the invasion secret not just from us and our allies, but from the better part of the Gadgerene Empire itself. That's astounding. Javitz must be apoplectic about that."

Meggy cleared his throat and fiddled with the trimming of his high-topped boots. "He's pretty much blaming you, Timo."

A few seconds went by before Meggy dared to look up again. Timo's face was a controlled blank. "Of course," he said.

"Well, we all thought you were dead. And there was that . . . problem with the Sessevian video."

"No, no, it makes sense. I was the one running operations in Kamerduk. But he didn't seem to be blaming me when he sent me on this mission."

"Right. About your mission . . ."

"It's simple, really. Figure out the connection between the explosion and the Gadgerene allies. Sorry, 'the O.F.'"

"Well, and to figure out what caused it in the first place."

"Of course. Have you got anything from the Lesser Knowledge people?"

"Nothing scientifically plausible. I managed to get some samples sent up to the Station. I don't think anything has come of that, either. Maybe there will be some news on the ground when we get there."

"Maybe." Timo sat back in the carriage seat and yawned. The light was hurting his eyes.

"You might as well take a nap while you can. It'll be a couple of hours yet."

"Thanks."

Timo had managed an hour or two of sleep on the floor of Chumber's nephews' house before Chumber had rousted him up and the two of them had threaded their way to the center of Deruffillum and Meggy Tollum's very exclusive apartments. He and Chumber had said goodbye standing outside in the gray pre-dawn light.

"I'll just be on my way then," Chumber said.

"Don't you want to . . ."

"He doesn't know who I am. And that's all right."

"You're a good man, Chumber. You're a great man of the Lesser Knowledge. Someday the world will know that."

"But not today, Tim. Remember your promise." There was an edge on Chumber's voice that was probably more than the morning chill. He was looking up at Timo with wide, hopeful eyes.

"I won't tell."

Now Timo closed his eyes and let his body sway with the jostling of the carriage. *"Who knows what complications have come up?"* Complications, indeed. Let Meggy think he was sleeping. Behind those closed eyelids his mind was churning. He needed a plan, and fast. It was going to have to be some kind of brilliant to explain away the buu blast and to stop the Gadgerene invasion. And save the world. And his career.

THEY WERE MAKING good time on the old river road when Meggy got an update on his link. The Gerts had offered the information that many of the ships had been loaded with bundles of Zimmer spires.

"Just what I was afraid of," Timo said. "Fire lances. Now that they have gunpowder, it's the logical next step. The Chinese used gunpowder in bamboo as a sort of disposable musket. It was the first step in the weaponization of gunpowder."

"How do Zimmer spires compare with bamboo?" Meggy asked.

"I'm afraid they're much stronger. We did some experiments. And if you coat the bore with skedge powder, a spire can be used for up to ten shots before it catches fire."

"Skedge powder?"

"It comes from mineral deposits in the Great Gadgerene Desert. They've used it for centuries to get a sort of mother-of-pearl finish on their jewelry boxes. But it's also a pretty good flame retardant. We have to assume they've figured this much out."

"Or just been told by the O.F. What about bullets?"

"They have lead mining in North Gadgerus, but we've kept a close eye on it. We haven't noticed any increases there. But the Gadgerenes are very skillful at rounding rocks into near-perfect spheres. I think that's what they'll go with."

"Jewelry again. It's good to have you back, Timo. And on the ground with us."

"I've done a pretty poor job as a field agent so far. It's not as easy as I thought."

The carriage stopped. The bleating of sheep and hearty greetings and conversation between Meggy's driver and some locals informed them that their road was blocked by a passing flock. Meggy put his head out the window and called out in his best foppish voice, "I say, Parlum, are we going to be . . . Oh, sheep again! How very vexing! Don't they have any roads without sheep?"

"I'm afraid not, Your Lordship," the longsuffering Parlum sighed. There was some chuckling and low-muttered commentary in the background.

Meggy sat back in his seat, checking the arrangement of his magnificent wig as he did so. "Is something amusing?" he asked crossly, still in full-blown aristocratic mode.

"You're good at this," Timo said, keeping his voice low. He leaned on the window ledge and took in the scenery. The sheep had kicked up a cloud of dust, making every break in the trees a portal for a hazy sunbeam. A shepherd boy was strolling away to the edge of the woods to fetch an errant lamb. The rest of the flock was milling aimlessly around the elder shepherd, who was still in easy conversation with Meggy's driver. "Nothing happens very fast here," he observed as he sat back in his seat. "Well, not until now."

Meggy nodded. "They're not bad people, you know, these Dabbians. They're a cranky lot, but they can be big-hearted sometimes too."

"I know."

There were a few other carriages parked when they pulled up at the Big Swide Inn. But inside, only a pair of locals were present.

"Why, good Mister Seez," Meggy pronounced, taking a stance amidst the tables and surveying the room with one hand stylishly on his hip, "Wherever has your clientele gone?"

"The customers, you mean? Ah!" Argum had been making damp circles with a rag, and now he slapped it on the counter. "All the bigwigs have gone up to the Duke's big house in the woods."

"Big house in the woods?"

"He means the Duke's lodge in the Night Forest," Nonesuch, one of the customers, offered. "You know, by the lake."

"It was the Distinguished Gentleman's idea," Nonesuch's companion Chapper added.

"That was no gentleman," Argum growled. "He was a *wizard.*" The proprietor of the Big Swide Inn, whose livelihood depended in good part on a determinedly cheerful disposition, had packed the maximum amount of venom allowed by Leeban voice into that last word.

"No," Nonesuch said, thinking hard, "He said he was a . . . Canceller."

Chapper brightened as a new thought struck him. "That makes sense. He sure cancelled the party here."

"Chancellor?" Timo asked.

"Could've been that, too," Chapper allowed.

"Long silver hair, deep voice?" Timo asked.

"That's the fellow," Nonesuch said. "And chock full of ideas! He got everybody into Come-to-Teas."

A moment of puzzled silence slipped by. "Committees?" Meggy asked.

"That's it, 'committees,'" Chapper said, pronouncing the new word in a mincing, singsong High Shalk accent.

"Do you know him?" Meggy asked.

"We met on the boat. And you are right, sir." He was addressing Argum. "He is a wizard."

"No! Where was the pointy hat then?" Nonesuch argued. "And the sparkly stick?"

"They don't wear that get-up anymore, Nunny," Argum said. "What will you two gentlemen be having, then?"

"I don't think we have the time . . ." Timo began.

"Two pints of Diddlyum's," Meggy said grandly, plopping his ample posterior into one of the many available chairs.

MEGGY'S CARRIAGE DIDN'T get them very close to the turning-off point. The Cart Road, hardly more than an extra-wide path here in the middle of the Night Forest, was blocked up for a mile or more with carriages. "I don't know who half of these belong to," Meggy said as they threaded their way down the row.

"Don't these belong to the Lesser Knowledge men?"

"Oh, they're here. But it looks like most of the aristocracy of Deruff has made it here, too."

Once the two of them turned off the road and entered the Night Forest, the single track turned into a well-trampled bog. "The boots I had on yesterday would have been much better for this," Timo said, looking woefully at his beribboned and buckled court boots, each now carrying a heavy load of black goo.

"Not really," Meggy said, slogging cheerfully ahead. "Once we get there, we'll find these boots to be much more useful. It's better to look smart than to be smart, after all."

They were still in the Night Forest, not even into the Sulphur Swamp proper, when they began to hear a sound quite unusual to the area: the ringing of axes. Soon they came upon a group of men felling and stripping straggly Black Gum trees. Meggy and Timo looked on in dumb silence for a few moments before an older fellow noticed them and strolled over. He smiled a knowing smile and tipped his cap.

"Good day, your lordships!" he said. "Sorry for the noise. The Big Hole is still a long ways down that path there. You can't miss it." The man was wearing a smart brown jacket with "cups"— upturned shoulder pads—marking him as one of the Baron's own overseers. He cast a quick, appraising eye over them and added, "Or young Trab here can show you the way and carry your things."

"What?" A wispy lad paused his wrestling with a vine-covered branch to gape at them.

"That won't be necessary, my good man," Meggy said. "We know the way. But may I ask, what does that strip of blue cloth on your jacket mean?"

"Oh, this!" The older man beamed and just touched the cloth without looking at it. "I'm a committeeman!"

"So ... You are in charge of this ..."

"The Timber Committee. Yes, yes. It's very ..." he screwed up his eyes in thought. "*Critical* for the *establishment* side of things, you see."

"What are you building?" Timo asked.

The older man and a couple of his crew laughed. "*We* aren't building anything!"

"We're the *Timber* Committee!" another man said.

"Of course! Quite right!" Meggy seemed to have caught their enthusiasm. "The *establishment* side. Always good to be thinking of the future. Pray don't let us keep you from your excellent work."

"Thank you, Your Lordships." The older man tipped his hat again and turned to his men, pointing and shouting out a string of largely unnecessary orders.

Meggy and Timo walked on along the now very wide and well-trodden path.

The deforested area around the Big Hole had an almost festival air now, what with all the aristocrats scattered about in their rainbow-hued finery. They seemed to be separated into groups. One group was strung along the perimeter of the Big Hole, setting up poles, for which there seemed to be a great deal of bother as to the height. Two other groups were gathered at different points on the rim of the Big Hole, engaged in some activity that had all of them peering over the edge. Another group seemed to be slowly circling the edge of the forest wall, gathering samples of the flora.

Close at hand, a large group of laborers was at work with axes and saws. They were fashioning the Black Gum trunks into usable lengths of timber. A couple of teams of grogies were dragging the finished logs to the near edge of the Big Hole. There the largest group of men by far, gentry and laborers alike, were bustling about what was clearly a sizable building in the making. Next to that a great tent had been erected. As they watched, a boy emerged from the entrance of the tent and set off running toward the group at the edge of the forest. He had a small satchel slung over his shoulder. They noticed another lad breaking away from one of the groups at the edge of the hole and running toward the big tent in the same fashion.

Timo and Meggy looked at each other. "It was just three days ago I was here," Meggy said.

"I take it none of this was here then?"

"Not a bit of it. I didn't think Dabbians were capable of this . . ."

"Speed?"

"Cooperation. The old nobles especially make it a policy to go it alone in every way possible. I've never seen this many aristocrats in one place before. Not even at the Archduke's balls."

"I suggest we go to the big tent first."

It was a large, round tent, originally white, one of those the Baron used for summer fetes on the lawn. The sides were rolled halfway up and the brightly-trousered legs of a milling crowd were visible as they approached. One mellifluous voice rang out over all others: "The Committee of Artifacts is now complete! Congratulations, gentlemen. Discharge your responsibilities with wisdom and thoroughness, and future generations will be greatly in your debt. Viscount Tarum, I give you the emblem!"

"Hurray!" and "Good show!" and "Yip, yip, yip!" sounded from the crowd as the better part of them began tromping out the tent opening. These Dabbians had not yet learned the gentlemanly "Hear, hear!" appropriate to such an occasion.

Timo and Meggy waited outside as the new committeemen filed out. Last of all was the grinning Viscount Tarum, a broad purple ribbon pinned to his lapel. As they passed into the shade of the tent, a boy dodged around them and ran up to the man dressed all in black and standing in the precise center of the tent. It was not the Chancellor.

"Ah, here it is at last. Thank you, young man." Derving Vale patted the boy on the head absent-mindedly as he perused the slip of Winding Tree bark he had been handed. The boy stood by in rapt attention. Derving produced a pencil and scribbled a line or two on the bark. "Off you go, then," he said. He smiled benignly as the boy sped off toward the door, once again dodging around Meggy and Timo. His gaze met Timo's and the smile vanished.

To Timo, Derving seemed to . . . flicker. One moment he was his normal, wizardly self. Then, just for an instant, he was shorter, his suit was rather dusty, and he had a startled, almost fearful look on his face. Timo closed his eyes and turned away. He felt as if he were falling. The sensation passed a moment later, and he looked up to see Meggy performing his sweeping, courtly bow and Derving responding in kind. Names were exchanged. Timo's confusion was gone. He was happy to see that these two liked each other. Everything was going to be fine.

"Lord Timden! How pleasant to see you are all right. Somehow we missed seeing you when we disembarked."

"I . . . took an earlier landing."

"Ah. That explains it. We came here directly, of course." Derving launched into an explanation of the committees. Timo was a bit surprised, and grateful, that Derving didn't pry any further into the events of his night on the ship with the Empress. But then, a wizard doesn't pry and is never confused or at a loss for words.

And a wizard is an excellent host. Derving led them outside, to the construction, "The Instruction Center," as he explained.

Future visitors will be wanting the specifics of the Great Light—precisely when it occurred, how high it was estimated to be, its effect on the local flora and fauna, et cetera, et cetera.

"And what caused it," Meggy added.

Derving became grave. Meggy and Timo and the growing knot of on-listeners became grave as well. Birds stopped singing and the sun may have dimmed slightly, too. "It is all very well," Derving intoned, "that people apply themselves to such questions. The gods have left us free to ask, to search, to test. You Lesser Knowledge men (at this word, Timo and Meggy felt a twinge of shame) have your ways. But what if you never find it? What if the cause is not within the compass of our small, Leeban existence?"

He seemed to lock eyes with each of his listeners, one by one, as his question weighed upon their consciences. "Drebbell the Farseeing saw it all centuries ago. The *cause* is quite simply the end of the world."

"Hold on here." Meggy glanced about, startled and a little embarrassed that he had spoken this out loud. "Um, begging your pardon, Your . . . Wizardship. But if it's the end of the world, why are we building this house? There won't be anyone . . ."

"An excellent question. Many scholars have puzzled over the precise interpretation of the events Drebbell described. Some are difficult to understand *literally*. The rivers turning to syrup, for instance. Snake Trees. It may be that the Ladder signaled the end of the *age*, not of the world itself. There may very well be a great change afoot. After all, if the Ladder has brought legions of Sky Folk to the world, who can say what *they* might be up to?"

At the mention of Sky Folk, Timo and Meggy exchanged a surprised glance. Derving saw it all and made a mental note to inquire into Lord Tollum's background as well. "In any event," he continued, "We build, we preserve, we commemorate. The Great Knowledge must be passed on." He eyed a group of workmen heaving a timber into place on a low wall. From there his gaze wandered up, as if admiring the lines of the great edifice-to-be. His listeners did the same. "It will be magnificent," he said, a little hoarse with emotion.

He assured Meggy and Timo that a place could be found for them on one of the "quality" committees.

"But how did these committees get formed in the first place?" Meggy asked. "We never felt the need for them before."

Derving smiled. Someone chuckled. The circle of listeners— and the circle was growing moment by moment now that Derving had been spotted outside the tent—relaxed in a quick outward ripple of smiles and knowing glances. And then all eyes turned to Derving.

"That was before the arrival of the Chancellor," he said, with some show of modesty, giving all to understand that this was a vast understatement.

"He sorted us all out," someone in the back piped up.

"It's what Chancellors do," Derving said.

"Is the Chancellor here now?" Timo asked, looking about.

"Certainly not," exclaimed a young gallant at Timo's elbow. His red ribbon was affixed to his swooping lapel with a jewel-encrusted pin. "He's with the Prime Committee. You know. Up at the Lodge."

"Ah, would that be at the Baron's forest lodge? The one by the lake?" Meggy asked.

"Naturally."

"That's where we need to go," Meggy said to Timo. A mild gasp went up from the crowd.

"It's all right," Derving said, raising his hand to restore order. "This man is a friend of the Chancellor's." To Timo he said, "I will provide you with a scrip."

"Thank you," Timo said, with only a slightly too-long pause. "Shouldn't we see what's going on here first?" he asked Meggy.

"Of course, you should," Derving said firmly. "You must. Now, let me see." He glanced about. The young dandy with the red ribbon cleared his throat. "Of course. Lord Barrowmill here is a Committee Liaison. He can make the necessary introductions."

Young Lord Barrowmill took the discharge of his duties as Committee Liaison quite seriously. It couldn't be enough to simply walk them around and make introductions. They needed to know, first of all, who the Committee Chairmen and Vice-Chairmen were. And their titles and families. And then came the lengthy—and somewhat muddled—description of each committee's terribly, terribly important work.

The men setting up the poles and fussing over their height were in the Measurement Committee. In addition to the poles, their work involved clattering about the area with *very special* rods of a precise length (derived from the Chancellor's own foot!). Also a lot of string, which seemed to have a particular attraction to the buckles on Lord Barrowmill's boots.

And around over here, leaning out over the side, was the Aquatic Committee. A frame of sorts had been anchored in the ground, and a pair of compound pulleys, the action of which defied all Lord Barrowmill's attempts at explication, had been used to lower a rowboat to the water's surface far below. There a gentleman and a farm lad were seated: the gentleman dabbling at the oars from time to time and the lad raising and lowering a weight on a rope. Up above, one man was calling out fathoms while others furiously jotted down the numbers and made calculations. "Over ten rods deep here," one of them announced. "Ah!" said Lord Barrowmill.

Next was the Wall Committee, also leaning precariously over the side of the Big Hole. Most of them were observing and giving advice to a pair of young men who were suspended by ropes. Timo and Meggy crawled to the edge and peered over. The young men were at different depths—one about a third of the way down and the other nearly two-thirds to the water. Both were whaling away at the wall with pikes. The near one stopped his hammering for a moment and pried out a chunk the size of a fist. "That will be four-and-a-half rods" called out a fellow on his hands and knees next to the supporting ropes. The young man below took out a stub of chalk and marked his new specimen before putting it in a pouch. "Another rod down, then," ordered a stout man seated comfortably a few feet back from the edge. He had the purple ribbon.

On a sheet behind him lay a row of what looked like chunks of glass, each marked as to the depth at which they had been quarried. They came in every color. Some were nearly uniform, while others were shot through with streaks. "Have you found a pattern?" Meggy asked.

The stout gentleman furrowed his brow. "Pattern? No one said anything about a pattern. That wasn't in our charter, was it?"

"I'm quite certain it wasn't," Lord Barrowmill said and then brightened. "We'll be needing a Pattern Committee."

They visited other groups scattered about the area collecting samples of various things. Enthusiasm was high. Progress was slow, for each new find seemed to call for a round of spirited discussion.

It was already mid-afternoon when a lad came running up with a scroll of Winding Tree bark in his hand. "Begging your pardons, Your Lordships," he said a little breathlessly. "Would one of you be Lord Batherum of Tipstitch?"

Timo took the scroll and unrolled it. In florid script it read, "The bearer of this scroll is a credentialed Man of The Lesser Knowledge. He is accorded auditory access of the second degree with the Prime Committee."

"'Auditory access,'" Timo repeated. "So I may listen in, I suppose."

"But you won't be *on* the committee," Meggy added. "And you won't have the privilege of speaking. I suppose that is where the information will be, though. A pity I don't have access as well. I should know some of the people there." By this time they were walking back to the path leading to the main road. "Committees! Rules of order! I never thought I would see it in this Society. How could the Duke allow all this? This Chancellor of yours has remarkable powers of persuasion."

"He's a wizard."

"That's another thing I don't understand. Wizards are none too popular in Dab. They all left during the war, you see. Still some hard feelings about that. I can't see how a few magic tricks could change everyone's opinions so quickly."

"Didn't you feel it?"

"Feel what?"

"You didn't feel it? They . . ." He wanted to say, *"They cast a spell,"* but Meggy was already eyeing him with a bemused expression. "They are able to exert an influence on people near them. They make people like them. Believe in them. Want to follow them."

"Oh, I've heard of this. It's called 'Allure.' Some sort of hypnotism technique, supposedly. Wait, you're saying these wizards have hypnotized the entire Society of Lesser Knowledge?"

"I don't think its hypnosis."

"Well, it's a good thing it doesn't work on us."

At the road, Meggy told his driver, over Timo's worried objections, to go on back to the Big Swide Inn and wait for word from them there. "The road from here is still blocked off," he explained to Timo, "and of course, we'll be staying at the Baron's lodge tonight. Or failing that, at the big house at least." They set off on foot.

Once clear of the carriages clogging the road at the turnoff to the Big Hole, it became a pleasant enough walk. The road here was narrow and meandering and overhung with trees. The Night Forest had its name because of the vine cover, and many of these vines were in flower at the moment. A near-constant fugue of bird calls sounded from every direction. Many paths led away into cool, deep shadows. Meggy whistled a tune as he swaggered along, marking the downbeats with his tall dandy's walking stick.

"What song is that?" Timo asked.

"It's called 'Billium's Missus.' I'm afraid the words are rather vulgar."

"A drinking song?"

"We have hundreds of them. It is the true flower of Dabbian culture."

"I guess the Diddlyum's Milkmaid *was* something to sing about."

"Now you're catching on, Lord Timden."

"Shh." Timo stopped and waved a hand to make Meggy do the same. He pointed to the bend in the road ahead. After a moment they heard a voice. A woman. And she was making no effort to preserve the rustic peace of the Night Forest.

"Pretentious prigs, the whole lot of them! All they know how to do is talk. Not a one of them can even tell you how a counterslip ratchet works, I'll wager."

"I'm certain this evening's Committee Circular will afford us ample opportunity for addressing the more practical issues, Your Ladyship. Oh, and how *does* a . . ."

The woman, who had been keeping a vigorous pace, stopped abruptly upon rounding the bend and seeing Meggy and Timo. Although she was wearing all the layers and adornments demanded by Dabbian aristocratic fashion, her clothing seemed subdued, almost modest compared with what they had been seeing all day. Her shoes allowed her to walk normally on the rough track, and her sensible hat did not pose even a mild threat to her walking companion. In fact it did little more than shield her head from the sun. Her companion caught up with her and abruptly stopped his speech.

"Marchioness Damberell! Count Spood!" Meggy exclaimed, and took a few seconds to execute an elaborate court bow, including the latest Strammang Pivot and cane swizzle-and-tap. "How delightful to encounter you in this sylvan setting!"

"Ah . . . Lord Tollum, is it not?" the count managed after a moment's thought, and shuffled his feet and nodded his head. He was encumbered somewhat with the bulky Emanation Box in his arms. "And . . ." His eyes went from Lady Damberell to Timo and back again. She gave the barest shrug and continued eyeing the newcomers with cool detachment and an expression that flickered between disdain and private amusement.

"Allow me to introduce my cousin, Lord Timden Batherum of Tipstitch." Again, a flourish of cane and buckles and laced cuffs. Timo bowed.

"Lord Tollum has told me much of your work in the Lesser Knowledge, My Lady, My Lord," Timo said. Lady Damberell kept her lips in a stately semi-frown, but she could not suppress the twinkle of amusement in her eyes. No doubt it was the Middle Shalk accent.

"And the two of you are bird hunting, I take it?" Meggy inquired. "How . . ."

"Certainly not!" Lady Damberell thundered, nearly making poor Count Spood drop his Box.

"Just a stroll, you see," Spood said. "Just some fresh air before dinner."

"Of course," Meggy said smoothly. "A great benefit to the digestion, I find."

"The blasted committee has invoked 'Privilege of Party' or 'Prattling' or—whatever the nether gods . . ."

"Apartment, My Lady," Spood said. "Privilege of Apartment."

"Thank you, Nebbling. I can't be bothered to learn all their weaseling terminology."

Meggy stepped forward in an earnest show of sympathy. "Oh, Lady Damberell! Lord Spood! I would have wagered my lands that the two of you would be on the Prime Committee! Running the thing! Oh, the very idea!"

"Do you really think so?" Spood asked. "Because I've wondered sometimes when I've been explaining a very particular point if whether they were really . . ."

"They are besotted with wizardry!" Hathet Damberell had fire in her eye. "I banished the crowsuits from Frolirillum as soon as I had the chance. They know nothing of value. They produce nothing. They only prey on men's vanity. The weak-willed seem to find them irresistible."

"Oh?" Timo peeped.

"And now they have the Hafswide Society of Lesser Knowledge under their thumb! And it was such a fine Society, too. Such lively discussions." She turned to Spood and her expression softened a bit. "So many original minds."

The count had been peering intently at some strings in the corner of the Emanation Box. It took him a moment to realize he was the object of anyone's attention. "Excuse me?" he said, looking from one person to another. Something in the Box caught his eye and his gaze swiveled to the Box's corner once again. He pivoted slowly, waving the device in a high arc. His mouth was slightly ajar, as if he were about to sing along with whatever distant quaver his Box was receiving.

"A new species of bird?" Timo whispered.

"No bird. This is another . . . I don't know what they are. They've just appeared the last few days. Very low. And . . . patterned."

"What sort of pattern, Nebbling dear?" Lady Damberell asked gently.

"Complex. Repeating. But low—below what we can even hear. Nothing a bird . . . ah, I must be wrong." He blinked and shook his head. He had stopped with the Box held chest high, pointing at the treetops. He grinned sheepishly at the others. "It seemed to be coming down from the sky," he said. "Of course that's . . ."

"It was coming from that direction, you say?" Timo asked. "You're sure?"

"That was the indication."

Timo ran several paces back on the road. He stopped at the opening to a path and craned his neck to see where it led.

"Are you all right, Lord Batherum?" Lady Damberell asked.

"Splendid! Quite! Tell you what. I'll meet you all back at the lodge. I have to . . ." He couldn't keep from looking down the path even as he spoke. "The fact is, you see, I really, really like birds!"

He ran into the forest.

Chapter 15 • TOURISTS

IT WAS HARD going. This path had been tracked by russerveebs—a kind of short-legged, long-bodied deer, fond of twisting under branches and through thickets. Timo crouched and thrashed his way along a shadowy green tunnel. But the direction was right, as near as he could tell.

In a few minutes the track dumped him onto a real path, and he could walk upright again. He turned his head to listen. It was late afternoon and the rich insect and amphibious life of the Night Forest was stirring to full, communicative life. Buzzing, creaking, croaking, chirping, whistling, and whining assailed him from all sides. At least the sound of his own movements shouldn't be too obvious. He turned left and took off in a cautious walking jog.

This path had a lot of twists too, and at every turn he paused just a moment to peek around. A quick flash of blue between the trees ahead made him snap back and go into a crouch. A bird? A moment later he heard laughter. He wriggled under a lush canopy of ivy and waited.

In a few seconds they began filing by. He counted eleven of them, Leeban as nearly as he could tell, dressed in the colorful and impractical fashions of the aristocracy. They were talking eagerly in Dabbian, but with an odd lilt to the accent that he couldn't quite place. The one at the front of the line was attempting to describe the lay of the land around the Big Hole, and suffering many interruptions and good-natured raillery for his pains. It was an altogether unruly group. They plucked at the bushes as they passed, or whacked them with sticks. One of them leaped to snatch at a bug and tumbled into the fellow in front of him. Laughter ensued, followed by insults, followed by more laughter.

They passed by, and the creature sounds of the Night Forest returned. Timo peeked out. All clear. He began to make his way along the path as stealthily as he could, going back the way the strangers had come.

Long ago in his HIPI Academy days, he had taken a course in Survival in the Wild, which had included a few days on tracking. He hadn't thought about it since. Now he puzzled over every bush and twig he passed. They all looked about the same. And there were so many of them! He slowed to a crouching shuffle.

He needn't have bothered. It didn't take any woodcraft at all to see where the strangers had joined the path. They must have been charging along through the undergrowth three or four abreast here where they had spilled out onto the path, the ground was so broadly trampled and branches broken and vines torn. If these were fellow off-world spies, they were a poorly trained lot. Timo turned onto the newly made track.

A hundred meters or so along, he saw the light of a small clearing ahead. He slipped off the exposed track and approached through the underbrush. Still no signs of any people. He waited and listened. The bugs and all the other noisemakers of the forest seemed to be carrying on with no concern. He stood up and stepped into the clearing.

Actually he stepped halfway into the clearing, at which point he walked face-first into an invisible wall. He tumbled backward with a noisy rustling of underbrush. He lay for a few seconds, confused, thinking he had been attacked in some way. But no attackers appeared. He sat up.

Now he could see the signs. Here a branch was bent down at the edge of the clearing. There in the clearing itself a whole bush was flattened. In fact . . . He stood and peered into the open area. The clearing itself was a suspiciously regular oblong shape. This had to be a landing craft or elevator pod, cloaked.

He put out a finger and carefully pressed it forward until he found the hard, invisible surface again. No buzz, no rippling sensation, no momentary iridescence. So, not one of ours. Human cloaking technologies focused on force fields, as did those of most of the adversaries against whom he had been trained. And force fields always produced some sort of reaction. This must be an old, activated coating method of cloaking. Not the best, really. This would be susceptible to the sensing methods of even the more technologically backward Gass species.

He began to walk around the small clearing, reaching over and touching the side of the craft from time to time. As nearly as he could tell, it was uniformly smooth and featureless. An elevator pod. These were dropped from a low-orbit vessel and impelled and controlled primarily by anti-gravity, leaving no trace of their passage, at least no trace that Human Interplanetary Intelligence technology could perceive. The eleven people he had seen passing would have just about filled up a pod.

He tripped and sprawled into the undergrowth again. Something had caught him on the shin. He sat up and saw a snake undulating through the vines just before his eyes. He scuttled backward. The snake wavered slightly but remained poised in its downward passage. Its slender body was a dull green, and its eyes shone like jewels beneath sinuous yellow ridges that trailed well back on its head. Timo reached out and touched it. He laughed.

It was a Spang, a snake-fish from Neemnot mythology. Neemnots incorporated Spangs—and many other fantastic creatures—into their designs at every opportunity. You could always spot Neemnot vessels. They were the ones sprouting gargoyles and nymphs and magical beasties borrowed from a hundred other civilizations. It was a serious drawback in utility, but one they cheerfully put up with.

Now the noisy, unruly, unprofessional group that had passed him in the forest made sense. They weren't spies—they were tourists. Nobody knew what Neemnots really believed; they seemed to cheerfully believe everything. So here they were, out on a mystical lark, here in the hope that they might see somebody's—anybody's—ancient prophecy fulfilled.

The Spang wobbled when he touched it. That explained why it was no longer cloaked. It must have broken loose when he tripped on it, cracking its connection with the activated coating. He traced the body back to the vessel—well, to where it seemed to emerge from thin air. It curved in the traditional Spang gyre along the way, and it sported a smattering of brilliantly colored "jewels" among its scales, along with the distinctive yellow ridges. The Spang's mouth was perfectly round and smooth and slightly flared out. A buu jet.

Timo stood up and looked cautiously around. The insect chorus droned on, and the deep-shadowed stillness of the Night Forest encircled him. There was no indication his presence had been detected. He grabbed the Spang and wrenched on it. With a little levering back and forth, it snapped it off. And nothing happened. The pod remained cloaked. No alarms sounded. He hefted the Spang in his hand and smiled. The world was a good deal brighter. He had a plan.

IN THE BIG tent, The Purple Meeting was just winding up. Derving faced a semicircle of men comprising a good portion of the upper aristocracy of Greater Deruff. In one glance he counted a baron, a marquis, two counts and two viscounts among them. And every one of these resplendently costumed and bewigged gentlemen proudly bore a strip of purple cloth on his jacket.

One of them was giving a confused but enthusiastic accounting of the activities of the Timber Committee. His confusion was owing to moment-by-moment interruptions from the chairman of the Building Committee, who seemed to be working from a completely different set of figures.

"And from the Mazewood trees, we managed ten good logs suitable for floor planks or windows. I can tell you, the hauling and stacking alone . . ."

"Oh, well, about those Mazewood trees!" trumpeted the Building Committee chair in a derisive tone, ostentatiously producing a scroll and unrolling it.

Some of the other committee heads were beginning to glance around. The old fellow at the end, leaning heavily on his cane, seemed to be nodding off to sleep. "Thank you, Lord Saragum!" Derving broke in, "Splendid work! I knew the Timber Committee was exceeding all expectations when I saw the magnificent edifice of the Instruction Center rising before our very eyes this afternoon!"

The two antagonists gaped, first at Derving and then at each other. For a moment, both were speechless. Derving acted quickly.

"Great progress on all fronts today, wouldn't you agree, gentlemen?" Derving accepted the rumble of half-formed remarks emanating from the group as a sort of collegial agreement. "The Prime Committee is pleased—pleased!—with our efforts." He was holding up both hands as a sort of benediction. The gesture changed gracefully into one beckoning them toward the door. "And now the reward of our labor awaits us at the Great Lodge."

Lord Saragum raised one finger in a modest attempt to interpose another word, but he was rather roughly jostled by the others as they flocked toward the door. The wizard managed not to notice. Everyone exited into warm, bright sunshine. The committee leaders set off for their carriages. Derving paused to make one last survey of the great clearing.

Without giving it the least thought or effort, he assumed a dramatic pose—an imperious, black-clad figure standing on a slight rise, arms crossed, looking over—and gravely approving—both the fire-ravaged landscape and the industrious Leeban activity scattered across it. *Yes. Yes.* He seemed to be saying. *This great work* will *be accomplished.* Slowly he turned a full circle.

He paused and turned his gaze backward a few degrees. That group of men over there, by the Big Hole. They looked local. Certainly their clothes matched the garish standard of Dabbian nobility in these parts. But Derving didn't recall having seen them before, and there was something . . . odd. He watched awhile. They walked funny: just a little pigeon-toed, as if their shoes didn't quite stay on their feet. But how could they *all* have bad shoes? Now three of them stood with their backs to the Big Hole. They were smiling in an odd, self-conscious way. Another man, standing in front and facing them, looked over both shoulders and then made a quick motion with his hand out of sight in front of his chest. The little group broke up.

Back in his undergraduate days Derving had picked up many wizardly curses. Some were meant to cause harm to others. Some were so potent they were reserved only for grand ceremonial occasions. But some were just a way of blowing off steam—an eloquent, stylish way of course—a wizard must never be undignified. Derving, cursing wholeheartedly, was perilously close to being undignified at this moment. He bounded off the little rise and strode toward the visitors as rapidly as Leeban legs could go without running.

He singled out one of the men. "What are you doing here?" he hissed. "Why did you bring all these . . . these . . . Who authorized this?"

The man was aghast, wide-eyed. "I . . . I . . ." he said. And then he started speaking in the rapid-fire hoots and hums and whistles of common Neemnot. Derving's face turned red. He shook his head violently and rushed forward and slapped a hand over the other man's mouth.

"Shut up! Just . . . shut up! Before you destroy everything!"

Chapter 16 • THE LESS-THAN-PRIME COMMITTEE

THE SUN WAS setting and the great bell was ringing out the eighteenth hour as Timo trotted up the gravel sweep to the lodge. Duke Arumbeed called this grand pile a "lodge," and his titled guests obliged him by doing the same, but to the servants and townspeople it had always been the "Forest Palace," an object of local legend and the setting for a whole genre of scary bedtime stories.

The Seventh and Eighth Dukes of Haflum had planted massive oaks all around the original lodge—which really had been a hunting lodge then, just a place to get away from the women and wear comfortable clothes and scratch yourself when you want. Arumbeed's father, the Tenth Duke, actually had been an avid hunter and had expanded the building as far as good taste would allow. Arumbeed didn't give a twig for good taste. He loved building projects. To do anything with the palace would have been ruinously expensive, but here in the heart of the Night Forest, he had turned his peripatetic imagination loose.

Timo stopped and stared. "Rambling" was too kind a word for it. This place rambled with malice aforethought. It wove and ducked and branched out among the oaks. Where possible, it reared up to a height of three or even four stories, sprouting dormers and gables and cupolas in profusion. Over there was an arcade. This corner had a turret. He was going to have a problem just figuring out which of these entrances was supposed to be the front door. He spotted Derving hurrying up the steps of a more-or-less major landing. He followed him in.

This door opened onto a spacious reception room. A good many nobles were standing about in casual groupings with tankards of the Duke's beer in hand. But whatever conversations they had been having among themselves had all been suspended for the moment. In the center of the room, the three wizards were addressing each other. For an instant it seemed to Timo that he was watching some sort of play. It just seemed that the wizards were speaking a little too loudly and standing a little too formally and the expressions on their faces were all too composed. And the next moment it was all . . . perfect. He stepped into the room and into the now-familiar glow of devotion and contentment. *We have wizards.*

"We were about to become concerned," Shamgath said in his lilting Fengal accent. The onlookers chuckled at the subtle use of irony. *Wizards, concerned!*

"Eighteen o'clock by the Duke's bell," Gerund said. "The Prime Committee is already assembled, you know."

"I was detained by pressing matters at the Prophetic Site, Your Enlightenedness."

A couple of seconds ticked by before the Chancellor perceived that no further explanation was coming. Well, he could hardly expect an apology. Wizards, at least in the presence of commoners, are incapable of apology.

"Of course," the Chancellor intoned grandly, as if an important point had been proved. Raising his voice even more, he continued, "And now we need wait no further. The Prime Committee session is at hand! All those with auditory access may now take their place."

The three wizards wheeled about to face the great double doors now opening on the other side of the room, the Chancellor's cape gracefully accentuating the movement. A smattering of applause broke out.

"You're just in time," someone said. The face was familiar. Timo had to stop clapping to place it.

"Oh, hello, Meggy. Yes, you mean for the Prime Committee. Say, you know what … The scrip here just says, 'The bearer of this scroll' has access, et cetera. It could just as well be you."

"Why, so it does."

"You know these people. You should be the one …"

"Quite right." Meggy snatched the scrip and trotted across to where the last of the chosen few had already entered. One of the Duke's footmen frowned and bent and made a show of studying the scroll, still upside down to him. An instant later he straightened up, a satisfied smile on his face. "In you go then, Lord Tollum," he said. "I was wondering where you'd got off to."

For a moment, those left behind in the reception room had trouble meeting each other's glances. There was often an awkward silence when a wizard left the room. Everyone had the feeling that he had been on the verge of saying something terribly clever, but now he had forgotten it.

Dottie the serving girl was the first to speak. "The North Great Room is right through this hallway over here, Your Lordships.

Tables o' fancy little foods to eat, but not get full on." The room relaxed with a ripple of laughter. Dottie was nonplussed. "'Cause there's dinner after the Committee meeting, remember. Meantime there's plenty of beer in there, that way." She had been carrying a wide wooden tray and she waved it now in the direction of the hallway. "Thank you, sir. Y'Lordship." Men were setting their empty tankards on her tray as they passed, and she was dipping in a miniature curtsy with each one. "Ah, Lord Beedley, we have those little fishes with the big eyes tonight."

"Thank you, Dottie."

"This beer is marvelous, Dottie!"

"Glad you like it, Lord Garullum. We've got some other fine ones in there too. Oh, good evening, Your Lordship." She had come to Timo and now she gave a slightly lower curtsy, despite the tray full with tankards, and despite the curve of her saucy half-smile.

"A well-ordered good evening it is," he answered, gazing into the distance over her head, without thinking giving the coldly aloof, High Shalkin response to a greeting from a social inferior. Damn that bug. Once he was back in charge of his own operations, he would have to look into a programming fix. Make it easier to switch styles.

"Begging Your Lordship's pardon," she said quickly, curtsying for real now, her eyes down. Timo hated himself.

"I'm sorry, miss," he said. "I'm . . . Timden Batherum, of Tipstitch. Meggy Tollum's cousin."

"Ooh, Lord Tollum!" she cooed, smiling again. "He's a favorite around here!"

"I thought I was your favorite, Dottie," someone said.

"You are, too, Lord Nain," she said. And so the group withdrew to the North Great Room in somewhat repaired spirits.

Count Spood was already there, gravely contemplating an array of cakes and holding up the line.

"I've heard these are wonderful, Lord Nebbling," Timo said, plucking the first cake he came to and offering it.

"Thank you. Oh, hullo Lord . . ."

"Timden. Of Tipstitch."

"Right. Say, did you find the thing making the strange emanations?"

"I'm afraid not. But it was a pleasant stroll in the woods."

"Did you happen to hear any Chubby Wailers?"

"I'm not sure."

"Oh, you would certainly know if you had!" The Count was overcome with a high, hiccupping chuckle, and it took a moment for him to compose himself. In the meantime Timo surveyed the room. There was a rather large group in the corner that seemed to be engaged in something more interesting than polite conversation. Voices were raised. They talked over each other. They broke into laughter.

"I'm glad to see Hathet—Lady Damberell—has joined us again," Spood said.

"Who is the young fellow with the . . . hair." The group seemed to center upon a young man with a mop of flaming red hair. He was seated at a table and sketching rapidly on a bark as the others looked on and commented.

"That's just Lefton Steep, the Duke's . . . I don't know what to call him. The Duke's 'Maker of New Things.' Just a boy from the village, but quite clever in his way."

Spood and Timo drifted over and took up places behind the others. It seemed to be a boat of some sort that he was sketching. It was strangely rounded, with walls, and oars poking out of the walls, and a roof.

"I think the Duke has you this time, Lefton," someone said.

"It's absurd! Impossible!"

"It is only impossible until someone does it the first time," Lady Damberell said firmly.

"I am sorry, My Lady," said a short and wide gentleman whose flowing whiskers obscured his mouth entirely. "But in this you are mistaken." He spoke in a slow, rumbling bass and his pronouncement rolled to its conclusion with majestic finality.

"Oh?" said the Marchioness.

"Well," said the gentleman, taking her remark as a plea for him to continue. "The methods of philosophical inquiry guide us in such matters. You see, it is a *categorical* contradiction. A boat by its nature is intended to be *above* the water. The very words 'underwater boat' are an absurdity."

"That's what I said," someone volunteered. There seemed to be a ripple of assent.

"Just put a hole in it—and there you go!" someone else said. General laughter.

"Is that really what the Duke wants poor Lefton to do?" Spood asked. "Make an underwater boat?"

"It's for the Big Hole," Lefton said. "I mean, The Pool of Prophecy. They want to know what's down there under the water. I've sent a couple of the boys in swimming, but it's too deep for them. They can't stay down long enough."

"Of course not," said the bewhiskered gentleman. "We don't belong there." He was standing across the table from Lefton. He spun the bark halfway round to give Lefton's sketches a glance. "A pity," he sighed. He moved to put the bark back in its place, but Lefton pinned it to the table with his finger.

"Hmm," the boy said.

The group seemed to be breaking up. "Are there any of the little fish left?" someone asked.

"I think they're talking about fire mountains over there."

"Ah, they've brought that red beer I was telling you about!"

Lefton hadn't moved. "Have you thought of something, dear?" Hathet asked, almost in a whisper.

He turned the bark so the sketch of the boat was completely upside-down. "My boat turned over once," he said. "I ended up under it. It was dark. I thought I was going to die. I grabbed hold of one of the crossbars . . . and it didn't sink. It held me up. How did it do that?"

"It was made of wood, after all," Spood said.

"It wasn't floating on the wood," Lefton insisted. "It was sticking up. Hardly any of the wood was in the water."

"I think you're on to something. I've seen that too." Hathet said.

Lefton sketched the top half of a circle, with rippling water under it. He drew in the torso and head of a man within the half circle. The few who remained of their group gathered in closer.

"But if it isn't the wood, what is holding up the upside-down boat?" asked an earnest young viscount, too engrossed in the sketch to notice his wig was slipping to one side.

Timo was holding his breath. The Gass had a rule for any of their people on a Protected Planet, and it was a rule drummed into every spy before he was allowed planet-side, and zealously main-tained and referenced again and again in every report they had to file: you must never, never, absolutely never interfere in the scientific development of the natives. There was a humming in Timo's head. He was here, he was present in this moment, when a critical breakthrough in Leeban scientific understanding might . . . just . . . happen. They were so close. So close. And he couldn't say a thing. Somewhere in the room, people were talking loudly, servants were scampering to accommodate new arrivals. But here, gathered around Lefton's sketching, there seemed to be a sacred stillness.

"I think it is the wind," Lefton said.

"Wind!" the viscount scoffed. "It is closed off. There can't be any wind."

"The wind is already inside," Lefton said, not sounding at all sure himself.

"But there is nothing *there*," insisted an elderly gentleman. "As the poet said, (here he planted his feet, set his eyes aloft, and quavered) 'With tenderest caress, she let go young Holgroth's hand, embraced the wind, and welcomed the abyss."

In the silence that followed, Timo distinctly heard the viscount choke back a sob. Someone sniffled. Even Hathet seemed misty-eyed.

"Yes, well, but," Timo stammered. "Wind must be *something*. You can feel it." The others nodded. There were footsteps behind him. Perhaps if some others were beginning to take an interest, they might keep this line of thought going, reach the necessary conclusion.

"Oh," Hathet said. "If the wind is trapped inside, perhaps it is pushing against the water."

"We've all seen that in the storm!" the viscount said.

"But how can the boat go down?" someone asked. "What could push it under?"

"Perhaps if it were very heavy," said a female voice behind them.

"Yes," Lefton said with excitement, "heavy enough to carry the air down with it. But wide at the base, so it won't flip over." He sketched in some new lines.

So close.

"Young man, do you see what you've drawn?" It was the woman's voice again.

Lefton stood up, clutching the bark in front of him as if it were a magic mirror. "A bell!" he cried.

YES! YES! A diving bell!

"And we have one!" Lefton added triumphantly.

"But surely the Duke would never allow . . ." Hathet began.

"He would love it!" Lefton exclaimed. "The adventure! The audacity of it! His bell, the world's first underwater boat! Of course . . ." he sat down quickly. "We will need a means of suspending it out over the water. I'm afraid I've never . . ." He picked up the charcoal stub and waved it in circles over the bark.

"A cantilevered beam. That's what you need."

"A what, Lady Damberell?" Lefton asked.

"Here, let me show you." She took the charcoal and he slid the bark in her direction. With long, sure strokes she drew in a beam and a platform to anchor it.

Behind him, Timo heard the voice of Sand, the butler: "Your Majesty, if we had known, certainly the Prime Committee would have reserved a place for *you.*"

"This committee is more to my liking, I think." It was a woman's voice again, and with a sudden chill in his stomach, Timo knew where he had heard that voice before. That resonant, musical, and *commanding* voice. He caught a whiff of musky and wild perfume.

He didn't turn around. From the corner of his eye he saw a broad-shouldered young man in loose-fitting clothing. He was standing alone with his back to the wall. Timo didn't dare look his way. Directly in front of him, at the far end of the room, was a door to another passageway. A couple of gentlemen were having a private conversation close by it. Timo looked that way and smiled. He gave a little wave. "Oh, there you are," he said. He began walking that direction. "I've been looking all over."

As he got close to the two gentlemen, they looked his way with mildly startled expressions. Then both of them fixed their gazes over his shoulder and their eyes grew wide. He heard a heavy tread behind him. "Yes, him" the Empress called out. It sounded urgent.

"Perhaps a breath of fresh air," Timo said brightly as he passed through the door. He turned the corner and broke into a run. This passageway gave on to another. In one direction was a door cracked open and beyond it the pale light of evening. He caromed off the wall and flung himself into the door. He was outside!

He was on a wide veranda. Over there was a group of people in chairs. An elderly servant was pouring tea. They seemed frozen in place, all eyes on him. Beyond the veranda lay a stretch of lawn and a waist-high row of bushes, and beyond them, forest. He bounded off the veranda and leapt over the bushes.

He got halfway. It was as if he had run into an invisible net, a net that actively grabbed at his hands and feet. He fell onto the bushes, spilling over headlong on the far side, his feet still in the air, firmly caught.

He heard footsteps coming his way—not very fast of course; they didn't want to spill their tea.

"Is he all right?"

"I think so. His feet are still twitching."

"Not from around here, is he?"

"Poor stumper must've never seen handsyvines before."

"Someone should untangle him. Now, where did that servant get off to?"

Timo twisted around to look up. Against the background of the evening sky, he could see them now: thin, dark shoots reaching high above the bushes, each ending in a tightly coiled spiral. He began tugging at the vines holding his wrists. This seemed to make them tighten their grip.

The servant, who by this time in his life had perfected that stately, processional pace so sought after among households great enough to include a mostly ornamental upper tier of servants, finally arrived. He began gently picking at the vines around Timo's ankles.

"I think you'll need a knife," Timo said.

"That only makes them angry, sir," came the mild reproof.

Someone giggled. Definitely feminine. Another feminine voice spoke up: "Lord Batherum, you do have a peculiar habit of dashing off on a moment's notice." That was Lady Damberell.

"Has he done that here too?" Dalada asked. "How interesting. Bursts of nervous energy, perhaps?"

"Shalkin aristocrats are a tightly controlled lot, I've heard.

Perhaps some of them periodically just can't stand it anymore."

"Fascinating."

The small crowd of onlookers drifted away. The aged servant took a few more minutes to coax the bushes into letting him go, after which Timo had to walk a good distance around the outside of the handsyvines hedge before there was an opening wide enough to safely pass through. The Duke's bell rang, once. "The Prime Committee is concluded," a servant announced from somewhere inside.

It was very nearly nighttime now, and Timo was alone outside. Two moons were up and casting competing shadows. He mounted the steps of the nearest landing. A figure stepped out from the shadow of the porch. He saw the glint of gold.

"Please don't run away again, Lord Timden," the Empress said. Her gown this time was a striking blue, rather more concealing than what she had worn on her own ship, but still leaving no doubt as to the shape of the woman beneath.

"Good evening, Your Majesty." His conscious mind was at a complete loss; his bug's social protocols took over—he bowed.

"Are we such strangers as that?"

"I am sorry, Your Majesty. I was . . . startled to discover that you were here."

"Obviously." It was hard to tell her expression in the faint light, but her voice, at least, gave no hint of anger. If anything, it seemed tinged with melancholy. "My men were not trying to catch you, you know. You don't need to run from me anymore, Lord Timden."

"Your men were searching for me in the city."

"Well . . . yes. But not anymore."

"You didn't come here . . ."

She laughed. "It was a complete surprise finding you here. And rather a temptation, I must admit. I thought, perhaps the gods . . . Well, you know better than I what the gods are up to. 'Their ways are inscrutable, their punishments a blessing . . .'"

"'Their jests bitter,'" Timo said, finishing the proverb. By this time they were standing close. She was looking up at him with the faint moonslight shining in her eyes. After a moment's thought, she lowered her eyes and gave a faint nod of the head. It was almost a bow.

"Whatever your mission is, I won't interfere."

"My mission . . ." He was going to say something witty and flippant. Something the wastrel scamp of the Batherum clan would say at a moment like this. The slight turning-away of her head stopped him. "Thank you, Your Majesty."

"Dalada. My friends may call me Dalada. And may I call you Timden?"

"I would like that very much. Dalada."

"We should go in now, Timden. The bell rang some time ago."

"Of course. But wait. Please pardon me again for my vanity, but . . . Why are you here if you weren't looking for me?"

She was already through the door and into the hallway, gliding ahead of him with the light from the Toop lamps making her gold jewelry flash as she passed them. "There are others beside yourself on secret missions!" she called over her shoulder.

The Duke's magnificent dinner took up the rest of the evening. Timo was relegated to a distant table, sitting with a clutch of counts and viscounts. Meggy tried to get his seat exchanged so they could talk, but Sand the butler would have none of it. Every dinner's seating arrangement was a major work of diplomatic puzzle-solving. He wasn't about to mar the perfection of today's work.

The Empress Dalada, it seemed, was exempt from such considerations. She left her seat at the head table before the soup was half-finished and meandered freely among the other guests, greeting and chatting as if she were among her dearest friends. She settled at last where she wanted; a footman brought an extra chair and placed it next to Lady Damberell. These two, the only females in the room (besides the serving maids), carried on a lively conversation all evening, oblivious apparently to the stares of all others in the room. They whispered. Sometimes they laughed. It seemed to Timo they laughed the most when they glanced his way.

Chapter 17 • **A DEVIOUS PLOT**

"*FIRST WE NEED* a blacksmith's shop."

"You've come to the right hunting lodge then. Young Master Steep has his workshop off that way. And a morning stroll in the woods would be just the thing for the digestion."

Timo and Meggy stepped off the veranda and onto a gravel path that meandered through the grounds. Timo looked back.

"Don't worry about them. Everyone is at the other end of the lodge watching them take the bell down from the tower. We have the woods to ourselves. So what is this plan you've cooked up?"

"Let's get a little further away." The path to Lefton's workshop branched off into a thicket of young trees overlaid with whistle vines. This early in the season only a few of the long flowers were open, making more of a gentle sighing overhead instead of the thrumming chorus for which they were famous. Timo relaxed a bit. Not much chance of being overheard here. He pulled something from under his jacket.

"How the devils did you get a Spang down here?"

"It turns out it was a Neemnot elevator pod the Count was tracking yesterday evening with his . . . device."

"The Emanation Box. And you found the pod in the forest? Astonishing! They'll be wanting that back, of course."

"In time. What do you suppose would happen if this should be discovered by some local?"

"Oh, my gracious. What an Assertion of Fault this would make up on the Gassplat! Someone would be nipped for sure. And there would be years of sanctions. What do you have against the Neemnots?"

"Not a thing. But picture this: One of the locals brings this strange new object into the lodge. All the spies here know exactly what it is, even though it is horribly twisted and partially melted. They all call in: 'Never mind. Buu doesn't grow on trees in Calema after all. It was just a Neemnot ship that blew up.' And this includes whoever is spying for our friends, the Outside Force."

"Ah. And they call off the invasion. Nothing in Dab but sheep and tinsmiths after all. Very neat. But Timo, what if buu really does grow on trees?"

Timo shrugged and tried to give a sly smile. "*We'll* know to keep looking."

"I see. Hmm."

"You see a problem?"

"We don't know who the O.F. is, or how far their reach extends."

"What? You think they're in the HIPI? That's ..." Timo remembered the doctored video feed. "... highly likely. Damn." The two men looked at each other in puzzled silence.

"I trust *you*," Meggy said. "Do you trust me?"

"Mostly."

"That will have to do, I guess." He turned to continue their walk. "Shall we go to the smithy, then? I take it we have some twisting and melting to do."

LEFTON'S WORKSHOP DID have a small forge and a decent collection of metalworking tools. But nothing they tried had any effect on the Spang. The metallurgical properties of a buu jet—even a Neemnot version—were well beyond the current state of Leeban technology. Even the massive stone sledgehammer bounced right off the thing. And the rebound just about yanked the sledgehammer out of Timo's hands.

Meggy helped him up off the floor. "Maybe if we packed it full of explosives?" he suggested.

"Toop oil is the closest thing to an explosive they have in Dab," Timo said. "Well, until the Gadgerenes get here." They considered that prospect in glum silence for a moment.

"We could try Slobbervines," Timo said.

Meggy used his link to access the Earthplat secure knowledge database. "The HIPI doesn't seem to know anything about Slobbervines," he reported. "Are you sure this isn't just a local legend?"

"Try Mack. The Caleman Library."

It took a while for Meggy to find the HIPI's secure link to the Gassplat. He rummaged about in the Caleman Library for several minutes. It was a peculiarly quiet activity, this accessing information by link. Meggy's daydreaming gaze meandered to the corner of the room and fixed there. Timo watched Meggy's face, hardly breathing. The forge gave an occasional tick or creak as its temperature gently dropped.

"Nothing here on Slobbervines, Timo. Sorry."

"It has to be in there. It wouldn't be like Mack . . . Try 'Swamp Worms.'"

"Where do you get all this? OK, 'Swamp Worms.'" Another minute went by. "Hmm," Meggy murmured. And a moment later, "'Slime Streamers?' 'The flowers are known to release a combustible gas when buried in damp, acidic soil.' He has an illustration. Disgusting. Even the flowers. So . . ." He took a deep breath and turned to Timo, blinking hard. "What can you make with Slime Streamers?"

"A bomb."

"Oh, dear."

It was an unpleasant day's work. With everyone's attention diverted by the Duke's "Underwater Boat," they had no trouble procuring some knives and large sacks. With a few hours of tramping around the Sulphur Swamp—an impractical enterprise in their gentlemen's costumes—they had a fair heap of Slime Streamer flowers. They didn't seem very flowery. They were long tubes of a sickly yellow color, packed with viscous goo.

Under an awning in a far wing of the lodge, empty beer barrels were waiting to be carted back to the brewing wing. They took one and rolled it out to a sheltered place close by the work shed. They began layering in flowers and dirt, flowers and dirt. And in the center of the barrel, the Spang. As Timo dropped the lid on top, it seemed as if it had a little pressure pushing it up already.

"Now," Timo said, leaning on the rim of the barrel, "I seem to recall a report about a 'self-regulating drummer.'"

"Ah, yes. Lefton's little clicking box."

"The proto-mechanical clock."

"And, I take it, the timer for our barrel of mischief. Yes, I saw it in the workshop. He also has a variety of 'sparkers'—I believe they call them—for starting a flame."

"Well then. There we have our bomb. We'll give it some time for the flowers to decay. Then we'll set the timer and bury the barrel out here."

"'Bury'? That sounds like a lot of digging. I may be needed at another meeting that day." Meggy looked around. "But isn't this too close? Everyone in the lodge will hear it."

"That shouldn't be a problem. We'll make sure we're close enough to get here first and recover the Spang—hopefully a great deal the worse for wear. The locals will just chalk it up to Swamp Worms. And our fellow spies, once their orbiting plats have analyzed the data, will know that the blast came from a local substance and has a natural explanation." Timo glanced upward. "Hard to tell in these woods, but I think we have a few hours in the day. We should find our way to the Big Hole. Make an appearance."

"I was thinking it was time to return to the lodge and sample some of the Duke's excellent beer. No, no, of course you're right."

They began trudging along the deeply shaded path. "You know, Timo," Meggy said, "It's a brilliant plan and all."

"But too clever by half."

"Well . . ."

"I know. If we had more time, more resources, more people . . ."

"And more time."

"That too. But what else could make the Gadgerenes—and the O.F.—call off the invasion? If we can explain away the buu gas, Dab is of no interest to them. We have to try."

THEY PLUCKED SOME interesting plants along the way, and when they emerged into the clearing around the Big Hole, dirty and bedraggled and their arms filled with something strange, they looked like any number of other aristocratic enthusiasts. They dropped their loads with the Flora Committee and joined the crowd watching the men getting the Duke's bell into place. They were just about to swing it out over the water for the first time. It was very dramatic—the kind of work that called for a lot of shouting and arm waving. And heckling advice from the onlookers. It was difficult to hear each other.

"Does that beam look sturdy enough to you?" Timo asked.

"Some of these people have beer," Meggy said, looking around.

"Because I'm thinking it's just sticking out there too far."

"Where are they selling beer?"

"And what's holding the platform down? It just looks all wrong."

"No, no, it's quite the right thing. Beer helps the mind think of new ideas. I'll just have a look around, then."

This first use of the Duke's "underwater boat" was supposed to be purely experimental. They were going to ease the bell down into the water just a couple of feet and have some brave local lads swim under it. Then they would lower it a couple of more feet and wait to have the boys swim back out and report what had taken place inside the bell.

The crowd of onlookers became even more boisterous and argumentative as the bell was lowered. Bets were running in favor of a negative outcome. Lefton was down in the boat with the lads. Duke Arumbeed was planted off to one side with a few of his retainers, his shoulders back, his head high, a grim smile chiseled into his countenance. Only his left eye betrayed an occasional twitch. By the time the bell touched the water, Timo had leveraged himself to the edge of the Big Hole. He was tingling with excitement. Real science! Progress! The diving bell was not such an essential breakthrough in the great scheme of Leeban technological development. But the very fact that it was being done *this way*—experimentally, with more-or-less neutral observers—was deeply significant.

The men above let out the ropes, the pulleys turned, and the bell eased into the water. Lefton held up a hand and they stopped. The boat paddled closer. Lefton had a long pole with a hook on the end. He lowered the pole straight down into the water until the hook slipped under the edge of the bell, and then pulled it back. "Two feet, two fingers," he called out. He gave a sign, and the lads spilled off the boat on either side and swam under the bell. They lowered the bell again, inch by inch. Lefton took a second reading. Five feet, six fingers. Now the crowd grew quiet.

The water in the Big Hole was surprisingly clean. Timo could see the edge of the bell clearly. Perhaps a minute passed by. Shapes appeared in the water on either side of the bell. The lads were swimming out. The crowd above gave a brief cheer as they broke the surface and then quieted to hear what the lads were trying to say to them.

"It was great!"

"It was dark."

"We could breathe just fine!"

"The water did rise a bit."

"Then it stopped! It was only maybe three feet!"

Lefton had the bell raised back above the water. They brought the boat under the bell for another measurement. When it reappeared, Lefton was beaming. "Two feet, thirteen fingers!" he shouted. "The water rose inside the bell to only two feet, thirteen fingers! The underwater boat works!"

The crowd above—with the exception of those who had bet against success and were sore losers—broke into ragged cheering. Timo was among the loudest.

"Isn't it wonderful!" he said, turning around. "And to think we were here to witness it, Meggy! Meggy?"

Meggy at this moment was a good distance away. The wizards had shown little regard for the peculiarly Dabbian manifestation of the enterprising spirit, which sees every public gathering as an occasion for hawking food and drink. The beer merchant's tent was in the midst of a motley straggle of lean-tos and shelters hard against the edge of the clearing, as far from the Committee Tent as possible. Meggy bought a pint of Diddlyum's Woolly Sock, paid the deposit on the rusty tankard it came in, and found a shady spot among the trees. It was a convivial place. By this time in the afternoon, quite a lot of Lesser Knowledge dabblers had slipped away from their committees.

"Lord Tollum! What a pleasant surprise! Ah, I see you already have a Woolly Sock. I'm just discovering the wonders of the local brews myself. Sticktinyer.[31]"

---

31 Sticktinyer: "cheers" in Deruff.

It was Derving Vale standing there quaffing a Diddlyum's Milkmaid. He looked utterly natural doing it: elbow out, head thrown back, sun dapples glinting on the buttons of his coat, the rustic venue gauzy in the background. If Diddlyum had understood the concept of an advertisement poster, he would have chosen this.

"Your Lordship," Meggy said. Then he remembered to bow, spilling a cupful of beer in the process.

"I should think by now you could call me Derving. We're working together after all, on the Prime Committee."

"Yes. Yes! Your presentation on the Instruction Center was inspiring, by the way."

"Oh. You are very kind. But surely we don't have to talk Committee work on a lovely afternoon like this. How are you doing, Meggy? And your . . . cousin, was it? Lord Batherum? How is he settling in?"

It was a delightful chat there under the trees. Meggy had never felt himself so easy and clever and charming. His companion was an excellent listener. Somehow the sun had dropped noticeably lower in the sky by the time Derving excused himself with a graceful, self-disparaging remark. Meggy was left puzzling over the position of the sun. Then he puzzled over the emptiness of his tankard. Then he imagined the tankard filled again, and he smiled. The buzzing in his ears was very loud now. Funny he had never noticed these insects before. He would have to ask somebody about them. Because that is what we Lesser Knowledge men do. Somebody close by said something.

"What?" he said.

"I've been looking all over for you." It was Timo. He seemed to be cross about something.

"Is something the matter?"

"I've been looking for you for the past hour. And you've been here? Drinking?"

Meggy checked his tankard again. The evidence seemed to be against him. "I was talking with . . . Prime Committee people."

"Here?" Timo looked around. It seemed to be mostly petty nobles and their servants idling in this shade.

"They just left." *An hour? He had been talking with Derving an hour? What in the world had they talked about?* He knew it had been—he had been—terribly clever and fascinating. They had talked about . . . but even the feeling was fading now. "We had better get back to the Lodge," he said. "There doesn't seem to be much to do . . . Wait. Wasn't there something about a bell?"

CLOSE TO THE Lodge, they split up, Meggy going on and Timo stopping by Lefton's workshop to get the clicker and a sparking device. He opened up the clicker. It was actually a rather complex set of gears and levers. He wound it up to watch it go. Marvelous. Amazing precision for these handmade gears. It was clicking away, but the highly coiled mainspring did not appear to be unwinding at all. How long could it keep clicking? It could be days. This was no good. He couldn't unwind it. The barrel could very well be ready for blowing as early as tomorrow. He would just have to get everything ready now.

In one corner of the device was a small half-dome structure with a lever poised above it. Timo flicked the dome with a fingernail. The dome rang. By all the gods, Lefton. Not only did you make Calema's first mechanical clock, in one go you made the first alarm clock as well. This will be easy. There was plenty of wire in the workshop. Timo tied the clicker and the sparker firmly together, cocked the sparker, and carefully ran a wire between its trigger and the alarm's lever. He tripped the sparker several times getting the length just right. Every time he got a bright orange spark in his face. He had to blink hard to see again.

He got it set, and put the cover back on the Self-Regulating Drummer. The whole shed seemed to thrum with the ticking. Holding it, he could feel the tiniest jerk with each noisy clank, as if something alive were trying to get out.

He picked up a shovel from the corner and went out to the barrel's hiding place. He pried the lid off and staggered back, coughing. Slime Streamer gas was pretty pungent—like rotting fish with a hint of sulphur. Apparently the flowers were hard at work already. He held his breath and thrust the clicker down under the first couple of layers.

He was just pounding the lid into place with his fist when he heard someone calling. He stopped to listen.

"Oh Lord Baaatherum! Lord Batherum of Tiiipstitch! Looord Batherum!" It was a boy. He was strolling along and calling out in a singsong voice, stretching the words this way and that until they hardly resembled their original form. He sounded bored. He must have been at it awhile already. It didn't sound like he expected an answer anymore.

Timo hurried to the main path and there began walking in a more-or-less dignified fashion. "Here I am!" he called cheerily.

"Looord—what? Is somebody there?" The pitter-patter of small feet was followed by the appearance on the path of a skinny lad in the brown and grey livery of the Duke's own house servants.

"I am Lord Batherum," Timo said.

The boy removed his cap. "Your Lordship," he said, and then stood at attention and focused his gaze in the mid-distance. "In the name of the Inner Council, you are hereby. . ."

"The Inner Council? I've never heard of it. Is this more important or less important than the Prime Committee?"

"What? Well . . . It's the Inner Council *of* the Prime Committee, you see. So I guess . . . more important?"

"I daresay you are right. Oh, sorry. Go on."

The boy reassumed his announcing pose. "In the name of the Inner Council, you are hereby graciously invited to attend the Prime Committee in the capacity of Recognized Guest."

"Along with Meggy?"

"That's all the message I have, Your Lordship."

"What does a Recognized Guest have to do?"

The boy waved his arms in an exaggerated shrug. "They didn't tell me anything more, sir." A bell began to ring—a small, tinny thing, going madly and arrhythmically—really more of a clanking than a ringing. The boy shook his head. "Poor Guzzum really misses the big bell," he said.

"Oh. Is this the bell for the Prime Committee, then?"

'Yes, Your Lordship. Please hurry. The Distinguished Gentleman was most insistent."

"The Chancellor?"

"Oh, no, sir. The other one. The one that does most of the talking."

"Derving."

THEY SERVED WINE instead of beer at the Prime Committee. This was the main thing Timo remembered about the meeting. And the delightfully cool water with a faint scent of flowers.

They made many important decisions. Somebody—usually the head of some committee—would go on for a while. There seemed to be a special way of speaking invented just for these reports: a sort of deep-chested intoning accompanied by a faraway and exalted look. Extra points for complex grammatical constructions. At some point someone on the Inner Council would ever-so-politely break in and summarize all of it in one short sentence. Then the Inner Council would all nod and the Chancellor would say, "By accord of the Prime Committee . . ."

Then everyone in the room would say, "Let it be written!" That was the best part. Timo shouted as lustily as anyone. Then Shamgath, after giving his quill a mysterious twirl or two, would dip it in ink and write the sentence down in a book. Timo wasn't clear on the question of whether he, as a Recognized Guest, actually had a vote in these things or not. But Derving did glance his way from time to time and nod encouragingly.

The Inner Council consisted of the wizards, the Duke, a couple of other finely dressed men of high rank—and the Empress Dalada. She also smiled and nodded in his direction now and again. And then he blushed.

He was blushing, he told himself, because when she looked at him, the eyes of every man around him would turn to him as well. Once again he was failing to blend in with the locals. And Meggy, seated not far away, had to be noticing. Nine Principles indeed!

Chapter 18 • **LIFE AND DEATH**

TIMO WOKE TO a strange noise. These rooms at the Duke's Lodge were small but tidy. No, it wasn't an intruder. He heard it again. *Clackity-clackity-clack.* Oh, murds. What had got into old Guzzum to make him ring his wretched handbell at this time of . . . the morning. Yes, technically that was sunlight giving this room a cheery, rustic glow.

The whole place was stirring to life, some people even more reluctantly than Timo. These were aristocrats, after all. From well down the hall came the Duke's resonant voice: "This is the great day, Lord Tarum! Splat the Nat![32] Today we discover what is at the bottom of the Big Hole! What? Yes, yes, Chancellor, of course. The Pool of Prophecy. But what a day for the Lesser Knowledge, eh?"

Timo dressed in a hurry. With luck he could finish up with the barrel while everyone was socializing over breakfast. He felt certain he had estimated correctly and the thing couldn't possibly detonate until afternoon at the earliest. Still, his imagination was playing him a nasty trick. It seemed to him he could hear it clicking now, all the way from here. He peeked out his door a

---

32   A Nat is a sleep spirit, a gauzy little thing like a dandelion seed. This is one of those things morning people say. Usually too loudly.

couple of times before he saw the coast was clear. He slipped down the hall toward the storage rooms and the back entrance.

The Night Forest was casting up a fine, early morning mist. Timo emerged into a gold-tinged haze and a cacophony of bird calls and insect thrumming. Excellent. Not much chance of being heard or seen.

A teacup clinked. "Lord Batherum! What a surprise!"

Timo bowed. "Lord Vale," he murmured. Derving was seated at one of the porch tables.

"I had thought to get some fresh air myself," Derving went on. "But I don't believe the fresh air comes until later in the day." He gave a little shiver. "This entire, dreary country! Well. A moment to chat." Now the face he turned to Timo was radiant with bonhomie, and it seemed to Timo they were old friends well-met, co-conspirators on a harmless lark of some sort.

Derving gave a low, three-pitched whistle. A servant stepped out onto the porch two doors down, and the wizard waved his hands to signify a refill and another cup for his guest. "These chairs are surprisingly more comfortable than they appear," he said. Timo sat.

And on the porch they sat, and chatted on about . . . important things. Some of it had to do with the great work at the Pool of Prophecy, and some of it was simply profound observations on life and the nature of things in general. It was hard to recall the specifics. Timo knew only that he was clever and witty and his companion was fascinated and the tea was delicious and the morning slipped by much too quickly and Guzzum's clacking bell came as a complete surprise.

"I do believe the excursion is ready," Derving said, rising.

"What? The what?"

"The excursion to the Pool. We are all going together this morning so as not to waste any precious time. It was the decision of the Prime Committee, you know."

"Ah. Yes. I remember."

It was good in theory, this idea of going *en masse* to the site. For the wizards, the committee chairs and the more zealous committee delegates, every morning was spoiled by the aristocratic habits of the greater part of crowd. They were not morning people. They slept in and then complained that their servants hadn't wakened them. The servants were in on the game and took the complaints in stride. Then these masters dawdled over breakfast and chatted on the veranda. By the time they had got their carriages sorted out, their hampers of provisions laid in and their traveling companions chosen, it was well-nigh on to lunchtime.

On the other hand, this going as a group presented tremendous logistical problems of its own—chiefly of the social sort. It was all very good to say they would go by order of rank, but what about the committee chairs, or the members of the Prime Committee? And then a great many servants were required to go ahead and make things ready. The departures of these squadrons needed to be managed in such a way that they were essentially invisible. On this auspicious morning, it had to be the Duke, the Empress, and the wizards leading the great procession. One has a duty to the generations of painters to come. The composition of the scene must be suitably splendid.

And so for everyone else there was a great deal of standing around in the yard. Timo couldn't get away. Meggy was tagged to be somewhere toward the front. It wasn't until mid-morning that Sand the butler stepped to the edge of the porch, shuffled through a clutch of barks, and called out the next group of lucky souls, among them Lord Batherum of Tipstitch.

Once he was at the site, the old scientific curiosity kicked in. Today they were taking the diving bell all the way down. A new Leeban record for depth of submersion was bound to be set. Timo shouldered his way to the edge of the Big Hole. The Duke had provided the three "under boaters" with swimming costumes— sleek affairs in ducal grey, modestly cut to the elbows and knees. Brave lads!

At Lefton's insistence, the lowering of the bell was to happen very slowly and by stages. The boys had a rope going from inside the bell back to Lefton's boat, and they had worked out a system of long and short tugs to signal their condition. The descent to the first stage took all of fifteen minutes.

"What are they being so timid for?" an old fellow at Timo's elbow grumbled.

"It is all new territory. They have no idea of the effects of that depth of water on a Leeban body. Of course, it isn't until the ascent that the real danger . . ." Timo coughed and covered his mouth. After all, "the bends" hadn't been discovered yet. "Just being careful."

The old fellow wasn't listening anyway. "Let's see who's at the big tent," he said to someone else. Timo looked around. The crowd had thinned considerably. Despite the Duke's focus on the underwater boat, many committee chairs were discreetly rounding up their members.

There was a great deal of milling about and socializing. Now was a good time to slip away. Timo meandered among the groups, nodding and exchanging greetings, working his way to the forest edge and the main path to the Lodge. He took one last, quick look back at the bustling site. Nobody was paying any attention to him.

Alone on the path, surrounded by the shrieks and whistles and chattering of the Night Forest, he almost started to regret the explosion he had arranged. Almost certainly it would be powerful enough to kill some of these creatures. Well, he would just have to bury it a little deeper. That would take a while. He quickened his step.

By the time he reached Lefton's workshop he was almost running. He thrashed his way into the underbrush, heedless of the noise and of the branches whipping against his face and arms and clothes.

The barrel was gone.

No, that was a stupid idea. This was just the wrong place. He went back to the workshop and tried again, this time taking the path he knew he had taken before: here was the dead tree, here was the fat bramble bush, the muddy patch . . . No barrel.

He found himself sitting on the ground. Whether he had sat down or fainted, he couldn't remember. He was rather light-headed though, and his thoughts were coming up slowly, like chunks of meat in a boiling pot of stew—rising and turning and disappearing. He buried the barrel yesterday and forgot about it? Meggy had come and buried the barrel? This was the wrong workshop? Thieves stole the barrel? He had imagined the whole thing?

No, no, and no. This was certainly the right place. There was the pile of Slime Streamer branches. Here was the trampled ground. Here . . . He got on his hands and knees and examined a deep rut wobbling off on a new path. The rut went straight down on one side and was angled on the other. Of course. He and Meggy had rolled the barrel here on its side. And now, with the barrel full of Slime Streamers and dirt and too heavy to tip over and pick up again, someone had tipped it at an angle and wheeled it away, balancing it on the rim.

Timo rose to his feet, not taking his eyes off the wobbling rut. Slowly, with many false trails and restarts—tracking and all this woodsy stuff had been his worst subject at HIPI U—he threaded his way through the Night Forest.

The rut took him to a path they hadn't noticed before. It looped away, eventually making a broad curve back toward the lodge. Timo stepped out into the yard and pondered the structure in front of him. This was the back side of an old wing of the lodge, a single story, and that not in good repair. Wood shavings were scattered over the porch, and in the grass just off the porch, a pile of sticks.

No. On closer inspection, these were barrel staves. Some were broken, some were splintered. The rejects, then. So if this was the place for barrels . . . Timo took a deep sniff. Yes, there was a definite whiff of yeast in the air. This was the brewery wing.

A door latch turned somewhere down the way. Timo looked wildly around. Too far to the trees. He might just get around the corner of the building before being spotted . . . The door opened. He heard whistling—one of the bouncy tunes he had learned at Mellian's Bar.

"Ho there, my good man," Timo called.

The portly young man paused drying his hands on his apron, and squinted into the sunlight. "Oh, hello there, Your Lordship. Er . . ."

"I seem to have misplaced my room! Imagine that! I took a shortcut through the woods, you see, and I came out . . . here." Timo spread his arms to show the magnitude of his bafflement.

"This is the brewery wing," the young man said, not without a touch of pride.

"Ah, so this is where the magic happens! I do hope you have some more of that red beer on the make."

"We have all sorts, Your Lordship! You would be amazed. It's a first-rate operation in there, I don't mind saying."

"I'm sure it is. But where are all the barrels? I thought I saw lots of them just the other day."

"Those are the empties, away over that way by the dining halls. The full barrels are all down in the cellars."

"Of course. Couldn't very well leave those out in public view. They might just roll themselves away!"

The young man laughed with him and added, "Happens more often than you think. Mr. Sand sent us out to look for stray barrels just last night."

"Really? Last night? Did you find any?"

"Just a couple. One was way out in the woods there. It's got to be the local hires, having their selves a little frolic and . . . 'misappropriating the Master's goods.' That's what Mister Sand calls it. Now us Duke's people," here the young man straightened up and pulled the wrinkles out of his apron, "we've got more dignity than that."

"Certainly. So you brought the stray barrels back to the fold."

"Yes sir, Your Lordship. Locked up tight in the cellar."

"Ah. Excellent." Timo didn't allow his eyes to linger on the keys dangling from the apron's belt. "You say the rooms are off that way?"

"Yes, your Lordship. The rooms for the nobility, that is."

Timo strolled away aimlessly, letting his feet take him here and there, admiring the details of the architecture and the flowers on the hedge. It was purely by accident that every few seconds he happened to glance back and notice where the young brewmaster was.

The young man was in no great hurry himself. He stretched himself and sauntered over to a little garden plot along the hedge. He plucked a berry from a bush and popped it in his mouth. After a moment's thought he spit it out. He squatted beside a row of herbs and began examining the leaves and plucking some out, one by one. Soon he was holding a double handful of them in his apron. He heaved himself up and carried his treasure back to the door from which he had come.

As soon as the boy was out of sight, Timo hurried back. Just at the edge of the woods was a narrow sort of cottage, plain but spotlessly kept, with three doors facing away from the lodge, no windows, and a blue roof and doors. A well-worn path ran to it. There were other cottages just like it all around the lodge. They were all painted a brilliant white, and each had a roof and doors of a different primary color. The Dabbian term for these structures was "comfort house." No one ever mentioned them. Walking by, one pretended not to see them. They were privies. Outhouses. Timo found a spot behind a luxurious cascade of vines, with a clear sight of the three doors, and settled in for a wait.

The afternoon wore on. The Night Forest has a great wealth of insect life. Timo had time to get acquainted with many specimens. He twitched. He flicked. He brushed away. But he did not leave his hiding place.

Two other lads came and went in the next hour or so. Then another long pause set in. There seemed to be no activity at all at this end of the building.

The lodge door rattled and the young brewmaster stepped out. He crossed the lawn, hurrying a bit this time, and went to the closest door of the comfort house. He took off his apron, hung it on a hook, and went inside.

Timo tiptoed in as rapidly as he dared. Somewhere in the back of his mind, he thought: *If anyone is watching, they will know exactly what I'm doing. And they'll be having a good laugh.* Because by this time, with hours of built-up pressure of urgency and panic, he wasn't just tiptoeing, he was doing an elaborate, vaudeville pantomime of a tiptoe. But he was past caring about surveillance. The clock—that is, the proto-clock—was ticking.

There was no key ring. Each key had been made with a circular end, and all of them were looped onto the apron string and held in a single knot. Holding his breath, Timo gently closed one hand over all of them and went to work on the knot. These were all large, heavy keys, made of iron or brass. After dangling all day, they had pulled the knot tight. Without the use of both hands, Timo had to use his teeth. There. He leaned his head well back to pull the loosened string through the knot.

There were five keys in his hand. He couldn't take them all; the lad would notice immediately and sound an alarm. One key was longer and heavier than the rest, with a double row of squared-off teeth. It looked like just the thing for one of those massive cellar doors. He took it and threaded the others back onto the apron string. He did his tiptoe dance across the lawn and into the lodge.

He found himself in a broad hallway with a floor of smooth tiles. It was uncomfortably warm. Somewhere down the hall, someone was talking just a little loudly. His voice was raised over a rhythmic tapping or scraping. It was the sound of stirring. A kitchen then. Or more likely, a brewing room. That explained the heat.

A couple of barrels were standing nearby. He bent and sniffed them. Nothing. A gentle nudge confirmed these were empty. Beside them was a long, low pair of doors, held together with a massive iron box. His key didn't work on it. Well. This didn't look like a door for people. It probably led to a chute or ramp for rolling the barrels in and out of the cellar.

He went on down the hall, away from the kitchen, checking the doors. A storeroom with sacks of meal. A cleaning closet. Around a corner he found the right sort of door—thick timbers supported with iron plates. The keyhole looked right. It was a tricky business getting the key to fit right. But the mechanism turned easily. The door even popped open on its own.

Immediately Timo knew why. A puff of air hit him in the face and stung his eyes. He knew that smell. The cellar was full of slime streamer gas. Two steps down and he stumbled into a wall. These stone steps were rough and uneven and went down in a jagged spiral. Well, he could hardly bring a lamp down here now. He stumbled blindly down, trying to breathe as little as possible. His throat was on fire. What would this stuff do to his lungs?

He took one more blind step down and toppled forward onto his face instead. This would be the floor of the cellar, then. It wasn't entirely dark. There was a crack of light filtering down and around a wooden ramp some distance away. In a few seconds his smarting eyes could make out the outlines of barrels. There were lots and lots of barrels. It was a big room and it had tiers of barrels stacked to the ceiling. He would estimate there were ... He couldn't estimate. He shook his head, but the numbers wouldn't come to him.

Something's wrong with my brain.

He was struck with the sheer novelty of it. He thought perhaps he should sit and ponder the situation for a while.

I'm in trouble.

Right. He needed to hurry. There was something—a barrel, *his* barrel. He needed to get to it and take something out of it. He got to his feet and staggered forward, glancing off the barrels on either side like a man going the wrong way on a crowded street. Somebody was hissing at him. Maybe *he* could help. Timo lurched toward the sound, over by the ramp.

Nobody was there. No wait. It's this barrel hissing. And it stinks. Hey, it's my barrel. What luck! Out of all these barrels, I found it. He fumbled at the barrelhead. He probably should have brought some tools. The barrel suddenly shot up, over his head. No, wait a minute. He was just on his knees. Must've fallen. He grabbed the barrel by the rim and tried to pull himself up. He was too heavy. He was enormously heavy.

I'm going to die.

Well . . . darn. What a sorry ending. His life didn't even make any sense. What was the point of all this? Of everything? There's supposed to be a point.

At least his throat had stopped hurting. The cool stone floor felt good against his face. The hissing was getting far away. His eyes didn't hurt, now they were closed.

And up at the top of the steps, the door was still cracked open.

Chapter 19 • **THE BLAME**

FIRST THERE WAS the sound. It didn't seem like an explosion at all. It was more of a continual roar, coming from all around. The earth itself was crying out. It was writhing beneath him.

Timo opened his eyes and saw branches and vines waving like pennants. The sky above them was an unnatural orange. Something gigantic crashed down through the trees. It was the corner of a building—two walls and a roof, even a bit of a window. It lodged, tipped up against two trees, smoldering. It had pulled a network of vines down with it and now small flames burst out all along them.

Timo turned his head. He was close up against some sort of wall. In fact, the wall seemed to be leaning over him. Lucky for him that wall was there. Lucky for him because the wall was between him and . . .

The explosion! His barrel! He had been about to get it . . . But it blew up! And HOW WAS HE ALIVE?

He tried to sit up. The motion made him dizzy, and he wound up curled in a ball on his side. This time he was facing the wall. There was a step close by his head. Above it was a blue door. He was behind the comfort house.

The roaring had stopped. Now there were many smaller sounds: the crackling of hundreds of small fires, various thumps and rustling noises, whistles and whizzes. Debris was raining down on the Night Forest. All things considered, curled up in a ball behind the comfort house was about as safe a place as any. He gave it another minute or so, and the debris continued to rain down. That had been quite a lot more of an explosion than he had planned.

That's right. I planned it. The Spang! I have to get it!

He rolled over and got up to his hands and knees. The dizziness was fading. The debris had stopped falling, for the most part. The fires here among the trees seemed to be dying down rather than spreading. The Night Forest was a soggy place.

He heard voices—shouting, at some distance. He staggered to his feet, using the wall for support. Now that he was vertical, he could see that this wall really was tipped out, away from the lodge. The roof was mostly blown away. Still unsteady and leaning on the wall, he shuffled his way around the corner of the comfort house.

The lodge was still there. No, wait. Most of the lodge was still there. Closer on it was a smashed-in jumble of timbers, a good deal of it in flames. And this wing of it, the old, unkempt brewery wing, was clean gone. Nothing but a hole. He crept to the edge and looked down. The better part of the floor was gone, replaced by a tremendous, smoke-filled crater. There was a sound . . . He leaned over to hear it better. Yes, water—or maybe beer?—was trickling into the hole.

He couldn't see any barrels. All that beer. But no, he shouldn't be thinking about that now! What about the people?

Timo looked up and saw someone on the other side of the blasted cellar, in the opposite yard. The man's apron was black from smoke, and he was clutching at his shoulder. There was blood. His lips were moving but no words were coming out.

"What?" Timo called out. "Are you hurt? What can I do?" Someone, a boy, came running to the man. He shouted up at him, "Over there, Guzzum! You've got to go over there! There's water and stuff!" The boy tugged at the man's apron until he began to shuffle away with him.

Now there were people in the yard on Timo's side. Some were flinging buckets of water at the flames closest to the still-standing sections of the lodge. Some were carrying the furnishings out of the building. Mr. Sand was standing in an empty cart from which he was issuing commands in all directions:

"No, ladies, don't worry about the crockery just now! The hangings and the paintings first!"

"Matron Deebee, put the chairs out in the shade of those trees. There you have it. We'll be needing some blankets, too."

"Yes, lads, go ahead and use the wine buckets! They're the largest we have!"

Order was setting in. A calm, sonorous voice shouting a steady stream of directions, with excellent diction, has that effect.

Timo ran to lend a hand with the bucket brigade. He waved off their protests with a snarl. This was no time for privileges of class. With his height and strength, he was the best man for the front lines, and the lads gave a whistle when he flung a full wine bucket of water all the way up to the flames on the peak of the roof. Then the race was on to bring the big man fresh buckets. The lads cheered his every mighty throw. He wished they would stop.

"Has anyone seen Lord Beedley? Lord Beedley!" Miss Lum-bush ran out of a doorway with a ceremonial scroll in one hand and a cracked pitcher in the other. She waved the pitcher as she shouted, "He was just in the South Hall playing foolsticks!"

"I'm sure he's all right, Dottie," Mrs. Deebee called.

"It's just he's so very, very slow," Dottie said, pleading.

"I saw'm carried out the front, Dottie," a lad in the bucket bri-gade said.

"Oh, thank all the gods! Wait! Lord Nain! He was in the little kitchen!" She dropped the pitcher and scroll on the grass and raced for the nearest non-flaming door.

"Don't go in there, Dottie!" But even Mr. Sand's ringing com-mand couldn't stop her.

Every time he reached back for the next bucket, Timo cast an eye toward the chairs and blankets under the trees. They were filling up quickly with the injured. Lots of gashes and broken bones. Some burns. *How many dead?* He wondered. He didn't dare to ask. He tried to concentrate on the task of fighting the fires, but his mind kept snapping back to the cellar—the stink, the dark, that cursed barrel, the floor. He should have been blown to atoms. How had he ended up behind the comfort house?

A flood of new help was arriving. Everyone at the Big Hole had seen the great pillar of flame rising over the trees. The Duke was among the first to make it back, galloping into the thick of things on his black charger. He wheeled the horse about, shouting orders.

"Save the people first! Search every room! There's not a moment to lose! Form a bucket brigade! Stop the fires! Fetch bandages! Medicines! Tend the wounded!" It was a magnificent sight. An inspiration to all.

Mr. Sand quietly dismounted his cart, adjusted his jacket, felt the angle of his collar and strode over to the Duke, losing a smidgen of speed with every step. By the time he arrived, he had fully recovered his flat-footed chief butler's walk. He clasped his hands behind his back and awaited his master's pleasure.

With more men and buckets, the fires were soon put out. Room by room, the household staff searched out the rest of the lodge, assessing the damage and looking for survivors. They opened doors and windows and let the slight breeze begin to clear away the remaining smoke. They came out and delivered the time-honored Dabbian response in the face of all catastrophe and misfortune: "It's not as bad as all that."

The distinguished visitors waited outside, growing bolder and more impatient once the emergency seemed to be passing. Soon they were bold enough to send in their own servants to check on their belongings. Some servants re-emerged with armloads of things packed and ready to go.

"What's this?" said the Duke. "Lord Tarum, surely you're not being called away now? However shall the Committee of Artifacts manage?"

Viscout Tarum glanced uneasily about, but no one seemed willing to make eye contact. "It isn't just me, you know. Some of us have been talking it over."

"Well?" The Duke's smile was beginning to show the strain.

"It's a lovely forest and all, Your Grace, but . . . well, peculiar things happen here. I never believed in Swamp Worms myself..."

"Swamp Worms!"

"But *something's* making these fires in the ground." A couple of the others nodded and the Viscount grew a little bolder. "And if we don't know what it is, we don't know where it's going to happen next! It could be anywhere! Right under our feet!"

In a dramatic touch, he glanced sharply about at the ground at his listeners' feet, and of course, they looked too. Somebody gave a nervous chuckle, which died out too abruptly. Many significant glances were exchanged. *I don't know—what do you think? Beats me. What do you think?*

"Gentlemen . . ." Duke Arumbeed rumbled, spreading his arms in the classic oratorical manner.

"It is a fair question, Committeeman Tarum, and we are grateful to you for posing it."

All eyes turned to the source of these ringing words. Chancellor Undertower stepped into the circle. There hadn't been a circle before; it mysteriously formed in that fraction of a second when the Chancellor took one significant step forward *as if* he were stepping into a circle.

"Gentlemen," the Chancellor said—and all other voices stopped. Only the red-faced Duke seemed not to be in breathless anticipation of the Chancellor's next word. He may have been just a bit piqued by the fact that his "gentlemen" had had so much less effect. "The moment has come for an extraordinary meeting of the Prime Committee. I hereby declare a GRAND REVEALED SESSION!"

Naturally everyone cheered. A Grand Revealed Session! In our lifetime! A moment later they quieted down and leaned forward in hopes of an explanation. So great was the anticipation that no one even noticed Derving off to one side, frantically waving.

"We shall convene immediately! Here, in THIS . . . (he raised one arm heavenward) VERY . . . (he pumped his arm, and the open palm changed to a raised index finger; he held the pose for a beat longer) SPOT!" The arm swooped down and locked into place with the finger indicating a now immortal tuft of grass.

Everyone jumped back. The ground did not crack open however, and the thunderous cheering that followed was as much from relief as it was from celebration of the Grand Revealed Session.

The Chancellor went on to explain. A GRS must be held out of doors, and all Leebans great and small are granted auditory access. The usual rules of order were suspended. All Committee Members were free to speak out, but there was to be no petty squabbling, no rancorous debate. The very gods were present in a GRS. If all hearts were pure, they might even speak.

This quieted the crowd, and especially those Committee Members who were accustomed to speaking. For half of them, this was a moment of sober reflection. The rest were still trying to figure out what "rancorous" might mean, and if they had ever done it.

Meggy found Timo just as the GRS was beginning. His embrace was more than their cousinly cover required. "I figured you had come back here to check on the barrel," he whispered. "When we saw the tower of flame . . ." He could only shake his head and blink back the tears. "But Timo . . . The house?"

"Someone ordered a search of the woods last night and the barrel ended up in the cellar. I went down to try to disarm it. But then I . . . Wait, *you* didn't carry me out?"

A gentleman next to them cleared his throat. Timo and Meggy abruptly turned to face the proceedings in the center of the cleared space. Derving Vale was holding forth there, flanked by the rest of the Inner Council.

"Surely as sound, rational men of the Lesser Knowledge, you can perceive the differences. Drebbell's Ladder was no mere explosion. It was light, pure light! It reached to the very heavens! Now this . . . this . . . was merely some accident. Tragic, of course. But nothing . . . prophetic!"

"I beg your pardon!" The Duke was quivering with agitation. "Are you implying that this was some *brewing* mishap? Preposterous!"

A sort of gasp or moan passed over the crowd. Timo blinked and shook his head. Before his very eyes Derving had . . . flickered. He seemed to be gaining and losing a few inches of height. No, it was something to do with the light. It was as if the illumination that surrounded him—Timo had never noticed it until it just now—was blinking. And in those un-illuminated moments, Derving looked . . . frantic.

"No, no, I'm not saying *what* caused it, Your Grace! My point is simply that we should not make a false association based on the superficial characteristics of the two events."

"I wouldn't call that a superficial hole over there!" someone called from the back.

"Gentlemen!" This was the Chancellor. "Only Committee members have the liberty to speak out. We are not a rabble."

But somehow, even with three accomplished wizards working their Allure with all their might, things continued to slide out of control. Timo could sense the glow of happy certainty slipping away from him with every argument a local dared to voice. Fear was doing it. One mysterious explosion was a miracle. Two mysterious explosions were a threat to public safety.

Out on the fringes of the crowd, some began to turn away. Nobody made a scene; this was no demonstration. But the Inner Council, facing outward in the center of the crowd, could see what was happening. In a quiet moment, as everyone was digesting an elegant point Shamgath had just made about the sublime joy of good organization, the sound of carriage wheels could be distinctly heard. For just a second the entire Inner Council paused to listen. The sound grew fainter. The carriage was leaving.

The Chancellor had commandeered the proceeding in the guise of summarizing yet another dissenting opinion when the Duke himself interrupted him. "Look! It's the Underwater Sailors come back from the Big Hole!" The crowd turned to look, and a semblance of a cheer went up. "Lefton! Bring the cart over here! Yes, here in the middle! Now, gentlemen! Let's see what wonders these brave lads have brought us!"

They drove the cart right over the lawn, the crowd parting before them. Lefton stood in the front of the cart and held up what looked like a couple of grotesquely twisted metal sculptures. "Have you ever seen anything like this?" he shouted. Everyone surged forward for a better look. The pieces flashed and sparkled in the sun.

"This is amazing!" the Duke enthused. "This could be an entirely new substance!" They were, in fact, chunks of ironroot fused together at terrific heat—something unknown on Calema or for that matter anywhere else in the Gass. Meggy began working his way forward for a better look.

"And look at these!" one of the "underwater sailors" shouted, getting into the spirit of things. He was standing in the bed of the cart and holding aloft two large chunks of what looked like jagged glass, brilliantly colored. "These are scattered all over the bottom! And it isn't glass! We couldn't break 'em with a hammer!"

The lads in the cart were handing out chunks of glass and pieces of twisted metal, and these were being passed around. "Careful, there. We don't want anything to walk away now," said the Duke.

"Yes, we'll be needing all these things for the Instruction Center," Derving added. He was standing next to Lefton, handing down artifacts as they came to him. He seemed to have regained his aura now that the crowd was back in an agreeable mood.

"Oh, that's right. Here's a different one," Lefton said. He reached under the driver's seat and pulled out a less-twisted piece of metal. Timo could see the brilliant yellow ridges from where he stood. "Looks kind of like a snake, doesn't it?" Lefton said, offering it to Derving.

Derving shrieked, held up his hands in horror, and tumbled backwards off the cart.

"Catch him," Lefton called. They let him down easy to the ground. He seemed to have fainted dead away.

"Guess he's scared of snakes," Lefton said, absent-mindedly tapping the piece of metal on his leg.

Meggy had made it to the cart by this time. "Could you hold that a little higher, please?" he asked. "Some people can't see it."

Its gyre was somewhat flattened out and it was missing some jewels, but it was most definitely and unmistakably a Spang. "Now that is most peculiar," Meggy said, exchanging significant glances with some others standing nearby. "Wouldn't you say, Stum? Reeg?"

"A significant find, I would wager," Reeg answered. "What would you say, Stum?"

But Stum didn't answer. He was already making his way out of the crowd. Reeg was quick to follow. Several others of those who had pushed in for a closer look also began to discreetly back away.

Lefton crouched down over the front of the cart. "Lord Tollum," he said, almost whispering. "Is something the matter? Are people afraid of this thing?"

Meggy gently pushed the Spang away from his face. "It is a very significant find, Mister Steep. I have no doubt these men were just running off to tell others about it. Perhaps you can persuade the Duke to put it on display. Prominently, so all the Lesser Knowledge men can have a good look. But protected too, of course. Yes. That will be important."

By this time the Duke had come to his side. Lefton handed the peculiar object to him. "Extraordinary," the Duke said. "It almost looks . . . Yes, it does look like a snake. Or a fish. Chancellor Undertower! Come have a look! What do you think of this?"

The Chancellor took the strange object in hand and turned it this way and that, taking in all its features with a critical eye. "Hmm! Ah! Yes! Well, now!"

"Well?" said the Duke. "Did this Drebbell say anything about snakes?"

The Chancellor put one hand on his chin, the better to think deep thoughts, and gazed off into the sky. In a few moments, his eyes returned to the Duke and then darted to Meggy. "Derving is really our expert on the interpretation of Drebbell," he said. A low moan emanated from the ground beside the cart. "Ah, he seems to be coming around." He stepped over and proffered the Spang. "I say, Derving, what do you make of this?"

Derving scrambled to his feet, staggering backwards as he did so. His face was wild and unnerved. "It wasn't me!" he said. He turned and began running out through the crowd, heedless of those he was jostling, creating a ripple of disturbance that was visible even after his black coat had disappeared from view.

Chapter 20 • **HISTORICAL PERSPECTIVE**

MACK WAS ON the verge of setting a record. He was in his cubbyhole of an office, with no less than a dozen open Readers positioned about his head like a flock of pigeons. His fingers were flying over the keyboard. In a few moments he would wrap up the twenty-second Suspicion of Unsanctioned Visit Report of the day, shattering a record that no Planet Clerk had even thought of breaking for the past thousand years. He looked a fright. His skin was a pasty gray and seemed to be stretched too tight across his face. His hair had developed a thin crust of sneeg dust, a universal lubricant on the Gassplat that built up in untended ventilation systems. His hands vibrated in the air whenever he paused his typing.

The twelve Readers around him were open on all kinds of things: video feeds, old reports, maps, lists, and of course, multiple sections of the Protected Planets Code. Suddenly the room went red, and he had to close his eyes. When he managed to crack open his eyelids again in a painful squint, he saw that it was just the red dot signaling an urgent message. In all twelve Readers at once.

"TOP PRIORITY" said the Readers set on official Planet Clerk feeds. "BREAKING NEWS," "IMPORTANT," and "URGENT" said some of the others. And then followed scrolling text in the largest font the Readers could handle. Mack looked from one Reader to the other, trying to follow them all. He couldn't of course, but certain words swam in front of his eyes no matter where he looked. "Calema," "buu," "source," "proof," and, strangely, "Neemnot."

He clutched at one Reader close at hand and tried to make sense of it. He had to let go—his hand was starting to shake too much. But it wasn't bad nerves giving him the shakes this time. There was a powerful, foreign feeling welling up inside his chest. "HAA HAA HAAAA!" he said. His voice was a little creaky from disuse, but he was pretty sure this was laughter. One of those peculiar Human things that popped up to embarrass him from time to time.

Unu appeared on several of the Readers at once. "Have you heard the news, sir?" she said. "Calema isn't a source of buu gas, after all. It was just an accident with an unauthorized vessel. The Ministry says they have proof."

"YES! I KNEW IT! THERE'S NOTHING HERE, PEOPLE! JUST SOME STUPID NEEMNOTS!" Mack leaped to his feet, banging his head and knocking awry three or four of his Readers.

"Are you all right, sir?" Unu was sideways now but still speaking calmly from the nearest Reader.

"I'm great! I feel fabulous! No, wait. What is that? What is that?" He was standing stock still with one hand on his stomach, a look of concern on his face. "I'm . . . hungry!" he announced. "I'm REALLY hungry!"

"Very good, sir. Shall I bring you something?"

The news was all over Ninthwave®. The Neemnot government, of course, denied that any such disaster had happened with any Neemnot vessels. Then it said it was disinformation from some unknown enemy. Then it said it was looking into it and would cooperate fully with any investigation. And it was probably rogue elements of the previous administration.

Meanwhile, the Protected Planets Directorate had announced that the Special Assembly on the Status of Calema had been suspended. There was now to be an Urgent and Immediate (meaning within the next two or three months) meeting of the Protected Planets Code Subcommittee on Landing Craft Safety.

By the time Mack had eaten an actual meal, showered, and had a refreshing four hours of sleep, the Calema buzz on Ninthwave® had already peaked and was noticeably fading. A Torbor luxury liner had blundered into Bellow space. The Bellow navy's warning shots had been a smidge too close, and now the liner was tumbling toward the Bellow sun with its propulsion systems blown away. There was video. And breathless, moment-by-moment coverage. Ninthwave® had its next next big thing.

Mack sipped his tea and skimmed over the very backed-up queue of Urgent Communications from the Protected Planets Ministry. What a mountain of reports and memos and analyses he had before him! He would be working overtime for weeks. He smiled. He almost laughed again.

One of his Readers showed a flashing yellow dot. Some reminder he had left for himself. He gave it a tap. "Gadgerus Fleet Status" it said. There were many links. He opened the first, labeled "Satellite Surveillance." It was a wonderful, high-altitude photograph. You could see every ship as a tiny dash on the deep blue sea. The ships were close enough that their collective wake spread out along the way, a pale path trailing across the deep. Giving a wide berth to the shoals on the southeast coast of Shalk and pointing toward . . .

"What?" Mack shouted, making the teacup rattle. "They're headed straight for the Maybay! Why haven't they turned back? What are they up to?" He started for the door and realized he was still in his pajamas. He called Unu instead. "The Gadgerene Fleet is still heading for Dab," he said, trying to keep his voice calm. "What are they up to? What do we know?"

Unu's face was bouncing a bit. She seemed to be walking down a corridor. "Information is coming in from many sources now. I think we are getting a pretty good picture. Would you like to discuss it?"

'Yes! Of course! How soon can you . . ."

A bird whistled. His Reader showed Unu standing in the doorway. She was smiling up at him. She waited. "Oh! Sorry," he said. He waved the door open. Unu floated in, making the ninety-degree rotation to the room's gravity plate without spilling a drop of her tea. In her other hand was a stack of Readers.

The Gadgerene expedition had never paused or changed its course. In fact a second fleet was just leaving Sareemport, and by all the signs, it could be as large as the first. There were confirmed reports of reinforced Zimmer spires on board, as well as crates of rock spheres. And lots and lots of soldiers. The Sareem wasn't keeping it a secret anymore. The empire was mobilized for a major war.

"But why Dab?" Mack wondered out loud. "Doesn't the Outside Force know what's happened there?"

"We have picked up evidence of extensive extradimensional communication from the fleet since yesterday. Obviously the O.F. has its agents in the fleet, and they are aware of the latest developments."

"Wait a second." Mack had been leaning over the table, glued to the Readers. Now he straightened up and blinked at Unu. "'We?' Who's 'we'? The Gass doesn't do any spying on Calema."

"Certainly not. We only spy on the spies. But all together, they provide us with a pretty well-rounded picture of what is happening on the planet."

"Huh. How long has this been . . . Never mind. What do 'we' know about the O.F.?"

"Nothing. Which itself is something. They apparently have at least the surveillance capability of the Gass. They seem to have inside knowledge on everyone's operations."

"That's scary. So what is the well-rounded picture we have?"

Unu hesitated. "It takes a long time for Gass intelligence to announce any conclusions."

"Naturally. It must first be filtered through all the political concerns in the galaxy. So. What do *you* think?"

"I?"

"You. Unu. I'm guessing *you* have a well-rounded picture even if the Gass does not."

She hesitated again. Then she looked Mack in the eye, some inner troubling having been resolved. "They are not in control. The Outside Force. That is what the spike in extra-dimensional communications means. They were trying to stop the fleet. They couldn't."

"Good heavens! Who *is* in control then?"

"The Sareem. The O.F. handed him a tremendous technological advantage and convinced him that Dab was ripe for the taking. They didn't tell him about buu. Nothing has changed as far as he is concerned."

"Surely they can make up some pretext . . ."

"We may assume they did. Perhaps they claimed the Dabbian tinsmiths had some new machine to use against them. And that is why the second fleet was launched."

Mack pondered for a moment. "Do the Dabbians have a chance?"

"No."

"Well . . . You don't have to sugarcoat it, you know."

"Excuse me? Sugar . . . ?" She glanced at his cup of tea. "Ah. Sarcasm."

"I'm only Human."

Unu gave the tiniest of nods, looked away as if distracted, and smiled. It was the Corgurid way of gracefully dealing with someone else's embarrassment.

Maybe I'll never fit in here. "I'm sorry," Mack said. "So do the Dabbians have any idea the fleet is coming?"

"There is no evidence of any preparations. The Dabbians only just managed to fend off the barbarians in their last war. They won't have a chance against a coordinated, well-armed invasion, with superior technology."

"That's it, then." Mack stirred his tea and managed a rueful smile. "At least the O.F. won't get what they wanted."

"I don't understand."

"The Sareem is in control now. He doesn't really care about new technology."

"Then what does he want?"

"The world, actually. He believes it is his by right. He is a god, after all."

"He doesn't really believe that, does he?"

"Oh, his predecessors were sensible enough to believe it in a more-or-less metaphorical sense. But His Effulgence Akka the Thirteenth seems to be lacking the necessary . . ."

"Humility?"

"Imagination. He can't accept that there can be more than one way to be a god. The world is all wrong, as far as he is concerned. He wants to re-establish Plu Gadgerus."

"Isn't that just a . . . day?" In the Book of Days, the Plu Gadgerus was a reference point far in the misty past. All sorts of mystical calculations made use of it.

"It was the perfect day. It lasted the perfect length of time— twelve thousand years or one-hundred forty-four million years, depending on how you translate Old Gadgerene glyphs into numbers. In the Plu Gadgerus, the whole world was at peace. Leebs and all creatures worshiped the Sareem daily. And because of this worship, he was the Supreme God. Whatever he spoke, happened."

Below the window of Mack's quarters, Calema was a long, blue crescent. There were only a couple of hours of daylight left. "I must add a more thorough treatment of the Plu to the Caleman Library," Mack said thoughtfully.

"Meanwhile Akka the Thirteenth is taking the first step toward world conquest." There was something new in Unu's voice that Mack couldn't place.

"And with gunpowder, he will likely succeed."

"But I still don't understand, sir. Isn't that what the O.F. wanted?"

"Not at all. They just wanted to run the clock forward a little. Their plan all along was to speed up Accession, with their clients the Gadgerenes coming out as the dominant power on the planet. The last thing they wanted was the Sareem as the Supreme God of the world. It will be the new Dark Age for Calema."

"So hundreds of years of progress will be lost." Mack nodded in agreement. They both fell silent. Mack was already plotting the outline for his treatment of the Plu Gadgerus when Unu spoke up again. "It is a great evil."

Mack was a little dumbfounded. He had never heard a Corgurid use the word "evil." Their religion, as he understood it, was the high-concept, contemplative sort. The "look-at-a-leaf-and-see-your-self"—or the whole universe—sort of religion. "I guess," he said.

"And here we sit." There definitely was something new and strange in her voice. If he hadn't known better, he would have said she was *angry*. Sweet little Unu! She, the consummation of a million years of Corgurid enlightenment!

"Well, we're the Protected Planets Ministry. We don't interfere, we . . . protect." As many times as he had said these very words, and said them proudly, why did his voice sound so weak now? "Weaselly" was the word that came to his mind. "There isn't anything we can do, anyway."

"Mr. McAdoo." They had been speaking Corgurid, and his Human name in the middle of that sounded jarring and strange. She was standing with her feet planted, almost at attention. "I have a confession to make."

Mack had nothing to say to this. He waited like an audience before a symphony. Like an audience before a symphony that sees the percussionist pick up a big mallet and approach the gong.

"Mr. McAdoo, I am not a very good Corgurid."

"Ah, well," he murmured, "I'm sure it isn't all that . . ."

"I don't believe what everyone else believes."

Intimate secrets *and* religion! It was more than he could deal with. Mack broke into a cold sweat.

"We Corgurids say, 'The universe needs every atom to achieve the perfect balance.' By this we mean to include the atoms that make those ships. And that gunpowder."

"What do *you* say?"

"I say too much balancing is not good. If we balance all good with an equal amount of evil, there can be no joy, no love, no light. Only shadow."

"Joy?" "Love?" Corgurids don't even think *about this stuff.* "Why are you telling me this?"

"Because you are Human. You believe it too."

I've tried hard to overcome that. "Well . . . yes. We . . . I believe in right and wrong. There. So yes, I suppose I feel badly about what's going to happen."

"Wouldn't you like to do something about it?"

"What are you getting at?"

"Wouldn't you?"

"Okay, well sure, yeah. If I had miraculous powers."

Unu smiled. Mack felt the hair on the back of his neck stand up. "Miracles happen all the time, Mr. McAdoo."

"Call me Mack."

"Would you be very upset if a miracle happened to the Sareem's fleet?"

"You mean like . . . a bad miracle?"

"I'm sure it would be a good miracle."

"Now you're just playing with semantics. And why are we talking about this?"

"You are the Planet Clerk. You want what is best for Calema. Would you approve if a good miracle happened to the fleet?"

She was utterly serious. He tried to be serious too. "Well, all right. Yes. A good miracle would be a good thing. Of course."

Unu smiled. She stood up smartly. "I am pleased to hear you say that," she said. She had suddenly regained her Corgurid aura of serene attention to duty. "I should get to work now. Will you be going to your office?"

"I suppose. Yes."

"Then I suppose I will see you there."

ALL THROUGH THE day Mack kept an eye on the Sareem's fleet. The little black dashes kept crawling steadily across the North Shalk Sea. Until mid-afternoon. Then the little dashes in front split into two groups that turned left and right. Those in the middle turned outward and those in the back began moving forward very rapidly. It was an interesting puzzle, like watching a marching band unwinding itself into a new formation.

It didn't take long to see what the new formation was: a circle. *How did she do that? Do Corgurids have a way of calling Bungs?* He didn't know much about Corgurid technology. Come to think of it, he had never seen any. They seemed to get by without it.

About the time the circle shape became evident, his Readers began to go off with news bulletins and emergency messages. *Gadgerene Fleet Halted by Bungs.* And a little later: *Greatest Bung Circle Ever Recorded Traps Gadgerene Fleet.*

Normally Mack didn't pay any attention to the constant chatter of intelligence bulletins coming in from all the interested parties and from Gass Intelligence as well. Now he was very interested. And very worried. Every intelligence service on every plat circling Calema was convinced that this event had an outside cause, and they were working madly to find out who had done it. Here was enhanced video showing the North Shalk Sea and every single Bung in it. No ships, no whales, no fish, just Bungs. In the time-lapse, the fine shimmer of silver dots all over the sea suddenly coalesced into a single great ring, which then began to contract with astounding uniformity. It was eerily beautiful.

The analysts were beside themselves. *Bungs can't do that!* The back-and-forth calls by which a ring is summoned ("pips"—a word Mack was delighted to discover) just can't go that far. And a ring that big just isn't practical, in an evolutionary sense. Bungs shouldn't swim that far and that fast. Some of them were literally killing themselves to get there.

The fleet didn't have a chance. Mack found a video feed with which he could move about the scene and zoom in at will. He couldn't watch for very long. Smaller ships were getting rolled over. Larger ships were piling onto each other and breaking apart. And even then the battering wouldn't stop. Once he had zoomed in close enough to see the bodies in the water, he was done watching.

Much as he had wanted the Gadgerene fleet to fail, he had never wanted anyone to *die*. He felt sick and a little shaky. Did Unu really do all this? Sweet, kind Unu? And more to the point, did *he* have any complicity in it? It had felt for just a moment as if he were giving permission for something. He had always skipped over the vast sections in the Protected Planets Code dealing with obligations for reporting what one knows. He had never before known anything worth keeping secret.

Down in the North Shalk Sea, the Sareem's ships continued to disappear beneath the waves. No rescue came. The airspace over the fleet was saturated with the beams of dozens of detection systems. No elevator pod or landing craft could possibly be cloaked enough to get through all that.

By the time night spread over the sea, the darkness didn't really matter—there was nothing left to watch. The ghostly Bung-tracking feed showed them dissipating back to a fine shimmer of dots. A few hours later, new bulletins began to come in saying that the second fleet had turned around and was heading back to Sareemport. If there was still anyone with any doubts about the existence of the O.F., this should have convinced them. Kamerduk had got word of the disaster somehow, and somehow sent the message to the second fleet to come back home. The invasion, it appeared, was decidedly off.

When Mack finally opened the door to leave the office, the Gassplat was a noisy place. He had to stand against the wall for a minute or two to acclimatize. The throughway was unusually full for this time of night. The shops were bustling. Music and music-like equivalents were blaring everywhere. The rules seemed to be off for the night—one of the subtler social signals Mack had never been able to grasp. Most of the Corguridoid species had been aghast at the prospect of Partition and appalled at the idea of the reassertion of the Gadgerene Empire. Now, with these twin disasters unexpectedly evaporated, it was party time on the Gassplat.

Unu was in the shop across the throughway, a florist. Her back was to him. When she turned around, she had a small fern of some sort in her hands. Its many shades of green were brilliant against the soft blackness of her dress. She was wearing a dress. Did she normally wear a dress? If she did, Mack had never noticed before tonight.

She came to him. No, check that. They were now standing in the florist shop, which must mean that he had come to her. Then he should probably say something. Something. "Nice flowers," he said.

'It's a Raaza Fern. It seems appropriate for the day. A new beginning."

"I guess." Mack looked around them. "Everyone seems to have gone a little crazy."

"They are happy. It is a very special happiness; something they loved has been restored."

"Love? That's kind of a stretch, don't you think? Seems to me everybody was pretty blasé about their jobs here."

"It wasn't the job they loved. It was Calema."

"Oh." He looked around again, this time paying attention to the faces. There was certainly something different going on. The place was energized. People were greeting each other with some special emphasis. Mack had always made it a practice to avoid figurative speech, considering it an impediment to clear, honest communication, but at the moment he could only think of an absurd old Human metaphor: their eyes were "sparkling." He could actually see it now.

"Is that really true?" he said. "I didn't think they cared about this planet."

"They didn't think so, either. Now they know."

Somebody bumped into him. A Glag. "Sorry," he rumbled. Or it may have been a she. Hard to tell with the fur. He or she shuffled quickly away.

"It's all right," Mack called out. When he looked back, Unu was looking up into his eyes as if waiting for something.

Did you do it? That was the question ringing in his ears now. It was blocking out every other thought. He didn't dare to say it out loud.

Unu nodded.

Do Corgurids read minds? No, that was ridiculous! He was an educated man; a good part of his higher education had been on the long and brilliant sweep of Corgurid history. There was nothing in there about telepathy. But of course, she could *guess* what was on his mind now.

"You are an honest man," she said. "You must do what you think is right." She waited a moment, but he said nothing. "You must. Everything must be set right. That is in your nature."

"Unu . . . What are you telling me to do?"

"Do what is right."

"I don't know . . ." His voice trailed off.

"You know what is right."

"But what about you?" It came out as a whisper.

"Do I know what is right?"

"No. I mean, what will happen to you?"

She smiled. It was not her usual, working, benign and efficient smile. This smile took over her whole face and made her eyes . . . yes . . . sparkle. "It will be fine. Whatever happens to me. I am free."

He didn't quite follow that. The Gass Security Force and the uncombined might of at least a dozen intelligence services were raking over every tiny crumb of evidence about what had just happened. If he hinted to anyone that this Corgurid might have had something to do with it, her life would become a nightmare. Even if they couldn't prove anything, her career would be over. *Free* was just what she wouldn't be.

"We should . . . can't we talk about it?" He looked around them. "I think there is a diner down the throughway."

"I have a fern."

"Ah. Yes, I see. Maybe some other time?"

"Of course. Good night, Mr. McAdoo."

"Call me Mack."

"Good night, Mack."

It was the first time ever she had called him "Mack." It hit him hard. His name didn't sound at all the same when she said it.

"Good night, Unu." Well, she didn't actually hear that. By the time he thought to say it, she was out of sight.

Chapter 21 • **PRIVATE CONVERSATIONS**

MEGGY GAVE TIMO the word about the Sareem's fleet. They had lingered at the Duke's estate for the past two days, awaiting further instructions for the invasion.

"That's incredible!" Timo said. "Who could pull off a thing like that?"

"Nobody knows. There literally aren't any clues. For all anybody can tell, it was a spontaneous natural event. Naturally, our people are trying to figure out how we can do it ourselves."

"And now every time someone's agent has a bumpy sea voyage, somebody's going to file an accusation."

"Steady work for the people upstairs. Oh." For a moment, Meggy didn't know what to say next. It had been his duty to pass on to Timo the word that he had been demoted to field agent. Timo was to catch an elevator the next morning to the Earthplat, where he would get his link fixed. And get his new assignment, which, rumor had it, would be as remote and obscure a posting as Calema had to offer.

"It's all right, Meggy. I'm looking forward to having my feet on actual ground for a while. It isn't such a bad place."

It was mid-morning. The two of them had been strolling the spacious grounds of the estate in the fashion of idle aristocracy everywhere. "Excuse me," Timo said. "I think I need to say a farewell." He hurried away toward the grand entrance. A fabulously long carriage was pulled up there. Servants were carrying trunks and boxes out of the palace. The Empress, now in a relatively subdued traveling costume of deep red and black was standing to one side and directing the traffic. Lady Damberell was with her.

"Ah, Lord Batherum. I thought the Empress would make her escape before you had stirred from your bed." Lady Hathet did not bother to hide the note of disappointment in her voice.

"That would have been a tragedy indeed, Lady Damberell. Your Majesty." Timo took a few seconds to execute the swirling Middle Shalkin Bow and Serene Pose with Quarter Twist and Simper. He nailed it.

Lady Damberell scowled, and the Empress laughed. "I think I will miss this constant parade of excellent manners," she said. Lefton appeared, bearing an obviously heavy trunk. "Just here with the rest, Master Steep," she said.

"What? Surely the men of Fengal know how to comport themselves with a lady?"

"Oh, that they do. That they do. And not a terrible lot else, I'm afraid."

"You are about to change all that, my dear," Lady Damberell interjected, with some satisfaction.

"You are about to reform all the men of Fengal?" Timo asked. "What an ambitious undertaking! However shall you accomplish it?"

"Little by little. The key is *business*." This last word was delivered in a conspiratorial whisper, with her face alarmingly close to his and her fingertips brushing his chest. At the smell of her, he felt just a bit dizzy and he had the urge to close his eyes and drift away in a dream. He took a step back.

"Oh?" he said carelessly. "What sort of 'business' can do all this?"

"The business of new things!" Lady Damberell said. Dalada held up a hand to signal restraint, but Hathet was too full of zeal to notice. "The Lesser Knowledge is coming to Fengal. This woman is going to make her land the new capital of the Lesser Knowledge!"

"New things? What do you . . ." At that moment Timo took notice of the fact that young Lefton was still standing with them, and looking quite sheepish. Timo looked down. The trunk Lefton had lugged over was quite a lot more battered and rusty than all the others.

"Aha. Are you contemplating a journey, Master Steep?" The young man nodded.

"How could you possibly be induced to leave . . . Well, what am I thinking? The Empress can be terribly persuasive."

"It isn't like that, Your Lordship." Lefton's face was nearly as red as his hair.

"It is strictly a business arrangement," Dalada said. "I am constructing a grand workshop at the port of Suzurey, and Master Steep will have the charge of it. We will make items of the finest steel. Lady Damberell has contracted with me to ship in the raw materials we need, from Shalk and from Gadgerus."

"And then my ships will bring the finished pieces to my new workshop in Deruffillum," Lady Damberell went on. "There we will assemble the swiftest, smoothest-running carriages in the world. Everyone will want them. Even you, Lord Batherum. You'll see."

"I am quivering with anticipatory delight, Your Ladyship."

"They're going to be wonderful machines, Your Lordship," Lefton said. "Just loads of improvements. I drew up the plans on real paper for Her Ladyship. They're all so . . . *pretty!*"

A high, keening sound, like a small animal in agony, made them all turn. It had come from just inside the palace's open doors. It came again. "*Ooooh Lefton! Don't goooo!*"

"Oh, for pity's sake," said Lady Damberell.

A face slowly emerged on one side of the doorway. It was a normally pretty face, but at the moment it was twisted with wild despair. "It *is* her! It's that Queen!"

Lefton stepped over some baggage and held out his arms in a gesture of appeal. "Now Dottie, it isn't like that! I'm going to be working, you see! In a grand new workshop. With lots of fellows to help me." As he spoke he slowly approached her. Miss Lumbush remained mostly behind the door, as if ready to bolt at the first sign of danger. "Come on now. Come on out and give us a hug." Dottie shook her head. "I'll be back before you know it. You know me."

"No, Leffy, no! That strange, wicked country! All those women like . . . like . . ." A slender arm now appeared around the door and an accusing finger wavered in the air.

"Dottie!" He reached for her hand but she pulled it away. The face disappeared. A moment later a protracted, heart-rending wail echoed throughout the palace. It slowly lost volume as her feet carried her away to the inner rooms.

Matron Deebee's solid form filled the doorway. "Leave her be, lad," she said. "She's just a bit dramatickal at the moment."

"Oh. Dramatickal. Well then." Lefton turned away. He knew lots about metals, but female complaints were a fearful mystery to him.

"So . . . I think I understand now." A wry smile had appeared on Timo's face. "You didn't come to Dab on my account at all. Nor to the Archduke's, nor to Hafswide. You were looking for . . . tinsmiths."

"But finding you here added so much spice to the visit." Dalada's gaze was fixed on him, but for once it seemed more filled with affection than with lasciviousness. "Farewell, Lord Timden."

Timo bowed deeply. "Farewell, Your Majesty."

THE EARTHPLAT HAD been bubbling with activity all day, and Sol Javitz had been at the center of all of it. Everyone, it seemed, wanted to tell him something. Or ask him something. Or congratulate him on the thorough annihilation of the O.F. The rumor was that wily old Sol had kept this top-top-top secret weapon in his back pocket all along. Of course he was going to deny it! He was the Spy's Spy; he would stick to his story to the end, no matter what evidence came up.

Javitz played along, issuing bland denials along the way, slapping backs, handing out attaboys, opening up a bottle of the good stuff in his office with his inner circle. "We've all been under a lot of strain these last weeks," he pronounced. "Everyone has done just a phenomenal job. How about if everybody on the plat gets tomorrow off? How would that be?"

The only thing about Javitz' personal quarters that gave away his high rank was the simple fact that the rooms were so spacious. His few items of furniture and decoration were the best of their kind, but there was nothing ostentatious. It was not his style to brag. He entertained often; he was friends with everyone, including the heads of most of the other stations orbiting Calema. He had an astonishing memory for the personal details of everyone working for him.

But Javitz liked his privacy.

He got home and established security, which was a great deal more than just locking the door. A half-dozen systems, each the cutting edge of physical or informational safety from a separate civilization, powered up. Before he even took off his jacket, he sat on the plain but elegantly formed couch and listened. One by one, he identified every faint hum and buzz and tick in the place. Nothing unusual. He continued to sit very still.

"I hear you are to be congratulated." The voice came from beside him, on the couch. He glanced over. No one was there. He looked quickly away as a person filled in (this was how Sol would describe it) beside him. Watching this particular visitor materialize always made Javitz a little queasy. When he could sense the weight of another person on the couch with him, Javitz turned back.

"Hello Mr. Hill," Javitz said.

Mr. Hill was a pleasant-looking man—middle-aged, in good health but no athlete, with a face that was both friendly and commanding and an affable but brisk way of speaking that swept his listeners along with him. He might have been the CEO of a corporation, or a successful politician from some Human planet.

Javitz was pretty sure Mr. Hill wasn't Human.

"I have received plenty of congratulations already today," Javitz went on. "People seem to be fixed on the idea that I had a hand in the destruction of the fleet."

"A misconception you have done little to dispel. No, no, Sol, there's no need to apologize for that. It's a good tactic. In fact, we have encouraged the idea."

"Really?"

"A little mystery, a little hint of hidden powers—it's a positive thing in your line of work. We are always interested in your success."

There it was. The subtle reminder that *we own you.* Although Javitz had never been clear on who the "we" was. Mr. Hill had ever been his one and only contact. Javitz had been an operative for the O.F. for more than fifteen years, and he had yet to hear even a name for the organization. He had no idea how many there actually were, although it seemed clear they had operatives like himself among all the species operating on Calema. He was now resigned to the idea that he would never know who was at the core of the O.F. or what they actually wanted. But they had kept all their promises, and the money was good. The help in his career was great. He didn't want to know any more.

"Did you take care of that agent of yours, the one who was causing all the trouble?"

As if you didn't know. Mr. Hill had never asked a question to which he didn't already know the answer. "You mean Sjogren. Well, I sent him to the surface on the pretext of needing everyone's help. I gave him an impossible mission, and he was completely unprepared. By all rights, he should have failed miserably, been exposed, been demoted, been re-assigned to some other station."

"But he succeeded?"

"As far as we can tell, he didn't accomplish anything. There was an explosion in a house close by the spot where the buu burn occurred. A natural phenomenon, I am told. He was hurt in that, but not seriously."

"And then the Spang was discovered."

"Yes. What? Are you suggesting he had something to do with that? It was found at the bottom of the buu crater."

"We don't know what the connection is. The site was crawling with agents from all the interested species. No doubt there were many operations in play. What have you done about Sjogren?"

"I demoted him for the failed operation in Kamerduk. He's going to be a surface agent now. I'll keep him well out of the way of anything important, of course."

"Why didn't you just kill him?"

Mr. Hill's face still had the pleasantly bland look of a boss going over the quarterly earnings report. No, definitely not Human. "That would have brought on an investigation. That would have put a big spotlight on the Kamerduk operation. I didn't want to risk it."

"And he is a friend of yours." Still the non-committal expression.

"Yes, he is a friend." *No point in denying that.*

"I understand. We'll just have to keep an eye on him."

IT WAS ANOTHER slow night at the Big Swide Inn. The explosion up at the Duke's lodge had really taken the shine off the doings around the Big Hole, and it didn't matter what the Duke or all the Distinguished Gentlemen of the world had to say about it. It was plain as the nose on your face that the Sulphur Swamp was under a powerful curse and not fit for Leeban habitation. All those barons and counts and whatnot had practically stampeded down the highway to the Big City. The consensus around Hafswide was "good riddance to bad company." Argum Seez, ever the solid and agreeable citizen, cursed the bigwigs with everyone else, and with fine fervor. Still, he reflected as he polished the row of unused tankards for the third time tonight, these outsiders had paid with real coin and without haggling over price or wheedling for credit.

The tankard at the end of the row was an ugly thing. It was covered in large, luridly painted flowers, and cracked. It had been cracked for twenty years, Argum told the help not to touch it; it reminded him of something special. Now, as he came to the end of the row, he paused to admire his special, cracked tankard. He could see the light of the fire reflected in the polished glaze. He checked the reflection in the mug next to it. The angle of the reflection was about five degrees off.

"Goldie," he said to the big-boned girl with her elbows on the counter and her eyes on the street outside. "Take over here. I need to go check the books." He went back to his office. Someone was sitting behind his small table. Neither of them said a word until he had touched a few odd spots on the wall and all noise from the outside was snuffed out.

"And how are things at the Big House?" Argum said pleasantly, pulling up a stool.

"Almost back to normal. Down to just the regular spies, hanging around to keep an eye on each other. The Humans just left. Any news from above?"

"The Neemnots have issued another denial. Now they're saying the Spang might be real, but it was planted in the Pool of Prophecy by some enemy."

"Have they accused anyone?"

"They don't have a clue. And the word is their government isn't going to push the issue any more than this. They'll probably let it die away into a long, low-level investigation that will never reach any conclusions."

"Really?" The visitor seemed a little incredulous.

"They never wanted partition, either. They love Leeban magic so. The cooler heads at Neemnot headquarters seem willing to put up with a few sanctions to keep this little planet undisturbed. Your plan worked to perfection."

"It was the Humans' plan. I just helped it along a bit."

"Well, it was very resourceful of you. And brave. The Company has awarded you a Brick. It just came through."

"Oh, my."

"Are you all right, Dottie?" Argum looked about for a handkerchief. He had to settle for the slightly damp towel tucked into his belt.

"Thank you," Dottie said, taking the towel and dabbing at her eyes. "A Brick. I didn't expect that. Not at my station."

"The Company knows your heart."

"My heart loves the Company."

Sessevians make the perfect spies. Literally, they make them.

The entire species being a registered company, the personnel department has the resources for very farsighted planning, beginning at conception. Argum and Dottie had been designed for their station in Sessevian Intelligence, and here in Hafswide, they were perfectly content. They loved the Company. No Sessevian spy had ever been turned. Sessevian Intelligence had never been infiltrated.

Argum gave Dottie a moment to pull herself together and then said, "How did you do it?"

"The Stobbins lad found the barrel in the woods."

"He's coming along well, that one."

"I thought it was just a bomb at first. When I was emptying it out, I found the Spang. That's when I saw the beauty of the Human plan. Of course, it was also insanely risky."

"Well, Humans."

"Yes. I sent the Spang up on the next elevator, for some appropriate heat damage. I just managed to drop it into the Big Hole the night before the Duke's Underwater Boat boys found it."

"Perfect. Neatly done. Of course, the explosion didn't go quite so neatly."

"I couldn't prevent that. I did manage to get everyone out of that wing of the building in time."

"Including the very handsome Human spy."

"That was strictly professional."

"Of course it was, my dear."

"He had proved himself useful."

"Yes. We're still working on that. We don't know what the Human angle is here."

"They were trying to prevent the Gadgerene invasion."

"But the possibility of a cheap source of buu gas! Surely that would overrule all other concerns."

"It's a puzzle. *He* is a puzzle."

"Most unorthodox." Argum stood and took down a slender bottle of yellowish liquid. "We'll be keeping an eye on him. I have some dew flower liqueur I've been saving for a special occasion. Care for a glass, Dottie?"

"You know it's my favorite."

Argum filled a pair of small earthenware cups. "To The Company," he said.

"May it fill the universe," she replied. They nodded deeply to each other and took a sip.

"Marvelous," Dottie said. "So, is the secret of buu really safe again?"

"Our people think so. Of course, it will be a big part of our assignments from now on to make sure it stays that way."

The "secret of buu" was simply this: that it can be organically derived on many planets, not just Calema. All the known buu planets were highly restricted-access under various legal maneuvers. And all were Sessevian-owned. All buu production was Sessevian, although the appearance of competition was scrupulously maintained. The fantasy of perilous buu exploration in the interstellar plasma fields was probably the finest bit of marketing the Company had ever come up with. "The secret of buu" was ten thousand years old, and thanks to the peculiar Human spy, and Sessevian intelligence, it was still intact.

☄

MEGGY HAD HIS carriage driver pull in at the Big Swide Inn before making the run to Deruffillum. He said he had some gloves to pick up at a shop, but it was really to let his driver pay a social call to Goldie. Meggy was an indulgent employer.

Timo saw the sign for the livery stable at the far end of the street. "You know, I've never really seen Hafswide," he said, and ambled down the street.

Most shops in Dab had a tinkling bell on the door to announce a customer's entry. When you opened the door to this shop, it tapped a small whistle set on a swivel, and its wild spinning made a sound just like a bird call that Timo remembered from the Night Forest. *How very much like Chumber,* Timo thought.

No one was at the counter, but someone was hammering on something in a back room. *Tap tap.* "I'll be out in a second!" *Tap tap tap.*

The shop was small but tidy. Harnesses and yokes and bridles of the more decorative sort covered the walls and gave the place a manly scent of leather and the outdoors.

Chumber Sackman rounded a doorway, a hammer still in his hand. "Sorry for the delay, sir, I just had to . . . Tim!" The little man hopped over and gave Timo a hug. Timo was too startled to reciprocate, but Chumber didn't seem to notice. "I was worried for you! I heard about the fire and all."

"Well, thank you. Yes, I . . . made it out of the house in time."

"And came away with a fine new set of clothes, too!"

"What? Oh, these. Meggy gave them to me. But I just came by to tell you, Chumber, that the most peculiar thing has happened since the fire took place. Everyone is leaving. I think we were just about the last ones to go."

"No! All those grand Lesser Knowledge men brought together from all over. What a shame!"

"Yes, isn't it though. You wouldn't expect them to be frightened of Swamp Worms..."

"Swamp Worms indeed!"

"But old ideas die hard, I guess. Anyway, the next time you venture into the Sulphur Swamp, you'll be terribly lonely, I'm afraid."

"Oh. Oh!" A smile began to spread across the ample width of Chumber's face.

"Yes, you will have to carry on your seed investigations all on your own. In complete privacy."

"Ah, Tim. What wonderful news." Chumber breathed heavily a couple of times with his eyes on the floor, as if feeling a little light-headed. He put a hand on Timo's shoulder. "I knew you were a good man."

IT TOOK ABOUT two weeks, but the day finally came when Mack left the office on time. It wasn't that he was caught up. The queue of messages on his Readers was as long as ever, and he had reports to make and his own analyses he was working on. But the urgency that had gripped him ever since the buu crisis began, his old "work frenzy" as the Gassplat staff secretly called it, had somehow tapered off. The moment had come when he once again felt "done" for the day.

He entered his quarters and stopped in the middle of the room to admire the view. Gadgerus, Brogora and Melligar were still in sunlight. The Festival of the First Potatoes would be going on in Brogora. In North Gadgerus it was almost Getting a Wife Week—the time when many a young swain gave himself the "now or never" talk. It seemed to Mack he felt the crackling energy from here. And in Melligar they were launching the long boats into the western sea in search of the first-year dragons. These cruised mostly over the reefs close at hand, and were still careless enough to blunder into the fling nets as these were shot into the air. It was exhilarating sport, and the survivors always came back with marvelous tales.

So much life going on down there. So much striving, so much doing, so much hoping. And the Calemans would carry on, blissfully unaware of the danger that had come and gone. Once again Mack felt the swelling in his chest. This time, for just an instant, he had an inkling of what it meant. He was tired of just looking at the beauty and the life. He wanted to enter into it. Be a part of it somehow. That was a strange new thought.

And it was nonsense, of course. He was the Planet Clerk. He had to be up here.

The door whistled. It was Unu. "Yes? What is it?" Mack said to her image in the corner of the window. "I didn't forget something, did I?" Unu held up a small black case, a toolkit. "Oh, that's right, the sweeper." He waved again to let her in.

"Can you find it?" she said as her feet touched the floor plate.

"I think I saw it in the kitchen." He stooped to get a better angle. "There it is." He approached the appliance cautiously. It popped up off the carpet, hovered for a moment, and then darted for the corner. "What's this?" Mack said. "You haven't moved all week!" He made a dive for it and snagged it with one hand. He

hung on as it pulled him halfway across the kitchen. "Ha!" he said triumphantly from under the table, as he found the off switch and stopped the infernal humming.

He crawled out clutching the sweeper: a sleek oblong the color of the floor. As he held it and stood up, it gradually changed to the color of the wall. Every apartment had at least one sweeper. It was supposed to stay out of sight when people were around and whisk about only when the apartment was empty. You shouldn't even know it was there, and you certainly should never stumble over one, as Mack had been doing for the last several days. Mechanical things just didn't seem to like him.

"Let's have a look," Unu said, and flipped the wayward sweeper onto its back on the table.

"It's been very erratic," Mack explained. "Sometimes it just stops in the middle of the floor. It even ran over my feet yesterday. I think it's . . ." By this time Unu had the base plate off and had four or five important-looking pieces lined up on a cloth. She had brought her own cloth.

"Ah-a-ah," she said after he had left off speaking, and without looking up. This low, three-toned murmur was the Corgurid equivalent of "Mm-hm." She had never used it in Mack's hearing before. It wasn't professional.

He couldn't quite follow what she was doing; her small hands were moving too quickly. And it seemed to him that Corgurid tools didn't have any fixed shape. They bent and twisted and developed new appendages as she needed them. No, that couldn't be. She was just changing them out so quickly that it just looked that way. No, now he *definitely* saw that pick-like thing lose its

ninety-degree bend and gain three or four centimeters, right there as she was holding it.

"Yes? Have you noticed something?" she said, glancing up.

"No, no. I'm just . . . I'll just watch from over here." He took a step back.

"There. It's what I thought. The *something-something* wears against the *something else-something else* after the first ten thousand hours of service and needs to be *somethinged*."

"Oh, that," he said.

She put all the pieces back in. It looked to Mack as if she were just laying them in place, not using any force. And yet they stayed. *She's stronger than she looks.* She snapped the base plate back into place and casually tossed the sweeper away.

"Look out!" he said. But the sweeper activated just above the floor, levitated for a moment, camouflaged itself, and zipped into its cubbyhole next to the sink. Mack and Unu looked at each other.

"That should do it," Unu said.

"Thank you."

"It was nothing."

She turned to him as she said it. He was looking straight into her eyes. He had a funny look on his face; she couldn't place it. It was an intense and slightly worried look—but that was normal—but also forlorn and faraway and just a little . . . hopeful? "Thank you," he said again, with a special emphasis. She said nothing. "I'm glad," he blurted out, and stopped to take a deep breath. "Unu, I'm glad you are not a very good Corgurid. I'm glad you love Calema, too."

She moved toward him suddenly. They embraced.

If anyone had been looking on, it would have seemed much too quick and awkward, Corgurids being so much smaller than Humans. But to Mack it was perfect. He was holding another person and she was holding him. Something inside him came back together in that moment. Something he hadn't even known was broken.

Somewhere out in the universe a switch clicked over, and time started moving again. They let go, slowly, and not awkwardly at all.

"I have some dew flower liqueur," he said. "Would you like some?"

"From Calema? That would be lovely."

As he went to get it, she said, "Oh. Is that a Raaza Fern?"

He glanced at it, and smiled a little sheepishly. "It seemed appropriate," he said.

"Have you made a new beginning, too?"

"Yes. Yes, I think I have."